DEVIL'S TOWER

A LONE MCGANTRY WESTERN

WAYNE D DUNDEE

WOLFPACK
PUBLISHING
— EST 2013 —

Devil's Tower
Paperback Edition
Copyright © 2023 Wayne D. Dundee

Wolfpack Publishing
9850 S. Maryland Parkway, Suite A-5 #323
Las Vegas, Nevada 89183

wolfpackpublishing.com

Paperback ISBN 978-1-63977-430-2
eBook ISBN 978-1-63977-429-6
LCCN 2023940083

DEVIL'S TOWER

CHAPTER ONE

"Is everything satisfactory, sir?"

"No, not by a damn sight." Lone McGantry's response was so blunt it caused the undertaker to recoil almost as sharply as if he'd been struck.

"I–I regret hearing that," stammered the man, an elderly, anxious-looking individual clad in a swallow-tail coat that looked like it had seen nearly as many years as the old gent himself. "Whatever the problem, I assure you I will see that steps are taken to correct—"

Lone held up a hand, halting the man in mid-sentence. "The problem's got nothing to do with you or your workmanship," he said, moderating his tone as best he could given the barely controlled rage that seethed within him most every waking minute these days. "My dissatisfaction is with something bigger—the reason you had to be called on to do this job at all. What you did, you and the stone mason, appears fine."

The undertaker looked relieved. "I appreciate hearing that. I'll tell Conroy, the mason, also. He never met Velda, like so many of us around town who still remember her, but I know how much it saddened him to mark a passage of someone so young."

"Yeah. Too damn few," Lone grated.

The gaze of each man dropped to the tombstone just a few feet from where they stood talking. The stone was placed at the head of a recently covered grave located on the slope of a small, tidy cemetery on the outskirts of the town of Beddoe Springs, Kansas. It was the middle of an early spring afternoon, the air warmed by a bright sun in a clear sky. The freshly greening grasses poking up around the other markers and crosses were being stirred by a gentle southern breeze.

The marking on the tombstone the pair were looking at read:

Velda Beloit
Beloved Daughter
and Friend
1863–1888

"It's too bad you weren't able to get here in time for the funeral," said the undertaker, whose name was Dutton. "But the instructions you wired ahead were very clear and we followed them precisely once Miss Beloit's casket arrived on the train. Reverend Poole, who unfortunately has been called out of town for a few days due to a personal family matter over in Wichita, conducted a very nice service. He also knew both Miss Beloit and her father."

"Pass the word, I'm obliged to all," Lone told him. "As for me, I said my goodbyes to Velda in my own way before arrangin' to send her here to rest next to her father. I followed along to pay my respects one last time."

A few feet to one side of Velda's fresh grave, an older plot was marked with a weathered tombstone bearing the name TIMOTHY BELOIT.

"I learned long ago," said the undertaker, "that each person grieves and marks the passing of a departed one in their individual way. I have a hunch you'd like to be left alone for a while now, so I'll take my leave. Will you be staying in town for very long, Mr. McGantry?"

"Just tonight. Then I'll be moving on."

"Well you know where to find me. Before you leave, be sure to stop by. The money you sent for the burial and services was more than enough, so you have an overpayment refund coming."

Lone regarded that rarest of creatures. An honest man. Then: "You go ahead and keep it. Use it to have some sod put over her as soon as you can, so it won't be just dirt and mud when the spring rains come. And if you think of it from time to time, maybe place some flowers here. I–I don't know that she favored one kind over another. Also, as I recall, her birthday is sometime in September."

"I'll see to it, just as you ask," Dutton assured him after a slight pause. Just as Lone was somewhat surprised by the display of honesty, the undertaker was in turn caught off guard by this big stranger's unexpected show of sentimentality. True, he'd sent money and specific instructions for the Beloit girl's burial and all. But when he subsequently showed up in person, so gruff and hard-looking—tall, broad-shouldered, with a square, weathered face anchored by a prominent nose and flinty eyes that seemed to bore into you with almost as much impact as a slug from the Colt riding on his hip —such a man possessing a streak of sentimentality was hardly the first impression anyone was likely to have formed.

As he turned to start back to town, Dutton bid a final, "If I don't see you again then, here's wishing you safe travels ahead."

Lone acknowledged the words with a faint nod, said nothing in return. He stood still and silent, watching the man plod away toward the assemblage of buildings that comprised Beddoe Springs. At the same time, another man, a sturdily built gent wearing a dark blue shirt, black vest, and black trousers tucked into highly polished black boots, was striding away from the buildings and approaching the cemetery. The star pinned prominently on his vest and the thick mustache, also black, splitting otherwise plain facial features identified him as Amos Tucker, the marshal of Beddoe Springs. It was the marshal with whom Lone had originally traded telegrams to set up the arrangements for Velda's burial when her casket subsequently arrived via train. It was also the marshal who Lone originally sought out when he got to town himself, and was then steered to Dutton the undertaker.

Now it looked like the lawman was coming around to do some follow-up checking on things. Though they had spoken only briefly earlier, Lone had found Tucker to be amiable and competent-seeming.

By the time he got to Lone, he was breathing a little hard and sweating freely. He removed his hat and took a handkerchief from his shirt pocket. He used the hanky to mop his forehead and then wipe the inside rim of the hat before putting it back on. "Warm day," he proclaimed. "Afraid it's a signal for another hot blasted summer to come."

"Could be," Lone allowed.

Tucker cut a brief glance down at Velda's tombstone and then brought his eyes back to Lone. "Dutton have things taken care of to suit you?" he asked.

Lone nodded. "He did. I'm obliged for the job he done, and also to you for passin' along my messages."

"No problem. Least I could do," said the marshal. "Like I told you, I knew Velda from back when. Knew her dad, too, of course. Marshal Tim everybody called him. He wore the star for this town near twenty years. Toward the end, I expect you know, Velda was his chief deputy."

"Yeah, she was mighty proud of that. Until the night her pa got gunned down."

Tucker made a face. "Uh-huh. A sad night for Beddoe Springs. Sad and—another thing about it that always struck me—so doggone ironic. Then, after I got your telegram about Velda and a little later heard more details on how she died, the same thing struck me all over again."

"Not sure I follow you," said Lone, frowning.

"The thing about it, see," explained Tucker, "is that in the early years when Tim Beloit first took over as marshal, Beddoe Springs was a pretty rough place. I mean, it wasn't Dodge City or Tombstone or no such, but it had more than its share of rowdies and gun toughs. The whole territory was on the raw and wild side back then. And Marshal Tim might not have been what anybody would call a town tamer exactly, but he was nevertheless rugged and stern and came down hard on enforcing the rules him and the town fathers laid out. Plenty of skulls got cracked and more than a few who thought they had what it took to make their own rules ended up eating lead pills they couldn't digest.

"In time, things changed and the town started to grow and become a place where more and more decent folks wanted to settle. The rowdy old ways tamed down to a few Saturday night drunken brawls, a bit of pilfering here and there, and now and then a wife bending a skillet over her husband's head for sniffing the wrong pair of bloomers. Things like that. And then, out of the blue, after surviving all the mean years when bullets whizzed his way regular-like without ever leaving so much as a scratch...now here comes the ironic part...one evening when that kind of thing had long since quit happening, Marshal Tim 'fronts a pack of unruly out-of-own drunks who decided they wasn't ready to dry out overnight in his hoosegow, so they plug him dead as hell and ride off laughing. See what I mean?"

"Maybe," Lone grated. Then, sharply cocking one eyebrow, he asked, "But what's that got to do with his daughter?"

"Same thing. Don't you see?" The marshal spread his hands. "After Velda left here and rode down those skunks who gunned her dad, she went on to make quite a name for herself as a bounty hunter. One of the most dogged and most feared on the frontier. Naturally, that didn't come without putting herself at risk against plenty of bad hombres. I realize I'm telling you stuff you already know, but I'm getting to my point about irony. So after several years of all that risky bounty hunting, the report I got from the Carverton marshal—and you can tell me if I didn't get it straight, since you were there

—was that Velda was sitting down to a peaceful supper in a hotel dining room one evening when two cowboys playing poker in the adjacent hotel saloon got into an argument that turned to gunplay. They ended up killing each other but in the process a stray bullet passed into the dining area and struck down poor Velda."

Hearing this replay of the details caused Lone to suddenly go ice cold on the inside, clashing with the twisting, churning ball of rage that had for days been gnawing at his guts like a starving feral beast. He squeezed his eyes shut and a great rushing sound filled his ears, drowning out any more words from the marshal. He couldn't tell how long the rushing sound lasted, but when it eased up he opened his eyes again and saw that Tucker had not only stopped talking but was staring at him in a wary, somewhat slack-jawed manner.

He met Lone's gaze and said softly, earnestly, "I'm sorry. It was thoughtless of me to go to such lengths to make my silly, trivial point. You were obviously close to Velda, had been spending time with her of late. I should have spoken of the tragedy that befell her more reverently."

Lone took a deep breath, let it out slowly, raggedly. "It's okay. No words, one way or another, can change what happened or do anything to bring her back. Trust me, if there was a chance for that, God—and the Devil, too—knows I'd be doin' it and not just talkin' about it."

Now the wariness in Tucker's eyes changed, took on a flinty edge. "Yeah... That's what concerns me."

CHAPTER TWO

"A WALKING STICK OF DYNAMITE PRIMED FOR THE SPARK that's sooner or later bound to set him off. That's how the marshal of Carverton described you in a telegram he sent after he heard you were headed this way," Tucker went on to explain.

The muscles at the hinges of Lone's jaw bunched visibly. "Sounds an awful lot like a warnin'. From him to you, and now you to me."

"Warning is a strong word," Tucker countered. "More like a professional advisement, at least on the part of the Carverton marshal."

"That still leaves you passin' it on."

Tucker puffed out his cheeks, blew a short burst of air. "Okay. Call it a precaution, for lack of a better word. Hell, maybe it is a warning—but one *for* you, not against you."

"No offense, Marshal, but you're not makin' a whole lot of sense," Lone told him.

The marshal squared his shoulders and said, "Alright, I'll try to make the rest of this straight and quick. Even without that telegram, I could see plain enough after one look at you that you're a man strained barbed wire tight. And why wouldn't you be? Full of grief and hate and bitterness with no outlet for any of it on account of the drunken fools who killed Velda went ahead and killed themselves, too."

"So you're worried I might find some other kind of outlet here in your town, is that it?" Lone prodded.

"As a matter of fact, yeah, I guess it is."

"Why would that be? Is there something in particular here to give you that worry?"

"Something's gonna snap that wire, strike that spark. And the more time passes, the closer the likelihood gets."

Lone stayed quiet, waiting, sensing there was more to it.

Tucker dragged a hand down over his face, no hanky this time. "Okay. Here's the thing. The last few years Marshal Tim was in office, even after things tamed down like I told you about, his ways of handling things remained kinda rough. Not to the point of blasting anybody, I don't mean, nothing like that took place for a long spell. But using his six-gun as a club, laying its barrel alongside somebody's head at the first sign of trouble, he didn't ease up on that much at all. And when Marshal Tim hit a lick it was no love tap. He meant business."

"Let me guess," said Lone, twisting his mouth sourly. "It turned into another case of where the town fathers who loved it when he knocked around the rowdies and sent 'em all packin', gradually started gettin' uppity and nervous about the same tactics continuin' in what was now their proper little community."

"Something like that, yeah," Tucker admitted. "And I know, same as you're implying, it's not an uncommon story. There've been plenty of towns—too many—who hired a tough lawman to clean out the dirt and then swept him out like the last of the dregs when he'd finished doing what they wanted. As far as Marshal Tim, it hadn't got quite that far here in Beddoe Springs. Nobody was talking about getting rid of him, at least not yet. But more and more voices were being raised about his hard ways. When he got gunned, of course, all that ended."

"Big of 'em," Lone grunted. "I can see now why Velda shed this town and never came back. Maybe it was a mistake for me to have her brought here now, even if it was to put her to rest next to her pa."

Tucker shook his head. "Don't feel that way. Please. This is a good town, good people. You're gonna find a few sour apples anywhere."

"Then what's the point of you tellin' me all this? What is it you're worried I might run into that could set me off?"

"What I just explained," Tucker said somewhat impatiently. "The talk, folks bringing up some of those old stories and grievances about Marshal Tim. There's even a handful around who've still got ailments, leastwise they claim they do, from getting his gun barrel bounced off their skulls. Having Velda's body returned for burial, don't you see, is naturally the kind of thing to draw attention in a quiet, mostly boring town. And it's more than enough to set the tongues of every gossip and busybody wagging for a month."

"Jesus Christ on a crutch," Lone groaned. "Is *that* what's got your long handles in such a bunch? Worried I might overhear somebody makin' an unflatterin' remark about the old marshal and it bein' enough to set off this walkin' stick of dynamite I'm supposed to be?"

"You tell me," Tucker challenged. "Tell me you're not aching for somebody to give you a reason to get rid of what you're carrying around bottled up in you."

"If I was as close to that edge as you're claimin'," Lone grated, "then you might want to think about not bein' the one to push me closer."

But even as he said this, the icy coldness and the gnawing beast were threatening to clash again inside him. And in his mind's eye flashed all the faces, the harder the better, that he'd glared at over the past seven days, ever since Velda died in his arms, hoping to get a reaction from one of them that would give him reason enough to go for their throats.

"Good God, man. Look at you," said Tucker. "You're trembling like a leaf. You *are* close to the edge. And no, I don't want to be the one to push you closer—but I'd rather it was me than one of my unsuspecting citizens."

Lone realized his breathing had grown rapid. He willed it to slow down and then pinned Tucker with a level gaze. "You can rest easy, Marshal. I won't go over the edge in your town. In fact, I won't even stay the night like I'd planned. Let me have some time alone here, then I'll come in and get my horse and gear from the livery, be on my way."

Tucker's face took on a strange, almost sorrowful expression. "Though it might seem otherwise, I didn't come here with any intent of asking you to leave town. I got to admit, though, I think it's probably for the best."

A corner of Lone's mouth quirked up. "Like I've never heard that before."

CHAPTER THREE

IT ALMOST WORKED.

Lone almost got out of Beddoe Springs without any trouble erupting. Ironically (Tucker's pet word again), when it came it stemmed in no way from anything to do with either of the Beloits. The fury it unleashed from within Lone, however, was a different story.

As he told the marshal he would do, Lone remained out at the cemetery for some time before heading in to reclaim Ironsides, his big gray stallion, from the livery stable. While at Velda's graveside, he'd mostly just stood silent and still, running memories and a few regrets through his mind. A couple times he closed his eyes tight, as if hoping when he opened them again the tombstone would no longer be there and instead a still vibrant and living Velda would be somewhere close by. But it never worked. Every time it was just the cold stone left in front of him, and the only remnants of Velda were what was in the ground and the empty space beside him where she *should* have been. At length, he reached out and rested his hand on the tombstone in a final gentle caress. Then he turned away and started down toward the town.

At the livery stable, there didn't appear to be much activity going on and there was no sign of the proprietor who'd taken in Ironsides when Lone first got to town. But inasmuch as he'd paid in advance for a night's boarding and care and the layout of the place was small and simple, Lone saw no need wasting time looking for somebody when he could find Ironsides and his gear easily enough on his own and proceed with making ready to leave. He began walking down the wide center aisle of the barn, looking into the row of stalls on either side until he found the one holding Ironsides. He'd just reached it, at about the midway point of the barn's length, when he heard the sound of voices coming from down near the far end. Pausing to listen, it didn't take long to recognize that the conversation taking place wasn't a particularly friendly one.

"Come on now, gal," a harsh, somewhat slurred male voice was saying. "You need to face the fact that it's time for you to take the next step toward bein' a woman. You got to forget that limp you're afflicted with and quit thinkin' it makes you unattractive to anybody. To a man with some seasoning on him, it ain't no problem at all. The way the rest of you is fillin' out is real prime, and if you was to lay out on your back, like say on that pile of fresh straw over yonder—the proper way for a woman to present herself to a man anyway—then that bother-some limp wouldn't matter at all." Here a pause for a nasty, snorting chuckle. Then: "And I guarantee there wouldn't be nothin' limp about me neither was I to lay down with you and give you the pleasurin' you're so ripe and ready for."

"You take your filthy talk and your disgusting notions and get out of here right now, Oscar Weems," responded a slightly quavering, young-sounding female voice. "You're drunk and talking out of your head. So you and that drooling moron of a cousin leave immediately and this one time I'll hold off reporting you to my father and the marshal."

Lone had heard enough of the exchange to know full damn well what was going on. When he left off Ironsides, he'd met the liveryman's daughter to the extent of trading nods with her as she took the big gray's reins and led him away. She looked to be about sixteen and had the makings to be rather pretty if not for her carelessness in grooming and attire. Her deformed right leg, apparent even in baggy trousers, and the pronounced limp she walked with added up, in Lone's judgment, to a case of very low self-esteem that accounted for her lack of effort in presenting herself better. And now, from the sound of it, some miserable wretch was attempting to take advantage of her misery and vulnerability.

As Lone proceeded past Ironsides' stall toward the source of the voices, the man called Oscar spoke some more.

"You ain't gonna report nothin' to nobody," he sneered. "You know why? Cause you like the attention, that's why, you little tease. And besides, who else in this shitpot of a town is gonna give a mousy little crip like you even the time of day?"

"Your time of day, you fat tub of guts, is plumb used up. The young lady clearly asked you to leave and, since her father owns this place, what she says in his absence is what counts. So best you and that other belly-draggin' slob you got sidin' you hightail it on out while you're still able to walk."

Lone gave this command upon reaching the final stall at the end of the barn and quickly sizing up the scene within. As he'd expected, the livery-man's daughter was crowded up against the back wall, trying to put on a bold front but looking every bit the frightened, cornered animal. Facing her, doing the cornering, were a pair of heavyset hombres with thick shoulders and bulging bellies. They had on battered, short-billed caps and were clad in bib overalls and work shirts that marked them as miners or freight workers who'd apparently been laboring over shots of redeye and schooners of beer inside some local saloon all afternoon. One was taller and appeared a bit younger than the other, the whiskers on his unshaven jaw tinted a rusty reddish color. The older of the pair, Oscar, the talker, had splotchy dark whiskers that looked like smears of coal dust.

At Lone's words, Oscar's fleshy, dark-whiskered face whipped around and from it flashed a fierce scowl. The sight of the tall man standing in the mouth of the stall, feet planted wide and shoulders spanning equally as wide, did nothing to diminish Oscar's drunken aggression. His bottom lip curling down, displaying a row of crooked yellow teeth, he growled, "Whoever the hell you are, mister, you better turn around and light a shuck outta here if you know what's good for you. What's goin' on here ain't none of your stinkin' business."

"Don't quite see it that way," said Lone. "Thing is, I've got a horse stalled in this barn and he's kinda fussy who he shares space with. He pure don't like pigs or polecats, and that ain't what I paid money for when I put him up here. So that makes even more reason for you two to clear out."

Now Red Whiskers turned and curled his lip. "You got a real smart mouth, don't you? But I guess you ain't so smart upstairs between the ears. You *wantin'* to stick your nose in our business and get it mashed all over your stupid face? Is that it?"

Lone felt the iciness and the gnawing beast inside him start to align, this time getting ready to surge together. He said, "What I want—no, make that what I wanted at the start of this—was simply for you two to leave the girl alone and get out of here. But I got me a hunch we're past that now."

Red Whiskers' brows writhed like furry snakes above his eyes and his expression wrestled between being anger and surprise. "What the hell? You think you got some kind of say about anything me and my cousin take a mind to do?"

"Reckon you missed the part before where I gave you the chance to walk out while you was able. That's the chip I'm callin' in now."

"Are you loco? Two to one odds? We'll break you into pieces and leave 'em scattered like horse apples," crowed Red Whiskers.

"Not so fast, cuz," piped up Oscar. He pointed. "This hard-eyed son of a coyote is packin' iron. We ain't. Those six in his wheel changes the odds considerable."

Red Whiskers glowered at Lone anew, still fired up but now also with a trace of tentativeness. "Gun courage, eh? So that's what's been drivin' that mouth of yours. Well me and Oscar are just a couple of workin' stiffs, freight loaders. We don't go heeled." He held up two cabbage-sized fists. "We do what needs doin' with these, and there ain't much we can't handle with 'em."

"Like bullyin' fragile young girls and threatenin' to force your way against their will?" Lone grated.

"There's plenty of women around who don't have to be forced to find out what a real man can give 'em," muttered a sullen Oscar. "But that don't mean there ain't still some fresh blood what needs a little extra persuadin'."

"Fresh blood," echoed Lone. "That's a real interestin' choice of words." He slowly unbuckled his gun belt, stripped it off, then held it out to one side. Addressing the liveryman's wide-eyed daughter, he said, "Come take this, girl. Go find your pa and the marshal. Somebody might want to fetch a doctor, too. By the time one gets here, I expect there'll be some work for him."

CHAPTER FOUR

THE GIRL SKIRTED AROUND THE HULKING COUSINS AND reached Lone. She took the gun belt, cast a furtive glance up at his face, then hurried away down the barn aisle as fast as her impairment would allow.

As the sound of her departing footfalls faded, Oscar's mouth stretched into a wide, sly smile. "So you've interrupted our fun with the little crip. For now. We'll get back around to her again someday. She ain't goin' nowhere. But in the meantime, you meddlin' bastard, you're gonna have to pay a price for causin' the delay."

"A *steep* price," Red Whiskers added menacingly.

Lone sighed. "You gonna just keep talkin' mean to me, or are we gonna get to something that amounts to something?"

"Yeah, we're gonna get to it. Right about now!" declared Oscar.

The two brutes moved in unison, advancing on Lone in a way that made it clear they'd done this kind of thing before. First they spread apart nearly as far as the stall space would allow and then they converged on Lone in a V-pattern that put him at the point of the spear. He waited, poised with balled fists, until the last second. When they were close enough to make simultaneous lunges for him, he bent suddenly at the knees and hurled himself under their reaching arms and into a diving roll that carried him past them and deeper into the stall. He sprang back up several feet behind them.

As Oscar and Red Whiskers turned to face him again, wheeling around with angry curses, this time it was Lone who made the lunge. He leaned in as soon as they were partially turned and immediately swung a slashing backhand blow that crashed his right fist to the side of Oscar's jaw and throat, knocking him staggering to one side with flailing arms.

Instantly twisting his torso in reverse, Lone swung his left fist in another hard backhand, this one hitting Red Whiskers square in the mouth and pounding in his teeth. Continuing to twist full around, Lone followed with a straight, nose-smashing right that sent a twin stream of blood squirting and also sent the big man staggering until he slammed against the opposite side of the stall.

Lone rushed after him. He realized he had little or no chance to come out on top if he tried fighting both of these brawlers at the same time. That meant he needed to quickly and thoroughly eliminate one of them. And since the punches he'd just scored gave him a pretty good start on dong that with the younger, bigger, stronger one, it was something he had to press to the fullest.

When Red Whiskers fell against the rough wooden boards of the stall's wall, his knees buckled partially and he sagged there for a moment with blood streaming down his face, his eyes blurred and watery. Lone threw his full weight at the man, raising a knee as he came in and ramming it into the younger cousin's ribs. He heard bones crack along with a great gush of air being driven from lungs. Keeping his knee in place, using it as a balancing anchor, Lone rained down blows with first his right and then left, hammering them into each side of Red Whiskers' face and neck, pounding his head hard back against the unyielding wooden wall.

The beast inside Lone was galloping wildly now, jets of frosty air snorting from its nostrils and filling Lone's own lungs, making his pulse beat faster. This was it. The outlet. The unleashing. Lone was going over the edge and ready to take bodies and souls with him.

Feeling he had Red Whiskers fairly well subdued and at the same time realizing he couldn't afford to ignore Oscar too much longer because the single blow he'd absorbed wasn't enough to have taken him out of the fray for very long, Lone pushed off the younger cousin and turned back to face the older one. And a faceful of him—of his flying foot, to be exact—was what he ended up receiving. Luckily, Lone's turning motion, combined with a reflexive backward jerk, came just in time to save him from getting his head kicked off. As it was, the heel of Oscar's boot, hurtling at him in a high, vicious thrust, still struck the side of Lone's jaw with an only partially glancing blow that gave it enough impact to nevertheless knock him reeling.

Out into the middle of the stall Lone staggered, lurching, fighting to stay on his feet while stars and pinwheels exploded inside his head. Before he could get fully righted or his head cleared, Oscar came barreling like a charging buffalo. Leaning forward, chin tucked down, he planted one lowered shoulder into Lone's midsection and drove him back to the stall's rear wall. Oscar may have been the smaller of the two cousins, but he was still a big, heavy man and his full ramming weight slammed Lone hard against the rough wood. Spurts of dust and fine particles of accumulated hay and straw were rattled loose from between the boards. A great gust of Lone's wind was also expelled.

Oscar dug the toes of his work shoes deep into the packed earth of the stall's floor and kept ramming forward, pinning Lone in place with repeated slams of his shoulder, grinding him against the wall.

Lone clenched his stomach muscles as tight as he could and fought to suck some quick, meager gasps of breath. He couldn't gain enough leverage to shove back against the continued ramming and get away from the wall. Pounding his fists down onto Oscar's broad, meaty back had no discernible effect. Finally, in an attempt to keep from being relentlessly pulverized, Lone leaned forward as far as he could and got his arms wrapped partly around Oscar's torso down near his thick waist. Grasping his belt on either side and straining with a surge of fury and desperation, Lone lifted the big man's feet off the ground and flung him to one side.

Though he touched back down after being swung only a short distance, Oscar was so startled and disoriented by the maneuver it sent him staggering drunkenly sideways. This bought Lone just a few precious seconds, but it was enough to get pushed out away from the wall and turned to face Oscar as the latter fought to get rebalanced. Lone stood hunched slightly forward, left arm hugging his battered stomach and ribs as he sucked raggedly to try and catch his breath. But the fire of his bottled up rage still burned bright and hot in his eyes.

With fire blazing in his own eyes, Oscar came in another buffalo charge. This time, though, the target for his lowered shoulder was ready and didn't stay put. Sidestepping at the last second, Lone even added a chop to the back of Oscar's head as his momentum carried him past and the empty rush took him all the way to an abrupt stop against the other side of the stall. This awkward, fruitless attempt might have been almost comical if not for what happened next. Because leaning in a corner of the stall, hitherto unnoticed but located just inches from where Oscar had now thrust out a hand to brace himself, was a three-tined hay fork. The big man's eyes fell on this immediately—and when he spun back around he was holding it outthrust toward Lone.

"Now, you meddlin' sumbitch," he snarled, "you're gonna pay that price I told you was due for stickin' your nose in where it don't belong!"

"You bring that sticker into this, all bets are off," Lone warned him in an ice cold voice. "I been itchin' real bad lately to kill somebody. You don't amount to much, but you'll do for a start."

"You ain't gonna do nothing to nobody, not after I got this rammed through your gizzard and your blood is runnin' in the gutter with the horse piss!"

Lone quickly peeled off his buckskin vest and wrapped it around his left fist to create a lumpy, makeshift shield that he held slightly extended in front of himself. Rising up on the balls of his feet, holding his open right hand a bit lower and also somewhat in front, he began slowly circling toward the middle of the stall.

Oscar also shifted into a circling motion, moving to position himself in front of where the stall opened out to the barn's center aisle. This would have been a smart maneuver on a less combative type who might try to use that gap in an attempt to flee to safety. What Oscar hadn't yet figured out about Lone McGantry was just how far he was from wanting to avoid this fight.

They continued circling, until Oscar made a sudden thrust with the pitchfork. Lone blocked with his shrouded hand, knocking it down and away.

They circled some more. Oscar thrust again and again Lone blocked it.

Following up quickly, Oscar feinted and got Lone to over extend with a blocking, swatting away motion that gave Oscar just a fraction of a second's opening. It was enough for the big man to stab viciously and sink one of the fork's tines in the outer, meaty part of Lone's left thigh. Lone jumped back immediately, pulling his leg free from the sharp tip, and skirted away in a wider circle. The puncture hurt like hell and a thick worm of blood promptly began crawling down his leg.

Oscar laughed. "Maybe that's how I'll do it. I'll put a dozen or so pin pricks in you and watch you bog down from blood loss before I step in and plant the big one in your gizzard."

"You stupid fat pig," Lone sneered. "You can try bleedin' me out all you want, but that saggin' gut of yours will have you suckin' air long before you wear me down. Once I snatch that fork out of your hands, I'll make just one poke—and your Adam's apple will be danglin' on the middle point out the back of your neck."

From where he continued to lay sprawled as Lone had left him, unable to rise, Red Whiskers mumbled out of his battered mouth, "Watch 'im, Oscar. He's a tricky one."

"You just hang on," Oscar replied, never taking his eyes off Lone. "After I cut down Mr. Tricky, I'll drag him over and let you poke a few holes in him just for fun."

In the course of this exchange, even though Oscar stayed focused on Lone, he somehow failed to notice how close Lone had moved to the end of the gate that could be swung shut when certain animals needed to be kept penned in the stall. Currently bracing the gate open was a three-foot piece of two-by-four wedged under one of the cross rails. Spotting this, Lone's right hand flashed out and seized it.

Oscar's face displayed a flash of concern at this. But he quickly tried to cover it up with a counter display of bluster, saying, "What you plannin' to do with that—poke wood splinters back against these steel fork tines?"

"I was thinkn' of something more like this!" Lone responded, wasting no time putting the heavy slab of wood to use. This meant hurling it in a hard overhand throw straight to Oscar's face. The edge of the two-by-four hit on an angle, striking just behind Oscar's left eye socket and down over his cheekbone and the corner of his mouth. It bit into flesh and bone with a distinct *chunk!* followed immediately by Oscar's wail of surprise and pain.

As Oscar jerked his face away and staggered backward, Lone rushed after him. He knocked the threatening pitchfork prongs off to one side with a sweep of his shrouded hand while at the same time stepping in close and driving his right forearm against the side of Oscar's face on almost the same track as the bleeding welt left by the two-by-four.

Only stumbling back against the side of the stall kept Oscar from losing his footing and falling to the ground. But Lone gave him no chance to breathe. He rammed forward into the big man, pumping his left knee high and slamming it into the soft gut then an instant later crashing another forearm blow to the side of his face. The only trouble was the buckskin vest Lone had wrapped around his left hand. It had served its purpose well but he'd wound it so securely that now he was having trouble shaking it loose—and, until he did, he was fighting one-handed and the shrouded left was useless for grabbing the pitchfork that Oscar still stubbornly held on to.

With a desperate surge of strength, Oscar shoved out from the wall and drove Lone back a step and a half. Reacting instinctively, Lone twisted and threw his right arm up around the back of Oscar's neck, clamping on a headlock. Then, bending forward and twisting more, he dragged Oscar over his hip and dumped him to the ground on his back.

Pouncing immediately, Lone threw himself on top of the man, landing so that his knees drilled deep into gut and ribs. For all intent and purpose, the remains of any fight left in Oscar should have been driven out along with the great gush of air this forced from his lungs. But the tenacious bastard still gripped the pitchfork with both hands. He had no leverage for tying to use it, though, and as Lone finally managed to free his left hand he too was able to lock the tool's long wooden handle in a double grasp.

After that it was no contest. Oscar was too battered and too weakened to resist having the fork wrested from him. Once in full control—the rage still stampeding wildly within him—Lone held a length of the handle between his fists and bashed it down twice on Oscar's upturned face, flattening his nose and pounding in his mouth much as he had Red Whiskers'. Then, twirling the fork and raising it above his head with the tines pointing straight down, Lone was ready to finish it. Curling back his lips, he rasped though gritted teeth, "I warned you all bets were off if you brought this sticker into it, you sonofabitch!"

But an instant before the prongs started down, a gunshot roared out of nowhere and a bullet crashed into the ceiling directly above Lone's head.

"Drop it, McGantry!" ordered the voice of Marshal Amos Tucker. "I don't want to, but I'll plant the next one in you if given no choice!"

CHAPTER FIVE

LONE RODE OUT OF BEDDOE SPRINGS WITH THE SUN hanging low in the western sky. Because he knew enough about wound infections to realize that having the prong of a dirty pitchfork stuck in him had the potential for some nasty after effects if not taken care of properly, he hung around long enough to let a doctor clean and treat the puncture to his thigh. After that, there was nothing more to keep him.

The testimony of the liveryman's daughter—Margaret, her name turned out to be—about how the two drunken cousins had been harassing her and then threatened Lone when he intervened was enough to exonerate Lone for the actions he'd subsequently taken. Yet the expressions on the faces of most of the crowd that gathered following the incident—including those of Margaret, her father, and Marshal Tucker, even as they were outwardly voicing their gratitude—clearly appeared unsettled by the degree to which Lone had punished the pair. A couple of voices from within the throng could actually be heard grumbling about criminal charges for "such savagery." And although Tucker's deputies quickly silenced them and herded them away before that kind of dissent could grow, the marshal's stiff attitude sent the unspoken message that Lone's departure would be more welcome than ever.

So depart is what he did. Purposely avoiding another pass by the cemetery, he pointed Ironsides due north and they rode beyond sunset then on through the calm, quiet night.

Calm and quiet. Good conditions for reflecting and, at last, thinking ahead some. Lone had done plenty of thinking in the recent days since Velda's death...remembering, grieving, aching, hating...but hardly any of it had been forward looking. It was almost as if he hadn't felt like he had any right to think past the loss of Velda. Like too big a part of him had been lost, too.

But that was no good. He knew better. He'd endured loss before. Hell, as an infant orphaned by the Indian massacre of his parents, he'd practically been *born* to loss. The baby son, no first name known, of the McGantrys, newly arrived homesteaders to the territory, he was the lone survivor who eventually had that distinction turned into what he was dubbed—Lone McGantry—by the army wives who raised him at Fort McPherson. And the rage and bitterness he'd grown up feeling toward those who had robbed him of a true family were not much different than what was seething inside him now over the killing of Velda. From the first day he was old enough to ride out with soldiers from the fort he was hell bent on killing any and every Indian that came in sight. And, God knew, he did kill many. Until he finally came to realize that the war party responsible for the death of his parents was long gone to the mists of time and distance and all he was doing was committing blind slaughter. And that wasn't who or what he wanted to be.

Yet now he teetered on the brink of wanting to act the same. In the interim, after ceasing his crazed Indian killing days and continuing on as an army scout then a wanderer throughout the frontier, he'd killed other times. More, no doubt, than many would think necessary. But always, the way Lone saw it, as a matter of self-defense, survival. And yes, revenge on some occasions. But in those cases his targets were clear and deserving.

That was the maddening part about what he was trying to come to grips with now. The careless lowlifes deserving to pay for what happened to Velda were already dead—killed by their own stupid, drunken hands. Leaving Lone with a bone deep ache, an emptiness, multiplied by two. First, the emptiness of Velda being gone; second, the emptiness of being unable to do anything to avenge her.

The fight with Oscar and his cousin had released some of the bottled up rage. At least for now, clearing his head sufficiently to make room for the forward thinking he was beginning to do. On the matter of nearly killing Oscar, Lone was of two minds. The man was a pig who would be no loss to the world. Still, since he'd had nothing to do with what happened to Velda, would it have helped any if Tucker hadn't been there to stop that pitchfork from plunging all the way down?

Probably not, Lone decided. Except for one final thing he'd had to say on the matter to Tucker and the liveryman: "You're left with those two rabid bastards continuin' to be alive and in your town. By their own words, they've still got designs on Margaret. If you're too stupid or gutless to run 'em out and keep 'em out, that poor girl may pay the consequences. If it comes to that and I ever hear about it, you'll be seein' me again someday."

That was the best he could do under the circumstances.

———

Shortly before sunrise, Lone stopped to make camp beside a small, nameless creek. He stripped down Ironsides, let him drink his fill after he'd cooled some, then staked him to graze in a patch of nicely greening creekside grass. Next he built a fire over which he cooked a pot of coffee that he drank along with some beef jerky and stale biscuits. His eating and sleeping over the past several days had been mighty sparse, and he was starting to feel it. He was also feeling the effects of his tussle with the two bruisers in the livery stall, causing him to add a healthy dollop of whiskey to his second cup of coffee.

When he was done eating, he spread his bedroll and lay down to grab a couple hours of rest. To his surprise, he fell asleep quicker and more deeply than he had in a long while. He didn't wake until the morning sun was high and warm on his face.

Lone built another fire and cooked some more coffee. To go with it he fried half a dozen strips of bacon that he ate with the last of the stale biscuits. After cleaning and re-packing the gear, he took time to change the dressing and apply some doctor-provided medical salve to his leg wound. It didn't show any signs of fresh bleeding or inflammation, nor was the pain particularly bothersome, so he figured the healing was coming along satisfactorily.

Once Ironsides was saddled, Lone was on the trail again. He had his destination now settled firmly in mind. Came down to it, there really was never much doubt where he'd head for. The same place he and Velda had been on the way to when they made their fateful stop in Carverton. The closest thing Lone had to calling a home since his days at Fort McPherson— where he always seemed to gravitate back to in between his wanderings.

North Platte, Nebraska, originally established as a rail head on the UP's westward-expanding main line, had quickly grown into a center for cattle ranching and then, in recent years, had continued to grow to include an increasing variety of other businesses and industries. Located in the heart of the Great Platte River Road, at the confluence of the Platte's north and south tributaries, it was only a short distance west of Fort McPherson. This resulted in a number of soldiers from the fort settling in the nearby community after their service was done. Among these was a gruff old sergeant named Sharples and his wife Adeline. A childless couple, the Sharples had played a major part when it came to taking in Lone and helping to raise him during his formative years at the fort. Though he was grateful to all who'd participated in caring for him, the Sharples stood out as his favorite; especially the tender, caring wife.

Years later, when he was cutting a wide swath across the frontier as a civilian scout for varying outposts, he heard how Mrs. Sharples, now widowed and generally referred to by most everyone as "Ma Sharples," was still living in North Platte and running a popular boarding house there.

First chance he got, Lone made it a point to swing by and say hi. The old feelings of fondness and familiarity were instantly there again, for both of them, and ever since Lone had been returning to North Platte to visit Ma between his bouts of wandering.

He'd been anxious for her and Velda to meet one another. He was confident they would have hit it off. Now, unfortunately, that could never be confirmed for certain, but he still held fast to the belief. He had of course told Velda all about Ma. As it turned out, he would have to settle for doing the same in reverse— merely *telling* Ma about Velda. He only hoped he could successfully convey the specialness of her, some measure of all the things that had captured his heart.

In recent years, Ma had grown steadily pushier about encouraging Lone to find a good woman and settle down. Recalling this brought a wry smile to his lips. Whatever shape his and Velda's life together might have taken, he highly doubted most people would have termed it "settling down." Whether they would have continued jointly in her bounty hunting pursuits or gone on with his wandering between adventures they had never really defined themselves. Just as the word "marriage" had never specifically been spoken. All they'd really determined was that they intended to be together for whatever came next.

But what came next was tragedy. Leaving Lone on his own once again. Lone...alone. He'd never really minded that as a destiny before. He'd accepted it, even embraced it to a degree. Only now it was different. Such a notion felt empty, unfulfilled.

In Ma, he knew he would find solace. He didn't want to impose on her, yet at the same time he knew she would not view it that way and would in fact chide him if he *didn't* seek her out under such circumstances.

Ma would help him find his bearings once again.

Little did Lone know, however, how many twists and turns the course would take before that could happen.

CHAPTER SIX

LONE ARRIVED IN NORTH PLATTE THREE DAYS LATER, JUST as dusk was settling. He'd pushed Ironsides steady, but not overly hard. After the first day out of Beddoe Springs he'd stopped to re-stock his trail supplies and had gotten back to eating better and more regularly. Staples of bacon, beans, and coffee, augmented by some canned fruit and a fresh batch of pan biscuits. Lone was a good trail cook when he took the time, but that didn't mean he wasn't looking forward to some hearty helpings of Ma's superior fare. And a soft pillow to lay his head on for a change.

These things were very much on his mind when he reined Ironsides to a halt in front of Ma's boarding house. The ride through town hadn't revealed much in the way of change since he'd last been there eight months earlier. But he was about to find out that initial assessment wasn't quite accurate.

The first indicators of this came after he'd dismounted, tied off Ironsides, and started up the walk to Ma's front door. Lying in a patch of grass off to one side of the walk, he noted a large metal ring or hoop, such as kids rolled about and played with. In its center was a large, lumpy, leather-encased round ball. On the other side of the walk sat a wooden hobby horse with a realistic-looking saddle attached to its back.

Lone frowned. He'd never known Ma to board out rooms to anyone with children before. He continued up the walk for a couple more steps before coming to an abrupt stop at the next thing he noticed. Missing from the front porch railing where it had been attached for all of the years Lone had been coming here was the neatly engraved wooden sign that read: SHARPLES' BOARDING HOUSE.

Lone looked around, feeling an eerie sensation run through him. What the hell was going on? Had he somehow mistakenly stopped at the wrong house? But no, this was the right place, damn it; the same walk he'd walked up a hundred times before, the same front porch and front door. Only...

Muttering an oath under his breath, Lone proceeded on in long strides. Up the front steps, across the porch width, to the familiar oak door. After rapping his knuckles on the heavy wood, he heard voices speaking inside. Nothing unusual there—except some of them definitely sounded like children.

The door opened and a man he had never seen before stood there. Middle-aged, stocky build, well barbered, wearing a white shirt with black suspenders, holding a dinner napkin in one hand.

"Yes? Can I help you?"

After a bewildered pause, Lone said, "I'm here to see Ma. Ma Sharples. I'm an old friend."

The man in the doorway blinked. "You must have

been out of touch for a while. I'm afraid Mrs. Sharples no longer lives here."

A sudden fear gripped Lone. He fought an urge to grab the strange man by the shirtfront. "You don't mean...?"

"Oh no. Nothing ill has befallen her," the man said quickly. "All I know is that she gave up the boarding house for some reason. I moved to town a short time after—along with my wife and five children—and we bought the property from the bank. With a family as large as ours, the size of the house was very appealing."

"Is she still in town?"

"As far as I know. I believe I heard she's staying at one of the hotels. But I don't know which one."

Lone stood silently, feeling somewhat stunned. All of this felt unreal. It seemed impossible that Ma would give up her precious boarding house, the rambling home she had shared with the old sarge before he passed. It was hard to imagine what would cause her to do such a thing.

The man in the doorway's forehead puckered. "Is there anything more I can help you with, Mr....? If not, I, ah, would like to return to supper with my family."

Lone shook his head. "No. No, I won't take up any more of your time. Thanks for the information."

Lone returned to the hitch rail and climbed back into Ironsides' saddle. His head was still reeling from what he'd just heard. He had to find out some answers, find out where Ma was staying and get the straight of things directly from her. In order to locate her and maybe find out a little more of the background on what had happened, he had a number of acquaintances in town he figured he could count on for that. His first choice, though, was Elmer Dalrymple, the marshal of North Platte. He and the marshal had developed a grudging respect for one another over the years, and thereby a friendship of sorts. Elmer, also a friend of Ma's, would have a handle on things and would level with Lone on what he knew.

Trouble was, when Lone swung by the building that housed the marshal's office and jail, no one was present. Considering the time, Lone figured Elmer was either home having supper or maybe out on patrol with one or more of his deputies. It was a weeknight, but North Platte was busy enough these days so that there was always enough local cowboys or drifters in town to pack the various saloons and present the potential for some form of rowdiness to break out.

Speaking of saloons, Lone's next choice for getting the scoop on things—unless he first happened to run into Dalrymple making rounds—was to visit the Ace High and have a chat with the bartender there, Art Watkins. Art had pushed many a foamy mug in front of Lone over the years and had a way of knowing all the talk around town that was worth knowing.

Having no luck spotting the marshal anywhere, Lone left Ironsides at the hitch rail out front of the Ace High and got ready to go in. From the sound of things, there was a fair-sized crowd on the other side of the batwings, having themselves a pretty good time. He climbed the three front steps and had just stepped onto the strip of boardwalk they accessed when the batwings flapped open wide and three obviously drunk cowboys came barging out. Lone shifted to one side to allow their exit. Once they were past, he proceeded to head on through the doorway.

Suddenly, behind him now, one of the cowboys whooped out a loud curse followed instantly by the ragged clattering of bootheels on wood. Lone wheeled around in time to see that one of the drunken trio had stumbled going down the steps and was staggering out of control, pitching forward and windmilling his arms wildly in an attempt to keep his balance. His efforts held him upright, just barely, but as he came off the bottom step he lurched hard to his left and fell heavily against the front shoulder of Ironsides, who was tied at the end of the hitch rail only a few feet from the steps.

The big gray, weary and somewhat irritable after a long day on the trail to begin with, was spooked by the unexpected jostling. In response, he rammed back with his muscular shoulder and at the same time swung his head around to take a hard nip at his tormentor. The cowboy, partly knocked back by the shoulder bump and simultaneously jerking away on his own accord from the gnashing teeth, once again fought to keep his balance. This time he lost. He ended up landing on his backside with a chunk of his shirt and some of the meat off his left triceps torn away by Ironsides' bite.

His two companions found all of this highly amusing and immediately broke into loud guffaws at his misfortune. But the stumbling cowboy himself, now sprawled in the dust, clearly did not see one damn thing funny about any of it.

He clambered angrily to his feet, face aflame with rage and embarrassment. First he royally cussed out his two pals for finding amusement in his predicament. Then he turned his ire fully on Ironsides. "You sonofabitch no-good hayburner! You ain't about to get away with takin' a chunk out of me and knockin' me on my ass," he declared. His right hand, trembling with anger, pawed at the six-gun holstered at his side. "I'm gonna blow them damn yellow choppers plumb out of your head and scatter 'em down the street like kernels of rotted corn!"

"You draw that smoke wagon and point it at my horse, you drunken bastard, the only thing'll get splattered out on the street is what passes for brains from between your ears."

This statement, made by Lone from where he stood facing out in front of the Ace High's batwings, rang loud and clear. The three cowpokes snapped their heads around to take notice of him for the first time. They saw the way he was poised and ready, like a coiled steel spring, a hard gaze returning their own gawking looks, his right hand hovering steady over the Colt holstered low on his hip, keeper thong already thumbed loose.

The woe befallen hombre at the heart of the situation—a moderate-sized number with a thatch of carrot-colored hair, wide set eyes under furry pale brows, and a small, puckered mouth above a jutting chin—was still drunk enough and mad enough not to be intimidated by the sight of this big, hard-looking stranger. Thrusting out his chin even more, he challenged, "Just who the hell are you supposed to be?"

"Made it plain once. But I'll say it again," Lone answered. "That big gray belongs to me. Your misfortune is your own fault, not his. I ain't about to stand by and see him mistreated over it."

"*Him* mistreated?" exploded Carrot Top. "What about me? What about this chewed-up arm and the way he knocked me down? That nag has gone loco, turned rogue. Everybody knows when a horse goes that route, the only thing for it is to put an end to 'em before they hurt somebody worse."

"That's a crock of shit, and you know it," Lone snapped back. "The gray only reacted the way he did because you slammed drunkenly into him. You're lucky he didn't switch around and club you with a hind foot."

"That might be the way you see it, but not me," Carrot Top insisted. "That wrong-headed nag needs to pay, and I aim to see he does!"

"Be a big mistake if you try," Lone warned icily. "And if you do, I guarantee it'll be the last one you ever make."

"Now hold on a minute," piped up one of Carrot Top's companions from where they stood a few feet off the other end of the saloon steps. He was a short, stocky specimen with sun-squinted eyes and a brooding countenance under a high-crowned, wide-brimmed hat that made his overall appearance look almost top heavy. Beside him, the third member of the trio was a somewhat portly Mexican with a round, fleshy face split by a drooping black mustache and capped by his own wide-brimmed, ornately decorated sombrero.

"Might be me and Gomez here had a couple laughs at the expense of our pal Dewey," the stocky one continued. "But make no mistake, stranger, we're still pards who ride for the same brand. So if you're pickin' a fight with one of us—'specially if you're threatenin' to throw lead—then you better be prepared to take on all three."

Lone was vaguely aware that the sounds from inside the Ace High had quieted down considerably, replaced by the scuffle of feet and a low murmur of voices as a crowd squeezed into the doorway behind him. But, sensing the heightened tension out on the boardwalk and the street beyond, no one pressed any farther. What Lone was more sharply aware of, though, was the icy, gnawing sensation building quickly in his gut. The hungry beast of rage that had been prowling in him ever since Velda's death—somewhat quelled by his recent bewilderment and new concerns over the situation with Ma, yet certainly never tamed—remained all too ready, anxious even, to break free. And it didn't take very much imagination for the rage in him to blur the image of these three drunken cowboys into that of the similar drunken pair directly responsible for killing his beloved. The beast howled louder than ever, its icy breath now swelling up into Lone's chest and threatening to push past all his restraint. He trembled with the urge to want to kill.

Responding to the words of the stocky hombre in the oversized hat, Lone rasped, "Okay. You had your say, now hear mine: You want in on this, you get the same guarantee I gave your pard."

The expressions on the faces of the three cowboys pulled tight and their torsos took on a rigid readiness. They shifted around so that all were facing Lone full on, menace gleaming in their narrowed eyes. Lone's fingers began to curl around the grips of his Colt...

That's when, from just a short distance down the street, a shotgun blast roared suddenly and tore attention away from everything else. Immediately following the booming report, a sharp, commanding voice called out: "Hackles down everybody! I mean *now*! Anybody tries to clear leather, he gets the next barrel all to himself."

CHAPTER SEVEN

SLOWLY, CAUTIOUSLY, STILL KEEPING THE THREE COWBOYS within the sweep of his eyes, Lone willed himself to relax some. The beast inside him eased off as well, retreating somewhere deeper down. For now.

The commanding voice that had called out was familiar to Lone. Unexpected perhaps, but nonetheless familiar. And reassuring because it belonged to one of the few men Lone had a measure of trust in.

As Lone and the cowboys stood waiting, the owner of the commanding voice strode into Lone's peripheral vision. Another man moved up close behind him. Both were brandishing double-barreled shotguns and on the chest of each a lawman's star glinted faintly in the rapidly deepening gloom of evening.

The front man, Chief Deputy Keith Overstreet, spoke again in his distinct voice. "Alright," he said, sweeping his blaster in a level arc. "All of you shuck your gun belts. Don't make me tell you twice. Then stand nice and still with your hands held out in plain sight."

Lone balked at the order, no matter who it was coming from. He hesitated until he saw for certain that the cowpokes were obeying, then grudgingly unbuckled his gear and let it slip to the ground. He aimed a glare at Overstreet to send the message he didn't much care for the treatment.

The deputy pointedly ignored him and instead cut his attention momentarily to the saloon doorway. "Art," he said, addressing the barkeep who was among the onlookers packed together on the other side of the batwings, "fetch a couple lanterns, will you? Then keep everybody else inside. Me and Tully got a job to do out here. All they need to worry about is getting back to their drinking."

A moment later Art emerged with a pair of glowing lanterns, one in each meaty paw. Overstreet stepped up to take one, Art hung on to the other.

"You see the start of whatever was taking place out here?" Overstreet asked.

Art shook his head. "Nope. None of us inside were aware of anything until it was already underway."

The lawman turned back around, splashed now in improved illumination. He was tall and lanky of build, crowding the thirty-year mark, sandy-haired with a handsome face, also slightly jut-jawed. Lone had seen all of this plenty of times before. But what he spotted now that was different gave him his next big surprise since returning to town. The star on Overstreet's chest was no longer that of a deputy—it was the badge of a full marshal. What the hell did that mean for Elmer Dalrymple? What had become of him? Lone wanted to immediately blurt out these questions only realized that now was hardly the right time. This matter with the three drunken damn fools had to be settled first.

Toward that end, Overstreet—now *Marshal* Overstreet—swept his gaze over the lot of them, including Lone, and said, "Okay. One of you merrymakers want to spit out an explanation for what me and Tully saw coming down the street—how you were squaring off to start throwing lead at one another?"

His gaze lingered somewhat on Lone, but it was red-haired Dewey who jumped on being the first to give his version of an answer. "It was all on account of him," he declared, jabbing a finger in Lone's direction. "Him and that loco damn horse of his!"

"You mean this gray here...Ironsides?" the marshal said.

Dewey scowled. "Wait a minute. You know that animal?"

"Familiar with him, yeah. Also know the fella he belongs to," Overstreet replied. "Can't necessarily say the same for McGantry, but I've never known Ironsides to act loco before. And he appears to be standing there mighty gentle right at the moment."

"Gentle? You call this gentle?" Dewey wailed, holding out his injured, still bleeding arm for the marshal to take a good look at. "See what that crazy nag did to me? Bit out a chunk near big as a fist. Then the sonofabitch knocked me down and tried to stomp me!"

"That's right, Marshal. Me and Gomez saw the whole thing," spoke up the stocky hombre in the big hat. "The three of us left the saloon together. Dewey came down the steps on the end near where that gray is hitched and, for no reason at all, the crazy critter went after him. Bit him, rammed him, knocked him down. Just like he said."

"*Si.* I saw same as Ralph," added Gomez.

"So what turned it into near gunplay?" Overstreet wanted to know.

Dewey cast a sullen look at Lone, then back to the marshal. "Naturally I got hot over bein' attacked like I was. I think that's understandable. Everybody knows when a horse turns mean and unpredictable that way, the only right thing is to put 'em down before they do worse hurt. So that's what I was fixin' to do, and I figure I had every right."

Overstreet's gaze settled on Lone. "Let me guess. You didn't see things quite the same. Right?"

Lone gave a faint nod. "Saw 'em a whole lot different." He paused a beat, then went on. "The three of 'em came out of the saloon together, like they said. All plenty liquored up. The red haired one—Dewey, I guess his name is—staggered goin' down the steps and fell hard over against Ironsides. Startled the horse. So, on instinct, he bumped back and swung his head around to take a bite at what was flailin' against him. Dewey ended up on his ass in the dirt. His pals even had a good laugh over it at first. But back on his feet, Dewey decided to try and take out his own drunken clumsiness on the horse. Should come as no surprise that I didn't look favorably on what he had in mind."

"No, I don't suppose you would," Overstreet allowed.

"Now hold on here, Marshal. Just because this fella is some kind of half-assed old friend or some such," protested Dewey, "you ain't gonna take his word over all of ours, are you?"

"Back off, bub. I ain't said I'm taking anybody's word

about anything," Overstreet growled. "But the idea of shooting another man's horse, no matter how much justification you figured you had, damn sure wouldn't have set well with me. I'll tell you that."

But Dewey wouldn't let up. "I only threatened a stupid damn hayburner. What about him? He's the one who said he was gonna splatter my brains all over the street!"

"I said what *passes* for brains," Lone corrected dryly.

"See? See how he is?" Dewey demanded. "He's the one who caused things to build to a face-off. First he threatened me, then both of my friends. What choice did we have but to stand ready to defend ourselves?"

"Same as I had when it came to defendin' my horse," Lone grated.

Overstreet held up a hand, palm out. "Enough. I've heard enough," he said. Before continuing, he raked a hard gaze over the four men he was addressing. "Because there were no shots fired or no damage done —except to you, Dewey—I'm gonna keep this simple. You're all charged with disturbing the peace. Dewey, the fine for you, Ralph, and Gomez is splitting whatever cost you incur for seeing a doctor about that bite. Then I suggest the three of you hightail it back to the Double B and get ready for waking up to morning chores with sorry-ass hangovers."

"What about him?" asked the one called Ralph, tipping his head toward Lone.

"He'll get a night in the pokey. And I'll take his horse into custody for observation."

Dewey frowned. "What's that supposed to mean?"

"I said it plain enough. McGantry stays as my guest for a while, you boys do your doctoring then get on back to the ranch. That'll keep you apart, give you all a chance to cool down. Far as the horse, I'll see to it he's kept an eye on, watched close for how he acts. He causes any more trouble, I may have to take action. He behaves, I'll chalk it up as a one-time thing. If McGantry sticks to habit, him and Ironsides will be moving on again before long anyway."

Dewey's frown pulled into a pout. "I ain't so sure that's an altogether square deal, Marshal. The damn horse—him bein' the only one who actually did any harm—gets off scot-free. That don't seem right."

Overstreet said, "If he's turned loco and mean, like you claim, then it ought to show up again soon enough. It does, he won't be treated easy."

But Dewey still looked pouty and unsatisfied. Until Ralph stepped close and put a hand on his shoulder, saying, "I think it's the best deal we're gonna get, Dew. And not too bad a one at that. I think we oughta see to that arm of yours then head on back to the bunkhouse."

"*Si*," Gomez agreed.

"That's good advice from your pards. Smart to listen to 'em," recommended the marshal. Then, addressing his deputy, he said, "Jeff, you tag along with these boys and make sure they stay on track. Let 'em fetch their horses from wherever they got 'em hitched. I want their gun belts stuffed in their saddlebags and kept there until they're finished with the doc and you've seen them out past the city limits."

"Got it," Deputy Jeff Tully replied with a nod. Then, to the three cowboys, "You heard the man. Let's get a move on."

Silent but still sullen-looking, his head hung chin on chest, Dewey shuffled off between his two pards. Tully followed a few paces behind, shotgun cradled in the crook of one arm.

After they were gone, Overstreet turned slowly and locked a flat gaze on Lone. "You and me got business over at the jailhouse, mister."

Lone eyed him back. "Suits me."

A long beat passed and then suddenly both of their mouths were stretching into wide grins. The marshal wagged his head in a forlorn way and groaned, "Jesus Christ, man, can't you ever just show up for a nice, peaceful visit and not immediately find your way into the middle of some kind of trouble?"

"Hey, at least this time I didn't bring it with me," Lone countered. "But a few of your citizens sure didn't waste any time providin' me some."

"Yeah, I noticed. Glad I did, before it got any farther out of hand."

"I suppose." Lone scowled. "But after all the changes I been runnin' into ever since I hit town, at least me bein' in a spot of trouble was something *not* out of place."

"Guess that's one way of looking at it. And yeah, I can see where you've got some things to catch up on," said Overstreet. "Reckon a fat-chewing session to take care of that gives us another reason to head over to the jailhouse. Come on. Pick up your gun belt, and also bring along that ferocious, man stomping, carnivorous gray stallion of yours."

CHAPTER EIGHT

Lone had been in the marshal's office at the front of the North Platte jail many times before. Far as he could see, it hadn't changed much—except, of course, for the person now sitting behind the desk with the marshal's star pinned on him.

"So ol' Elmer went and retired. I'll be dogged," Lone said, recapping the first of the updates he'd been provided so far.

"Yup. Left out just over a month ago," Overstreet confirmed. "I guess I'd seen it coming for a while. He still liked the basic work—dealing direct with folks, even the troublemakers—same as always. But the way the town has been growing and the city council and other interests along with it, meaning the demand for more rules and policies, some of them petty and just plain silly, not to mention the increased paperwork that came along with 'em...well, that was what Elmer got increasingly fed up with.

"The final straw, though, was when he got bad sick last winter. Doc had a fancy word for it, amounted to half-assed pneumonia. Elmer never really fully recovered. So, with his wife Mavis gone near two years now and the rest of his kin all back down in the Carolinas, where he originally hailed from, he decided to make the move. Said he was done with 'damn Nebraska winters', quote unquote, and was ready to finish out his days with a fishin' pole in his hand and the warm sun on the back of his neck all year round."

Lone lifted his brows. "If that's what he wants, reckon he earned it."

"You bet. He served this town well for a lot of years. Was a damn good husband and father, too. I think that was the hardest thing for him—leaving behind the graves here of Mavis and their daughter Marie. He went out to the cemetery regular-like to visit them."

"Yeah, I knew that," Lone responded somewhat huskily.

The mention of graves and lost loved ones hit him with a fresh pang of sadness. And the underlying bitterness that came with it. But that was too personal of a thing—and perhaps somewhat selfish in the moment—to get into now.

Upon arriving at the office Overstreet had heated up a pot of leftover coffee and poured a cup for both Lone and himself. Draining his, he stood up behind the desk and said, "Ready for some more?"

From where he sat in a straight-backed wooden chair hitched up in front of the desk, Lone sloshed the cup he held resting on one knee, indicating it still had some in it. "No, I'm good."

At the stove, pouring himself a refill, Overstreet said, "Suppose you're wondering why, with all the annoyances I mentioned, I went ahead and took the marshal's job?"

Lone shrugged. "Not really. Hardly any work comes without some amount of annoyance. Bein' a lawman is what you know, what you're good at. Seems logical you'd want to stick with it."

"Even more so now that I've taken on added obligation," Overstreet said, sitting back down.

Lone looked at him questioningly.

"Here's another change for you. You see, I've gone and got myself hitched."

Lone rocked back in his chair. "Holy jumpin'... I'm beginnin' to feel like I was gone for eight years instead of just that many months. Tarnation! Who's the gal— that little blonde you been moonin' over for so long, the one who used to clerk at Deckerman's store?"

"One and the same," Overstreet confirmed. "Mary-Lou, her name is. She's still clerkin' at the store for now. Will be until some additions to our family start turnin' up. We only tied the knot a few weeks ago. Elmer was my best man before he left."

"Sounds like congratulations are in order," Lone declared. Then, "Well, for you anyway. Lord knows what that poor girl has gotten herself into."

Overstreet gave a little laugh before replying, "At least she's over her reservations about marrying a lawman. That's what kept her from saying yes sooner."

"Bein' a lawman comes with risk sure enough. Just as sure that bein' married to one can weigh heavy on a woman. Speaks well for your MaryLou and how she must feel about you that she's willin' to sign on for it," said Lone. "So now part of your job is seein' to it you don't make her a widow."

"I'm all for that. It's one of the reasons me and Tully have got in the habit of packin' a pair of those"—the marshal jabbed a thumb to indicate the shotgun he'd been carrying earlier, now leaning over against the side of a gun rack—"when we make our night rounds. I discovered that just the sight of those shiny twin barrels squeezed tight together has a mighty powerful calming-down effect on even the tensest situation. Tonight's the first time I've had to actually fire a round so far this year. Some of our town fathers think carrying 'em the way we do is unnecessarily showy. But it ain't their asses on the line."

"To hell with them. You just keep rememberin' it's yours," Lone told him. He took a drink of his coffee. "As far as what happened tonight, you figure those three cowpokes got the message clear enough so's they won't come back around to try and make any more trouble?"

"Nah, they'll be okay. Probably on their way back to the ranch by now. Once there, come morning old man Barstow will spot they're hung over and will work 'em double hard to sweat any more foolishness out of their heads. Leastways for a while."

Lone took another drink of coffee. "Now, you really figurin' on keepin' me here tonight?"

Overstreet looked at him. "What do you think?"

"It's what you told the cowpokes. Others heard it, too."

"Anybody who listened close—and I made sure to choose my words carefully—heard me say 'He'll get a night in the pokey'. A little later I said you'd be my guest for a while.

"Well, I reckon this jawing session covers the guest part plenty good enough. Comes to a night in the pokey,

I never said exactly where or when. Don't have to be here and now. And it won't be a lie because I figure, sooner or later, somewhere or other, some duty-bound law dog is sure to have reason for throwing your naturally trouble making ass in the clink for a spell."

"Wouldn't be the first time," Lone grunted.

"So it's settled then," said Overstreet. "And before you ask, I've completed my observation of Ironsides and determined he's fine. I never believed for a minute any of that hogwash Dewey was spewing. It was clear he'd brought the bite and everything on himself, the way you told it."

"I appreciate all of that, Keith," Lone said measuredly. "But I don't want you to stick your neck out on account of our friendship and end up gettin' in a jam over it."

"You let me worry about that. My job is keepin' the peace in this town, and that's what I'm doin'."

Lone finished his coffee, reached forward and placed the empty cup on the front edge of the marshal's desk. Leaning back, he fixed a very direct gaze on Overstreet and said, "You probably can guess that I ran across another big change that I'd like to know some background on before I go visit a certain person."

The marshal leaned back in his own chair and heaved a sigh. "The situation with Ma Sharples."

"That'd be it. What the devil caused her to give up her boardin' house?"

Overstreet's mouth twisted wryly. "Interesting choice of words. 'What the devil'... It was more a case of *who* the devil. And I'm pretty sure Ma would have no argument with stating it that way."

"No offense, pal," Lone said, not fighting too hard to

keep the impatient tone out of his voice, "but I ain't hardly in no mood for riddles."

"Understandable." Overstreet leaned forward and put his elbows on the desktop. "Look, I can give you the bare bones. What I know, not any of the guesswork or speculation that's flapping on some tongues. I'll leave the details up to Ma. As close as you and her are, I expect she'll level with you more than anybody."

"Tell me what you can."

Overstreet expelled another sigh. "Okay. Last winter a fella showed up in town. Swain, Jack Swain, he called himself. A slick, smooth-talking sonofagun with big plans. An *entrepreneur*. Claimed he was fixing to settle in North Platte and really make his mark. Said he had money backers in Chicago ready to invest in whatever he recommended once he'd had a chance to look things over and get the lay of the land. Some folks were impressed by him, some weren't. All hat and no cattle was what a lot of us took him for.

"But there was one person who was spellbound by this Swain character practically from the get-go. When he needed a place to stay, Ma had a room available. That was the start of things going off kilter. In no time at all it became clear that Swain was charming her flat off her feet. They got so openly chummy that questions started being raised by some of the nastier minds around town about what might be going on after the boarding house lights got turned down at night."

Lone balled his fists and muttered a curse.

"In the meantime," Overstreet continued, "Swain appeared to be going on with his big plans. He visited with different banks, several established businessmen... 'Weighing opportunities' was the term he threw around.

What it seemed to boil down to was that he had a notion to put up a grand hotel, something to rival the finest ones in Denver or Omaha, an attraction to rail travelers and something to bring attention and more growth to our whole town. Somewhere along the way— and here's where she's gonna have to fill you in more— he convinced Ma to throw in with him, to 'invest' in his scheme. And, as it turned out, she went whole hog."

Overstreet paused, his expression turning pained.

"Go ahead. Cut to it," Lone said.

His voice tighter now, the marshal went ahead and told the rest. "So came the day when Swain went up town like he did most mornings, scouting and 'weighing', generally looking around. Gonna exchange some telegrams with his other backers in Chicago, he told Ma. But what he did instead was catch the ten A.M. westbound and leave town never to be seen again...*after*, that is, he cashed out all the money from Ma's bank account and sold the mortgage to her boarding house property."

"How the hell is that possible?" Lone growled. "What were the idiots at the bank thinkin'?"

Overstreet spread his hands. "According to Jeffers, the bank president, it was, quote, 'rather unusual', but all perfectly legal on account of a bunch of paperwork Ma and Swain had come in together and signed a couple weeks earlier. It gave Swain full access to any and all of her holdings.

"Why the heck Ma ever agreed to anything like that is something maybe she'll tell you. She ain't speaking much to anybody else since it all crashed down around her. She's staying at the Sinclair Hotel, hardly ever ventures out. My MaryLou has gone to visit her a few times—you know, to check and make sure she's okay.

But, like I said, Ma don't have much to say. A body can only imagine how distraught and humiliated she must feel."

"What about that bastard Swain?" Lone wanted to know. "What became of him?"

Overstreet grunted. "That's a good question. So far he's disappeared like a puff of smoke. I did some checking but wasn't able to determine much. The train ticket he bought was for Cheyenne. No sign of him actually going that far, though. Appears he got off somewhere sooner, only nobody took any notice of where or when."

Lone stood up. "Damn it all! What a mess for poor Ma. I'm gonna have to—"

He never got to finish, interrupted by a sudden commotion out in the street. First came the distant boom of a shotgun blast followed by shouting voices and the rapidly approaching clatter of horses' hooves. Overstreet also rose up and started around the end of the desk, reaching for his shotgun. He was jerked to a momentary halt by the bark of a closer gunshot and the crash of a bullet hitting the wall outside.

The marshal broke back into motion, snatching up the twin-barreled blaster and then promptly blowing out the lantern he'd lighted earlier when he and Lone first got to the office. As the room was plunged into deep shadows, he called to Lone, "I'll move up on the right side of the door, you take the left. Stay clear of that window!"

The two men converged on the office's front door, Overstreet brandishing the shotgun while Lone fisted his drawn Colt. Outside, the clamor increased. There was another shotgun blast, closer this time, with

Deputy Tully's voice hollering along with it: "He's coming for the horse! Watch out, he's crazy!" Immediately following that were two more pistol shots in rapid succession.

"Ironsides!" Lone hissed, grabbing for the door knob.

"No! Don't be so quick to—" Overstreet tried to stop him but it was a futile effort.

Lone yanked open the door and rushed out in a half crouch. Tully's shouted warning had given Lone a rough idea what to expect and all of a sudden it was right there in front of him. Some pole lamps had been lighted at sporadic intervals up and down the street, providing adequate visibility in the not quite full dark.

What Lone saw—with a quick, sharp-eyed sweep— was Deputy Tully approaching at a dead run, waving his spent shotgun wildly, but still more than a block away. Much closer, a horseman on a black gelding was coming at a hard gallop. It was Dewey Tibbs, the red-haired cowboy. His hat had blown off, his hair was streaming back, and he was wielding a six-gun.

At the sight of Lone, he hollered, "No goddamned nag is gonna make a fool out of me and get away with it!"

He was close enough then to start checking down the gelding. As he did, he extended his gun arm and began taking renewed, more careful aim at Ironsides, who was tied to the hitch rail out front of the jail. The big gray, spooked by the previous shots that had hammered close (one of them having creased a bullet burn across his rump, it would later be discovered), was straining and pawing frantically in an attempt to pull free.

Lone didn't hesitate. He dropped to one knee, raised and extended his own gun arm, cocking and aiming the Colt all in a single smooth motion. His finger stroked the trigger and his Colt's voice joined those of the two other guns that had already spoken within the past minute.

The .44 slug struck true, before Dewey was able to get another shot off. A splash of scarlet spurted outward in the middle of the red-haired hothead's chest. He flung his arms wide and somersaulted backward out of his saddle. His six-gun went spinning off into the shadows as the gelding, finding himself suddenly unencumbered by bothersome rider, galloped aimlessly away.

CHAPTER NINE

It was late by the time Lone finally made it to Ma's hotel room. She was waiting, expecting him after hearing about the shooting in front of the jail and his name connected to it.

Once they'd exchanged warm embraces and cheek kisses, she ushered him into one of two thinly padded chairs. He sat, placing his saddlebags on the floor beside him, leaning his Winchester Yellowboy against the wall. Ma settled in the other. She was a short woman grown somewhat stout in these later years, with iron gray hair and a mildly lined face. Lone quickly noted, however, that the lines appeared set deeper than he remembered from the last time he'd seen her, and the spark that was always present in her bright dark eyes was definitely somewhat dulled.

But it quickly became clear they hadn't lost any of their ability for sharp observation when Ma said, "Way I heard, you weren't injured in that gunplay earlier. Yet I notice you stepping with a slight limp. What's that all about?"

Lone's hand involuntarily touched his thigh where the pitchfork wound had healed to the point he hardly thought about it. "Old mishap from a while back," he replied to Ma's inquiry. "I didn't know it affected my walk any."

"It does. But then, considering all you've put your body and limbs through in your wanderings, it's a surprise you ain't walking with crutches or at least a cane. And that'd be from just the damage I know about. Was you to strip down for an examination, I bet your hide has more scars and creases than a little kid's picture puzzle."

Lone cocked an eyebrow. "Might be. But you seein' me stripped down ain't gonna happen, so no need to worry about it."

Ma chuffed. "Like I never have. Seen you stripped down, that is. Remember I saw you buck naked, you scamp, clear back when you was no bigger'n a loaf of bread."

Lone liked seeing a faint, though brief smile curve her mouth. From what Overstreet had told him, it was pretty certain Ma hadn't been doing much smiling lately. Unfortunately, lightening her mood—except maybe by offering some hope—wasn't his main purpose for being here.

"Speakin' of my wanderings, Ma," he said, his voice turning earnest, "I'm awful sorry I've been gone so long this last time and wasn't here when...well, when you maybe could've used havin' me around."

Her eyes immediately dropped and her expression took on an added sadness that was the last thing he wanted to cause. She was quiet for a long beat. Then her face lifted again and she spoke, in a low tone at first but gradually picking up intensity.

"I never welcome your long absences, and always like having you around. You know that. But in this case I...I don't know that it would have made much difference. You must have heard the basics of what happened. I fell under such a—a spell, is the only way I can say it. Like some silly, starry-eyed schoolgirl. God, I can't believe it about myself, Lone. At my age! Talk about no fool like an old fool. That snake Jack Swain charmed me and bespelled me so quickly and so thoroughly that, even if you'd been here, I don't know if you could have talked any sense into me."

"Well, there's no way of knowin' that now," Lone said. "But what I do know—and you darn well do, too—is that continuin' to beat yourself up over it won't do any good. Not for you, not toward fixin' the situation."

"I feel so ashamed for being such a fool."

"Anybody can get took in by a slick tongue," Lone told her. "You ain't the first, won't be the last. What matters is what you do next. I say quit feelin' ashamed and start feelin' mad. Good and pissed off. That's what I'd expect from the tough old gal I thought I knew."

Ma bridled, this time the reaction he was aiming for. "Why? What good would it do? I've still lost everything. No, worse, I *gave* it away. And, worst of all, that even included the money you've sent me to hang on to for you."

Over the years, in the course of his roaming ways, Lone had from time to time acquired amounts of money —payment for services, sometimes rewards, and so forth—which he intermittently forwarded to Ma for safe keeping. Money wasn't such a big deal given the drifting life he led out in the big wide open, under the sun and stars; and allowing the wrong type a glimpse or suspicion of it could even prove dangerous.

"That money was always yours to use if you ever needed it," he reminded Ma, though hearing of its loss didn't come without a sting.

"But I didn't use it in any way you meant I could or should. I placed it, along with rest, right in the hands of that snake Jack Swain and now he's gone somewhere in the wind with it."

"No," Lone grated. "He's *not* in the wind. He ain't no spirit or puff of smoke. No devil nor snake, neither. He's a human man. That means he leaves tracks, some kind of sign wherever he's been. That's what I do, remember? I'm an ex scout, a tracker. I mean to run the sonofabitch down."

Ma's brow puckered. "But, again, I say what good will it do? According to banker Jeffers and the marshal he didn't break any laws. The money he took and the deal he made selling the boarding house were all *rights* I allowed by means of the joint paperwork I stupidly signed with him."

"How came you to do that anyway?"

Ma made a sour face. "I just told you. Stupidity. Okay, at the time it didn't seem as empty-headed as it sounds now. It came about because his big money backers in Chicago started crawfishing on him over the hotel project he was pitching. Or so he claimed. I doubt now there ever were any backers anywhere. Except me, as it turned out.

"Anyhow, the way him signing jointly in on my hold-ings came about was a result of this story about the backers balking. Because his hotel proposal was shaping up to be so expensive, they wanted more buy-in from him. 'Earnest money' and 'collateral' and terms like that he tossed around. The problem with him meeting those demands on his own, he explained, was that most of his personal money was already tied up in other deals that it would be hard to pull out of."

"But," Lone said, wanting to move things along, "havin' joint access to your holdings would be a quick gain to give him something to meet those demands."

Ma nodded. "That's what it came down to. He never even actually asked. But I saw how it could solve the problem, so I offered. You have to understand, prior to that he'd already convinced me that my boarding house property would be the ideal location for his hotel. So, in a way, I was already sort of in on the deal. Plus...and here's something I've never mentioned to another living soul...Jack had proposed to me, we were discussing marriage. So, since I believed we were going to be joined by matrimony anyhow..."

"I get the picture," Lone said.

Ma regarded him. "I just wanted you to know that part. Hopefully it makes me seem a little less—"

"Don't say it," he cut her off. "Damn it, don't call yourself dumb or stupid again. You're not. This Swain, or whatever his true name turns out to be, is obviously an experienced flim-flam artist, a con man. Not likely you're the first person he's fleeced in some way or other. But, with any luck, we can damn well make you his last."

"You really mean to go after him?"

"You bet I do. What he did may not have broken any tidy little laws, but every right-thinkin' person has got to know it was flat wrong." Lone scowled darkly. "So if him takin' like he did didn't break the law, then neither should me takin' it back from him. Not that that'd stop me anyway. So while I may not be able to regain your boarding house, I still figure I got a chance at grabbin' a chunk of the rest. And, dependin' on how and where I catch up with him, I also plan to see that Swain gets his due, whether it falls inside those tidy legal boundaries or not."

CHAPTER TEN

AFTER LEAVING MA, LONE CHECKED INTO ANOTHER OF the Sinclair's rooms for the night. Once inside, he tossed his saddlebags onto a chair and leaned the Yellowboy against the nightstand beside the bed. Then he kicked off his boots, shrugged out of his buckskin vest, and sprawled out full on top of the bed. Suddenly he felt bone tired, exhausted.

What a hell of a day.

He'd arrived in town packing his own sorrow and grief, planning to tell Ma about Velda, about what might have been between the two of them and to receive some solace from the only source he'd ever seek such. But what he found instead was everything topsy-turvy and the steady, maternal anchor to his life struggling under the weight of her own tragedy.

He'd never even mentioned Velda to her. Now wasn't the time. He'd save it for a point in the future after some other things had been righted and he could present it in and of itself, giving Velda the focus and appreciation that was important to him, that she deserved. When Ma asked where he'd been for so many months following the incident she'd heard about where he had aided Buffalo Bill Cody in his involvement with the Indian Ghost Dance uprising, Lone had merely told her he drifted south for a spell to escape the mean winter.

The part about drifting south was true. What he didn't say was how Velda, who'd also been part of the episode with Buffalo Bill, had gone with him. Re-acquainting during the Ghost Dance matter after abandoning a smoldering mutual attraction in an earlier encounter, they decided to this time explore that attraction. And indeed they had. In hot, remote San Antonio, away from everything and everyone who might be a distraction, they had added to the heat with hours of passionate lovemaking. In between, they sampled various spicy food dishes and a variety of heady beverages. They attended dances and other festivities, and in the cool evening breeze they strolled hand in hand along the riverbank. Many afternoons they would ride out into the desert, away from the village, and find a lonely place where they would make love under the baking sun. By the time they were ready to return north, both were nearly as all-over brown as the locals.

Lying on the hotel bed with these thoughts running through his head, Lone realized that, for the first time, he was *savoring* them instead of replaying them through the filter of bitter loss. He wasn't sure what that meant, but it was certainly a better feeling than the other. He would forever cherish the memory of Velda, the good and special times. As it should be. He didn't want that part to always be tainted by an immediate thought of the gut-wrenching way it all ended. It was important to keep that part separate and, at some point, come to grips with it in a separate way.

Weary as he was physically, Lone's mind continued to grind.

Maybe, he thought, returning to this situation with Ma and striking out after Jack Swain might prove to be the quickest way—not through solace or the aching passage of time, but rather by focusing on a demanding task he'd set for himself—to come to grips with the torment. There was no denying that in the course of this evening's events there'd been stretches where, for the first time in weeks, his sadness over Velda hadn't been foremost in his mind. Not that she'd ever be far from his thoughts, he could never imagine that; but survival for any man who spent as much time in the wild as Lone did meant concentrating on the right thing at the right time.

Lone shifted restlessly on the bed.

His mind continued to churn, turning now to thoughts of Dewey Tibbs, the cowboy he'd shot. He felt no remorse for the killing. Ironsides' life had been on the line, perhaps his own, too, after he exposed himself in the doorway like he did.

The way Deputy Tully told it, he had succeeded without incident in accompanying Dewey and his companions out past the city limits following a stop at the doctor's. With them appearing to be continuing peacefully on their way, he'd turned back to resume conducting the rounds he and the marshal had been in the midst of when interrupted earlier. Tully didn't get far, though, before being interrupted again by the clatter of Dewey tearing back into town. According to subsequent testimony by Ralph and Gomez, the redhead had starting turning crazy mad almost as soon as the deputy was gone from sight. Even though they tried to stop him, he insisted on charging back to get even with the horse who'd knocked him down and made him look foolish. From there it had played out to the bloody finish Lone brought it to. So now Lone had done his killing, the thing the rage inside him had been snarling for ever since Carverton. But, curiously, though the rage beast in his gut seemed quieted, Lone somehow felt the shooting of Dewey had little to do with. The beast's craving wasn't yet sated. It had just gone dormant. Waiting.

Maybe, Lone mused, the beast would be unleashed once again to find what it craved when he caught up with Jack Swain. He finally drifted off to sleep at that thought...lips spread in a wolf's smile.

———

Lone woke ravenously hungry the next morning. He took time to wash up and scrape the whiskers off his face, then went in search of the hotel's dining room. On the way, he stopped and, with some difficulty, coaxed Ma into joining him. It marked one of the rare times she had ventured from her room since taking up residence there. Lone chose to take this as a sign that his presence and appeal to her fighting spirit, along with his intent to go after Swain, might help end her reclusive tendencies for good.

In the dining room, the staff and several other customers greeted Ma warmly and commented how good it was to see her again. Though she reacted some-what stiffly at first, it didn't take long for her to loosen up and begin responding almost as gregariously as her old self.

Lone was ignored during most of these exchanges, which was fine by him. He was busy working his way through the mound of scrambled eggs, bacon, and flapjacks that he'd ordered; all washed down by a tall glass of cold buttermilk and a carafe of coffee. Nonetheless, he noted the pleasantries being enjoyed by Ma and it was good to see.

When Lone's plates were at last emptied and he was down to a final cup of coffee, Marshal Keith Overstreet entered and approached their table.

"Well, good morning, Mrs. Sharples. Glad to see you," he greeted.

Ma smiled. "Good morning to you, Marshal."

"What about me? Don't I rate a good mornin'?" Lone asked.

"No, I'm not sure you do," Overstreet replied. "Not after shooting up the town last night and leaving a dead body in the street and me with a stack of paperwork I still ain't got finished."

"Then you oughta be at your office takin' care of business instead of interruptin' the breakfast of a poor innocent fella who was only defendin' himself and his horse."

"Maybe defending the innocent is what I am doing." Overstreet turned again to Ma. "Mrs. Sharples, I really should warn you about being more careful who you socialize with. This man is a rogue and scoundrel of the first order."

Ma's smile widened. "I'm afraid I already know that, Marshal. What's more—since I partly helped raise the scamp—I guess I'm guilty of being an accessory."

"Well then. This appears more serious than I thought." Overstreet pulled out a chair and sat down. He turned over the clean cup from the placement in front of him and pointed at Lone's carafe. "Anything left in there?"

Lone lifted his eyebrows. "Now *you're* gonna socialize with a scoundrel like me?"

"Got no choice. My line of work rubs you up against the bad as well as the good."

Ma took the carafe and poured some coffee into the marshal's cup. "I'll assume that makes me the 'good', since I admitted my sins?"

"You're plenty good by any standards, ma'am," Overstreet said earnestly. Then, "And don't let the pecking and pawing between me and this McGantry hombre fool you. Even though he tends to stir things up whenever he comes around, I've inherited from my predecessor what's called a grudging respect for him. Though, I gotta admit, I ain't ever tore-up sorry to see him leave when he drifts off again."

Lone chuffed. "Then you oughta be tickled pink to hear I'll be on the drift again practically before you know it."

Overstreet paused with his cup raised part way to his mouth. "How's that?"

"There's my travelin' gear," Lone said, pointing to the table's unoccupied fourth chair that had his Yellowboy leaning against it and his saddlebags hung over its back. "All I have to do is stock up on some supplies and make sure Ironsides ain't hampered by that bullet burn on his rump, then we'll be ready to hit he trail."

"To where?"

"He's going after Jack Swain," Ma stated, a mix of conviction and pride in her tone.

Overstreet said nothing right away. He took a drink of his coffee then lowered the cup, looking thoughtful.

"What's the matter?" Lone wanted to know. "I thought you never got tore up about me leavin'? No reason I need to stick around on account of that shootin' is there?"

Overstreet shook his head. "No, it's not that. Me and Tully were both eye witnesses—it was a clear case of self-defense. The business about Swain, though...his trail is five, almost six weeks old."

"I've chased down colder ones."

"Yeah, I remember. But you don't even know what he looks like."

"Not quite accurate," said Lone, reaching under his vest and into a shirt pocket. He withdrew a tintype and placed on the table in front of the marshal. The images captured were of a very happy looking Ma and a smiling, well-dressed man posed against a backdrop of decorative bunting. The man was a good looking rogue, much as Lone hated to admit it, with slicked back white hair, a smoothly shaven dimpled chin, and precisely razored sideburns.

"That was taken at the Ace High New Year's party," Ma commented somewhat glumly. "Why I didn't throw the blasted thing away, I don't know. But now, if it can be of some use, I'm glad I didn't."

"There's more. Ma found this left behind in Swain's room at the boardin' house," said Lone, holding out a second item he'd taken from his pocket. It was a business card for a hotel called the Wrangler's Rest in Belle Fourche, South Dakota.

After some studying, Overstreet said, "Well the picture is a good likeness of Swain, that's for sure. And the train ticket he bought for Cheyenne, even though he didn't go that far, would take him off in the general direction of Belle Fourche."

"Uh-huh. And between here and Cheyenne are a number of trails headin' up to that end of South Dakota." Lone paused, scowling in thought for a moment before adding, "There's still a stage run goes from Sydney to Deadwood and, if I ain't mistaken, it makes a stop where it crosses the UP line. If Swain was aimin' to throw off any pursuit with that Cheyenne ticket while really meanin' to cut north first chance he got, catchin' that Deadwood stage would take him up mighty close to Belle Fourche."

"Yeah, it would," Overstreet agreed. "But you're putting a pretty big stack of chips on that business card. Don't forget what a slick character Swain is. He might have left the card as another ruse or it might be a place he's already *been*, not necessarily one he's headed *to*."

"Yeah, and if chickens had lips they might not have to eat with their peckers," Lone said testily. "Doggone it, sometimes you gotta choose between overthinkin' a thing or goin' with your gut and actin' on what's in front of you. Me, I say what we got—*all* we got—points toward Belle Fourche. So that's the way I'm headed."

"I was just mulling things over. I got no strong argument against the way you lay it out," responded Overstreet. "You're the tracker, go do what you do and best of luck catching the varmint."

"Thanks for that. I'll take all the luck I can get."

Overstreet took another drink of coffee, then said, "In fact, you heading out right away might be a good thing for more reasons than just not letting Swain's trail get any colder."

"Why do you say that?" asked Ma.

The marshal sighed. "It's actually the reason I came around to see Lone this morning. You see, I expect some of the Double B crew—maybe Ben Barstow himself—will be coming to town sometime today to claim Dewey's body. You know how tight fellas who ride for the same brand can be, and that's especially true of the Double B riders. Ol' Ben is a tough task master, but he's fair and loyal to his men and they tend to stick with him a lot longer than most outfits."

"So you're afraid," said Lone, "that some of 'em might be showin' up with blood in their eye for me. No matter the straight of what happened. That it?"

"It's a concern, yeah. Like I said, why I came by in the first place. Naturally me and Tully will be around to keep an eye on things, but I wanted you to be aware, too."

"Damn it all," Lone swore. "Didn't we go through this once before with that Box 50 bunch? If cattle bosses care so much about their riders, then why don't they keep 'em on the damn ranch instead of lettin' 'em come into town where they're bound to get liquored up and run the risk of findin' trouble?"

Overstreet twisted his mouth wryly. "Not a bad thought—except for saloon owners and the cowboys themselves."

Lone took the tintype and business card and put them back in his pocket. "Well, it ain't gonna slow me down. I can't afford to let Swain's trail grow any colder waitin' around for some piss-burned cow pushers. If they think I'm runnin', tell 'em to make an appointment.

I'll be happy to accommodate any and all when I get back."

"Nobody thinks you're running," Overstreet assured him. "And by the time you do get back, it'll all be blown over."

"Just don't look for me until I've got Swain's scalp," declared Lone.

CHAPTER ELEVEN

LONE WAS ON THE TRAIL BY MID-MORNING. MA AND Overstreet were on hand to see him off. Tully was there, too. Because he felt responsible for allowing Ironsides to almost get shot, the deputy had developed a genuine fondness for the big gray. He'd taken charge of stabling him the previous night and had made sure the liveryman gave special care to the bullet crease he'd received. Came down to it, Tully was probably present more to see off Ironsides than Lone.

The day was warming nicely. Clear sky, only a hint of a breeze. Lone set his course west and at a slight northern angle, following the natural valley of the Platte's northern tributary. He rode south of the river and north of the UP tracks, allowing Ironsides the easy going of the flat, grassy ground in between. Due north, hazy in the distance, the rolling, treeless expanse of the vast Sandhills stretched on forever.

Lone had briefly weighed the notion of taking a train on the same Cheyenne-bound route that Swain had chosen. It would have covered the distance he had to go faster and easier. But it would present a problem for his plan to check out the locales of the train's scheduled stops in order to try and determine where Swain had gotten off and stayed off. The time it would take to thoroughly interview people at those locations would be greater than the brief stops the train made. So following the same route on horseback (with apologies to Ironsides for such a limited respite in North Platte) was the only alternative.

The miles fell away. Lone held Ironsides to a steady but moderate pace he knew the gray could easily keep up. They rode through scattered herds of cattle, varying in size with varying brands. A couple times Lone spotted riders off to the north, across the river, who watched him warily but with no sign of either aggression or friendliness. Once an eastbound train clattered by to the south and the engineer tooted his whistle at the lone horseman.

Having eaten a big breakfast himself and having been assured by Tully that Ironsides' livery stay had included a good feeding of grain and fresh hay, Lone rode on past noon. stopping only to let Ironsides drink from the river.

By the time the shadows of late afternoon were stretching longer and denser, they had neared the town of Ogallala, the first scheduled stop for the westbound out of North Platte. Lone considered not even taking time to check there since it didn't seem likely Swain would have made his departure so close. But Lone knew the law in Ogallala well, knew the marshal in particular to be a sharp-eyed individual who wouldn't have missed taking note of a dandy like Swain. So, just to be sure, he decided he'd go ahead and swing in for a quick check in the morning.

At a good spot with green grass for graze and a stand of cottonwoods for firewood, Lone reined up Ironsides and they stopped for an early camp. He stripped down and rubbed down the gray, then applied some salve provided by the North Platte liveryman to his bullet burn. It looked to be scabbing over and healing nicely. After watering the stallion, Lone staked him in the heart of the good graze.

Next he got a fire going and spread his bedroll. Over the fire he cooked a pot of coffee and fried half a dozen strips of bacon that he ate with some biscuits he'd bought from a bakery in North Platte. When he was done eating, he set a final cup of coffee on the grass beside his bedroll and crawled under the blankets. With no cloud cover to hold the day's heat, the night air was turning chill.

Lone sipped coffee and pondered things. He thought about the tintype in his pocket and wished that, somewhere along the way, he'd gotten a photograph of Velda. Not that he needed any device to envision her. He could bid her image to his mind's eye in an instant. Still, a photograph to carry, to perhaps show others when he spoke of her, that would have been nice. Something else that was nice was to be able to once again have pleasant thoughts of Velda without the dreaded darkness of how it all ended immediately infringing. That dark end would always be in his memory, too, but Lone was fighting hard to hold it in its place.

Another thing holding in place was the rage beast in his gut. It remained quiet, but nonetheless there. Waiting. Lone's strengthening hope and belief was that he could summon it once he caught up with Swain.

When the coffee cup was drained, Lone turned it upside down on the grass. Then he pulled the blankets up under his chin, lay his head back on his saddle, and slept.

———

As EXPECTED, the stop in Ogallala the next morning provided no information on Swain. But it was good to make sure, and also good to have a brief chat with a couple old friends. Lone kept it to a polite minimum, though, and was soon back in the trail.

The day was warming nicely once again with a few fluffy clouds in the morning sky and a soft breeze skimming over the land.

Lone hadn't gone very far before an old familiar feeling began prickling the hairs on the back of his neck. It hinted that someone was on his back trail. Just a vague sensation, nothing specific that he'd caught a glimpse of or could spot in any of the glances he cast back. Yet the feeling persisted. He'd experienced this kind of thing a number of times over the years. Sometimes it meant something, sometimes not. But it had turned out to be warranted often enough so that he'd learned never to ignore it.

Thoughts cut back and forth through his mind. Had he picked up a tail in Ogallala, or had someone been back there previously and he'd only just now become aware? Either way, who might it be? And why? Lone had made more than a few enemies in his time. Most of the worst he had dealt with permanent-like. But there was a handful of others still on the prowl who wouldn't hesitate to set his sun if given half a chance. Had one such perhaps spotted him in Ogallala—going unnoticed in return because Lone was too focused on his inquiries about Swain—and was now in pursuit to settle an old score?

Or, another possibility, might it be just another fellow traveler coming along on the same route with no kind of harm in mind? To test this theory, Lone cut Ironsides' pace almost in half and continued for a considerable ways. If it was merely a harmless rider back there, coming at a more reasonable pace, one equal to what Lone had been holding before, then he ought to close the gap between them and hove into sight before long. But that didn't happen. Whoever was back there (unless Lone's sense of such was in error this time) seemed to be purposely lagging in order to maintain a distance that kept him unseen.

Lone gigged Ironsides back to his previous pace. He swore under his breath. He couldn't shake the feeling and therefore grew increasingly convinced it *wasn't* a false warning.

The terrain began to change. The rise and fall of the Sandhills was reaching farther down through this stretch. Also some ragged rock outcrops began appearing intermittently. The river flowed in its deeper, age-worn channel, the tracks and the space in between followed the undulations of the landscape.

Lone's thoughts continued to grind. He damned well didn't like the notion of whoever was tailing him just hanging back there, biding their time, waiting to make a move when it suited *them*. To hell with that. *He* wanted control over how and when a confrontation took place.

But how?

If he turned around and rode straight back to challenge whoever was fogging him, they could meet him with an ambush.

If he stopped and simply waited, they might have the patience to outwait him. After all, he was the one with time working against him by virtue of the already too-cold trail he was chasing.

And if he took off hard, urging Ironsides to the formidable top speed he was capable of and managed to outrun/evade his pursuers for the time being—what then? If they were determined enough and had any tracking skill, he'd be left wondering when they might show up again. That would be even worse than now, when he *knew* (at least to the extent he trusted his hunch) they were back there.

As he gazed out ahead, seeing how the land grew steadily hillier and rockier, a vague possible solution started to take shape in Lone's head. Maybe, just maybe, if he stayed patient a little longer, this more rugged terrain might provide something he could work with.

A mile later he came upon what he was looking for.

CHAPTER TWELVE

THE GROUND HAD BEEN RISING ON A FAINT BUT STEADY incline for a ways. Now it came to a blunted crest and, on the other side, fell away to a long, markedly steeper slope than ran for several hundred yards before flattening out again. A low, ragged spine of rocks ran along the track side of the slope. Over along the river, three or four individual rock humps thrust up through the long grass.

A man heading down that slope would quickly drop out of sight to anyone on the trail behind. It would be a natural fading from view, nothing that might look suspicious or evasive. Nevertheless, it would most likely give the pursuers cause to hurry up a bit in order to again be able to spot their quarry. But that was okay. Lone figured the period of time they'd be unable to see him would be plenty for him to get ready.

Three quarters of the way down the slope, Lone swung Ironsides in behind one of the rock humps. Farther in, closer to the river, there was bramble that provided good concealment for the gray. Lone tied him there, pulled the Winchester Yellowboy from its saddle scabbard, then returned to the rock. It was as tall as him, sun bleached to a bone white color, deeply seamed in places by rain runoff, worn by the winds. Around its base tall grass grew.

Lone pressed close to the rock and dropped to one knee in the high grass. This positioned him so he was able to lean out slightly and look all the way up the slope. If and when anybody came over the blunted crest, he could quickly drop back out of sight. He jacked a round into the Yellowboy and waited.

Minutes ticked by. The sun, still more than two hours from its noon zenith, beat down hard. The rock hump grew hot to the touch. Lone lifted his knee for a moment and plucked away a stone that had poking up through the grass. Just hold easy, he told himself. Don't get impatient, don't start to question your hunch.

More time passed.

And then, finally, a head poked into sight up on the crest. Only one man, hatless, making a quick, cautious scan down the slope. After a couple seconds he disappeared. Half a minute later he showed himself again. Now he had his hat on and there was a second man beside him. Both were mounted. Over the crest they came and on down the slope they proceeded.

Lone had edged back behind the boulder. Sweeping off his own hat, letting the Stetson drop back and dangle between his shoulder blades by its chin thong, he eased forward again to watch the two horsemen draw closer. So these were the hounds dogging his trail.

Lone continued to study them. As they got nearer still he began to discern something familiar about the pair. And then he recognized them fully. It was their headgear that did it. The sombrero on one, the over-sized hat on the other. Damned if it wasn't Gomez and Ralph, the other two Double B cowboys who'd been with Dewey Tibbs back in North Platte a couple nights ago.

What the hell were they up to?

Whatever it was, it had a bad smell to it. And in real short order Lone meant to find out what was behind the stink.

When they were even with his position, he rose up and stepped out into plain sight with his rifle held at his waist and tilted meaningfully straight at the riders. "Mornin', boys," he greeted in a hard, flat tone.

Two startled expressions snapped around as the men they belonged to went rigid in their saddles and jerked their horses to a halt. Gomez muttered something harsh in Spanish. It might have been a hasty prayer inasmuch as a gun was aimed him. But more likely, Lone thought, it was something uncomplimentary about the man holding the gun.

The Mexican said nothing more and Ralph stayed silent, just glaring.

"You fellas are quite a ways off your range, ain't you?" Lone drawled. "You get lost lookin' for stray doggies or some such?"

The pair remained silent, their startled looks gone now, and Gomez joining Ralph in fixing Lone with a baleful stare.

"I can give you a chance to make your spiel, or I can choose to not waste any more time and just blow you out of those saddles," Lone grated. "Why are you two peckerwoods foggin' my trail?"

Ralph kept his mouth in a tight, straight line for a

long beat before answering. "We got no choice," he muttered sullenly. "Dewey was a popular fella at the Double B. Everybody there—including Boss Barstow—blames us for not doin' a better job of backin' his play when he went up against you. They wouldn't listen when we tried to explain how he took off crazy-like and never gave us a chance to stop him or join him, either one."

"*Si*," Gomez agreed, now looking mournful.

"So the only choice we had," Ralph went on, "was to let ourselves be run off in shame or to come after you and square things."

"There's other cowboyin' jobs," said Lone. "Seems you wouldn't have had to go all that far to get away from the blame of the Double B crew. Would've been a sight better choice than the fix you're in now, wouldn't you say?"

"Only because things didn't go quite like we aimed," Ralph admitted grudgingly. His glare returned, eyes narrowing even tighter than before. "Then again, maybe you ain't holdin' the pot-winnin' hand you think."

Lone cocked an eyebrow. "Oh? How so?"

Ralph cut a quick sidelong glance over at Gomez, then brought his eyes back. "You havin' the drop on us ain't no guarantee you got the whole bulge," he said. "You try pullin' that trigger, what's to stop us from pitchin' out of our saddles and goin' for our own shootin' irons? You might get one of us, but that'd still leave the other a chance to throw some lead in return. You can only shoot and crank in a fresh load so fast. What have we got to lose?"

"Only your lives, you jackass," Lone told him. "If I'd

certain sure wanted you dead, I'd've started shootin' as soon as—"

But it was no use. Ralph had whipped himself—and Gomez, too—into feeling trapped and desperate beyond reason. At some unseen signal they threw themselves into motion, kicking free from their stirrups and lunging off the far side of their mounts as they clawed at the guns holstered on their hips.

Lone instantly fired the Yellowboy and sent a bullet ripping into Ralph, the rider closest to him. The slug hit just above his right rib cage and angled out through the left side of his chest, taking the top part of his heart with it. Ralph was dead before his body hit the ground.

With practiced speed Lone levered home and fired a second round. But all it did was slice empty air above the saddle where Gomez had been. The Mexican proved as quick and agile as a cat. He landed on the ground, went into a roll to get clear of his horse's stamping feet, came to a stop on his stomach with gun drawn and extended at arm's length in Lone's direction. The gun barked, spitting a bullet out under the horse's belly. The shot smacked against the rock hump a foot from Lone's head and went ricocheting away with a sharp whine.

Lone pitched forward onto his own stomach, flattening down the high grass and slamming the butt of the rifle to his shoulder. He swung the front sight trying to lock on Gomez.

The determined Mexican rolled over twice more and, as soon as he stopped, clear of his horse now, snapped off another shot. This one sailed close above Lone's head.

When the Yellowboy spoke in return, it was on

target. Red flame licked from the muzzle and the round it hurled struck square in the center of Gomez's forehead, punching a red-rimmed hole like a bloodshot third eye. His head gave a single jerk then his body went flat and limp, totally still.

Lone pushed to his feet, automatically jacking a fresh round into the chamber. He walked slowly forward, stopping to stand over the two men he'd just killed. He gazed down first at Ralph, then Gomez.

Wagging his head, he said in a raspy whisper, "Damn fools... *God*-damn fools! It didn't have to go this way."

CHAPTER THIRTEEN

Lone finished dealing with Ralph and Gomez by tying the bodies face down over their saddles and swatting the horses back in the direction of Ogallala. In spite of feeling somewhat remorseful for having had to kill the hapless pair who'd been berated into coming after him, they nevertheless had given in and thereby brought it on themselves. Lone had neither the added time to lose nor the inclination to break a sweat burying them. It was highly doubtful they would have done any such for him if things had gone the other way. Hell, more like they might have cut off his ears or maybe his whole head to take to the rest of the Double B crew as proof of a successful mission. As an indicator of who the horses' grisly riders were, Lone tucked a note in the waistband of each carcass that read: BUSHWHACKERS WHO GOT WHAT THEY DESERVED.

After that, Lone rode for three days without incident.

He swung Ironsides into every town they came to that was a scheduled stop for the UP westbound and showed the tintype of Jack Swain (with Ma's half bent back out of sight) inquiring if anyone remembered seeing him. There were none who did.

Only in the town of Lodgepole did Lone run across an old timer, a UP brakeman, who was on medical leave due to a bad case of the shingles but remembered seeing the man in the photograph on one of his last runs before the brakeman got laid up. Unfortunately, the old gent had no recollection where Swain left the train.

Late on the third day, with a thunderstorm brewing off to the northwest, Lone arrived at the remote layout that served as a watering stop for trains and a way station for stagecoaches on the Sydney-to-Deadwood run. The place was an assemblage of sun-beaten, wind-tilted structures made of mostly sod walls supported by wood framing. Nothing particularly attractive or inviting maybe, but with the storm rolling in, Lone had in mind to be staying the night regardless. He and Iron-sides were weary from pushing steady and deserved at least shelter from the rain plus whatever other accommodations were available.

Lone dismounted and tied the big gray to the hitch rail out front of what appeared to be the main building. The place almost had a deserted look, but light shining dimly in some of the windows and the sight of horses in the corral and pole building out back indicated there must be somebody around.

Lone went to the front door, carrying his Yellowboy and saddlebags, and entered. A little bell over the front door tinkled when the door swung inward, announcing his arrival. The chime was hardly necessary in this instance, however, inasmuch as there were three people

—a man, a woman, and a teenaged boy—seated at a table in the middle of the room. The impression Lone got was that they had just sat down to an early evening meal. All faces turned to look at him, expressions showing neither surprise nor particular warmth.

Until, that is, the man—a husky specimen with a thick shock of coal black hair swept back atop head and a full beard of the same—stood up and greeted, "Welcome, stranger. Come in. My family and I are just sitting down to supper. There is plenty, and you are welcome to join us if you like. Be you traveling alone?" He had an accent that Lone judged to be Russian.

As for the offer to supper, Lone's gaze had already appraised the fare on the table. Beef, cabbage, potatoes, fresh-baked rolls. Everything looked, and smelled, delicious. You bet he would care to join!

"I'm travelin' alone, just me and my horse," he replied to the man's query. "I'd be honored to share in that fine lookin' meal, but first I'd like to get my animal inside somewhere ahead of the storm. I'll see to him myself if you'll direct me to a suitable place. And I'll be more than happy to pay for his shelter, maybe some hay and a scoop of grain?"

"For that there is no need," the bearded man rumbled. "Shelter from mean weather and a few bites to eat, neither for man nor beast, is something that should come at a price. My son Ingmar will stable your animal and see to its needs."

The boy stood up. He was tall and lean, sturdy-looking, and perhaps closer to twenty than Lone had first took him to be. He was of fair complexion, not at all like the ruddy-cheeked man, and his bowl-cut hair was the color of butter. The stout woman still seated at the table had long, braided hair of the same color. Though the man had referred to them as his family and had called the boy his son, Lone couldn't help being a bit curious about these mixed physical traits.

"I hate to take the lad away from his supper," he said. "I'm fine with carin' for my own horse."

The man wagged his head. "For a guest in my house that is not acceptable. Ingmar is young and strong and well fed. He can stand to have his meal delayed for a few minutes."

"Yah. That is fine," said Ingmar. He spoke with an even thicker accent that sounded different from his father's.

"If you are worried about Ingmar's skill with animals," said the latter, "you need not be. He has a fine touch with horses. Yours will be well cared for by him."

"All right," Lone relented. Then, to Ingmar he added, "He's right out front, you can't miss him. Big gray stud called Ironsides."

"Ironsides. Yah."

As Ingmar was going out the door, the blonde woman got to her feet, saying, "I will get our guest a plate and some utensils. Invite the man to sit, Gregov." She spoke with the same thick accent as the boy.

"Hold, woman. First we must complete introductions," said the man. Then, turning back to Lone, he stated, "I am Gregov Rostek. This is my wife, Ursula. You met our son Ingmar. For a long time, I ran this station as a lonely person. Last year, through a service that arranges such things, Ursula agreed to come from Sweden to be my wife. She was a widow, Ingmar her son. Now we are blessed to have each other, and I could not be prouder of Ingmar if he was my own blood."

"You're a lucky man," Lone told him. "You have a lovely wife, a fine son."

Ursula blushed and actually did a little curtsy.

"My name, by the way, is McGantry," Lone added. Then, grinning, he added further, "My only family's Ironsides. Probably best not to bring him in for a full introduction, him not bein' housebroke and all. But you heard enough about him to get the general idea."

"Yes. Yes, indeed," said Rostek, grinning, too. "Come, friend McGantry. Sit now. Sit, and Ursula will fix you a plate."

In a matter of minutes, they were all settled around the table enjoying the food that proved every bit as delicious as it looked. Ingmar returned to rejoin them and was full of enthusiastic praise for what a magnificent animal he'd found Ironsides to be.

Smiling agreeably, Lone allowed, "Yeah, me and him have been together quite a spell. He's never let me down."

Their table talk drifted to other things. Rostek explained how, since no trains or stagecoaches were due through until the following afternoon, the family was taking their supper somewhat early because they planned to devote the rest of the evening to speech lessons. He said, "You may find it amusing that I, who still often struggle turning my native Russian tongue into the proper words even though I have lived in this country for many years, am trying to help Ursula and Ingmar convert their Swedish to English. It makes for an interesting though sometimes frustrating challenge. But it is good time spent together and we continue to make progress."

Lone nodded. "Sounds like you're doing pretty good

to me. Heck, I was bred and born in this country, and I mangle proper English regular-like."

That got a polite chuckle in response but Lone wasn't sure Ursula and Ingmar really got the self-deprecating humor. A little later, as the conversation began to lag some, Lone decided to bring up the reason behind his being there.

"I been travelin' for a time on the lookout for a fella," he announced. "I know he came west on a train out of North Platte, headed for Cheyenne. But he never made it that far. I'm wonderin' if there's a chance he might've stopped off here." At this point Lone took the tintype from his pocket and handed it to Rostek. "That there's a pretty good likeness of him."

Outside, the growl of the approaching storm's thunder was growing steadily louder and closer and the light of early evening coming through the windows was considerably dimmer than normal for the time of day. As he took the tintype and examined it, a similar gloominess suddenly settled over the previously open and friendly countenance of the Russian.

He lifted his eyes from the picture and gazed at Lone. "Is this man a friend of yours?"

Lone took a beat to consider his answer. Then: "No. Not hardly. As a matter of fact, he's a scoundrel I don't have particularly kind intentions toward if and when I catch up with him."

"Is he an outlaw then, and you a lawman on his trail?"

Lone shook his head. "No, I'm not a lawman and the fella there hasn't broken no law, leastways not in any official way. But all the same he took advantage of and caused harm to a friend of mine, an elderly lady unable to retaliate for herself. Like I said, she's a friend. I aim to do some retaliatin' on her behalf."

Ingmar reached out and took the picture from his father. His eyebrows immediately lifted and he rattled off an excited string of words in some language Lone couldn't understand. Rostek nodded solemnly in response. Ursula took the tintype next. Her face also showed somber recognition but she made no comment.

Rostek's gaze returned to Lone. "Yes, that man did get off the train here. He sought lodging for a night, awaiting the Deadwood stage that came through the following day."

"How long ago?"

"Just short of four weeks." Rostek paused, then heaved a sigh before saying, "But you need not be in a hurry with your continued pursuit."

"Why do you say that?" Lone wanted to know.

"Because the man you seek is no longer on the move. North of here, not too far from a town called Bayard, the stage he was on got stopped by robbers... they shot and killed the man in your photograph."

CHAPTER FOURTEEN

LONE STAYED THE NIGHT AT THE ROSTEK'S WAY STATION. In the morning, Ursula insisted he remain long enough for a hearty breakfast while Ingmar saw to it that Ironsides got another helping of hay and grain. The lad then saddled the gray and had him waiting when Lone was ready to leave. The former scout thanked the family sincerely for their hospitality and then did some insisting of his own when it came to leaving payment as a token of appreciation.

The sun was barely an hour old in a still partly cloudy sky when Lone rode out, pointing Ironsides north toward Bayard. The morning was considerably cooler than the previous string of days had been, the storm-battered landscape still wet and shiny-looking with the early rays of sunlight streaming down on it.

As he rode, Lone's thoughts roiled and tumbled inside his head much like the night's lightning-illuminated storm clouds. He'd wrestled with those same thoughts through most of the hours he'd tossed restlessly on the sleeping pallet laid out for him in a corner of the station's main room. The crash and rumble of the storm hadn't kept him awake, but the news he'd received about Jack Swain surely did.

If the report of Swain being robbed and killed was factual, where did that leave Lone's mission to catch up and hold the cur accountable? Not that he doubted the word of the Rosteks, but it turned out that most of what they'd related was second hand information. Yes, they had seen the man in person for the duration of his stay at their place, but the rest of what allegedly happened they got from stage drivers who passed through on subsequent runs.

It was Gregov who suggested that, since there was a lawman up in Bayard who had been involved with the follow-up to the robbery, Lone might want to go and talk directly to him. A suggestion now in the process of being taken.

Another aspect to all of this that was grating on Lone was the bitter irony (Amos Tucker's pet word again) of it. If Swain was truly dead, killed by stage robbers, then it would mean once again—just as the drunks who'd killed Velda had killed themselves before any other justice could be exacted against them—yet another wrongdoer had escaped direct punishment (at the hands of Lone or otherwise) for his misdeeds. The only difference was that nothing done to Velda's killers after the fact would have brought her back; in this matter with Swain, while nothing done to him would save Ma the humiliation she'd suffered or likely regain her boarding house, at least catching up with him might have salvaged some of the bank funds he took. What was more, while Lone was encountering nothing but futility when it came to getting back at those who'd harmed his loved ones, he had in the meantime managed to kill three men of minor consequence. Three killings that had done little to satisfy the craving of the rage beast still lurking inside him.

———

IT WAS the middle of the afternoon when the town of Bayard came in sight. It was a small community in the midst of the grasslands sprawl located south and west of South Dakota's Black Hills and north of Nebraska's Pine Ridge region. It was a cluster of twenty or so wood frame and sod structures, its handful of businesses supported by surrounding cattle ranchers and a few farmers.

Said businesses, Lone noted as he rode in, included two saloons, a general store, a bank, a cafe, a combination leather goods repair and livery stable, and a blacksmith shop. He saw no sign of a sheriff's or marshal's office. The clanging of steel coming from the blacksmith shop near the end of the street where he rode in caused him to steer Ironsides over to it.

The shop was a long, low building made of weathered gray wood. One half of the double doors in front was propped open and through it Lone could see a man working a red hot chunk of steel on an anvil, a glowing, smoky forge not far behind him.

When Lone reined up next to a watering trough just outside the open door, the man working at the anvil spotted him. He paused for a moment with his hammer raised and called out, "Be with you in a minute, mister."

Lone climbed down from his saddle and waited.

After the smithy had whacked the piece of steel half

a dozen more times, he set aside his hammer, held the piece clamped in a pair of tongs and plunged it into a nearby tub of water. Leaving it there to sizzle and steam, he removed the leather gloves he was wearing and strode out toward Lone. The fellow was tall and lanky, with a beak nose separating pale blue eyes set in a narrow, sweaty face. A prominent Adam's apple bobbed up and down in a somewhat elongated neck and the forearms jutting out from the rolled up sleeves of his shirt rippled with hard, stringy muscles.

"Afternoon, stranger. What can I do you for?" came a friendly greeting.

"For starters," Lone replied, "I'd like to water my horse after he's cooled some."

"Absolutely. Help yourself. Nice lookin' animal, by the way."

"Thanks."

The smithy took a hanky from his pocket and wiped the sweat from his face. "Don't recall seein' you around before. We don't get a lot of visitors to our little town 'cept those passin' through on the stage runs. We're real welcomin' to anybody stoppin' by, though."

Lone smiled thinly at the hinted question. "Sounds like a friendly place. Sorry I won't be hangin' around very long. But I got hammered pretty good by that storm last night," he fabricated, "so I'm hopin' to find a sight better accommodations for this night. Somewhere I can get a hot meal, a bath and a bed for myself, and a place to stall my horse."

"We can fix you right up. We got all those things." The lanky man took a minute to also wipe his hands on the hanky, then clenched it in his left and thrust out his calloused right palm. "My name's Pribitt. Lyle

Pribitt. As you can see, I'm the blacksmith hereabouts."

Saying, "My name's McGantry," Lone reached out and shook the hand. As expected, he was tested by a strong grip.

"Better go ahead and let your horse have his drink," Pribitt suggested. "While he's doin' that, I'll point out where you'll want to go. Guess you can spot the cafe and livery for yourself. Far as a bath and a place to sleep, both of the saloons have upstairs rooms where you can get those. The Prairie Palace also has, er, a couple of entertainin' girls, if you know what I mean. If you want to *just* get some rest, 'spect you'll find things quieter over at Finnegan's."

"Thanks for the tip." While Ironsides lowered his head into the trough and slurped noisily, Lone looked around and made another scan down the town's stretch of businesses. This time he noticed a doctor's shingle that he hadn't spotted before, but still nothing that indicated where he'd find the lawman Rostek told him was here. Turning back to Pribitt, he said, "Happens I got me a matter I been wantin' to discuss with somebody representin' the law. I was hopin' you might have such here. But it don't look like it, eh?"

Pribitt's eyebrows lifted in a look of mild surprise. "Hold on a minute." After stuffing the hanky back in the pocket it came out of, he pulled aside the leather apron he was wearing and dug into the front pocket of his trousers. With the apron pulled back, Lone had cause for lifting his own brows a bit when he saw the Remington hogleg holstered on Pribitt's hip. When the blacksmith produced a tin star and held it out, Lone's brows shifted a notch higher. "What do you know,"

Pribitt said. "Looks like you might be in better luck than it first appeared."

Lone was momentarily at a loss for words.

"I don't flaunt it much, especially not when I'm blacksmithin'," Pribitt explained. "But, yeah, Bayard does have a lawman. In the form of me. I don't rightly consider myself a sheriff or marshal or anything like that. More of a constable, I guess you'd call it. Anyway, a couple years back, the folks in town decided we oughta have somebody to kind of keep things tamed down if and when the need came 'round. I'm the one who got stuck—oops, I mean had the *honor* of bein' elected to the job."

Lone grinned at the man's candor. "At least you have that in common with more than a few other town marshals I've met—the feelin' of gettin' stuck with your duties."

Pribitt shrugged. "Aw, it ain't all that bad I guess. The wife likes the few extra dollars it brings in each month. And the work mostly amounts to thumpin' drunk cowboys who show up and try to drink one or the other —sometimes both—of the saloons dry. Reckon you know what that leads to. Them startin' to feel too big for their britches, then some other liquored-up ranny decidin' to try and show 'em they ain't. So it ends with my Remy barrel rapped on the noggin of one or both and a night in the drunk tank. Until next time. About the only thing else that chaps me regular-like are snooty travelers who roll in on a stagecoach and act like they're too good for our little town. Thankfully they don't usually stick around very long. So I seldom get to give any of them a rap, much as I'd sometimes like to."

"Maybe you should give in to that urge once in a

while," Lone said, his grin taking on a crooked slant. "Have a little fun with the great honor bestowed on you."

Pribitt eyed him. "Probably a good thing you don't plan on hangin' around too long either. I think you'd be a bad influence on me."

Lone's expression turned serious. "Speakin' of the stagecoaches that come through, the thing I wanted to talk to you about, in your constable role, has to do with a passenger on one of 'em. That is, he *was* on a stage headed here. From what I've been told, he never quite made it this far. Leastways, not alive."

CHAPTER FIFTEEN

"Yeah, that's him," Pribitt said, making a sour face as he studied the tintype of Jack Swain. "A-course he didn't look quite so dandy when I saw him, what with a bullet hole in one ear and his nice silver hair all blood splattered. But it's the same fella, no doubt about it."

Lone took the photograph back, saying, "But no identification or anything was found on his body?"

"Nope. The robbers picked him clean," Pribitt replied. "Their big score was the money belt he had on him, the one he fought and died tryin' to hang on to. But they took everything else, too. That's why we had to bury him with just a wooden marker sayin' 'Unknown' on it. You gonna want to have that replaced now with his name?"

Lone grunted. "The only thing I'd care about doin' to his grave would involve what most folks leave down the hole of an outhouse. And Swain ain't even worth the added bother to do that."

The two men were seated in what Pribitt called his

"constable's office." It was located at the rear of the blacksmith shop, a narrow room reaching across the width of the building. One end of the room was sectioned off by some thick iron bars set close together and running floor to ceiling; an opening had been cut out for a barred door held closed by a chain and padlock. This was Pribitt's drunk tank, currently unoccupied. At the other end of the room was a wooden table strewn with papers. Two wooden chairs had been placed on either side of this and these *were* currently occupied, by Lone and the constable.

When Lone had brought up the stagecoach robbery and the killing of Swain, Pribitt announced it sounded like official business that should be discussed in its proper setting. So he'd halted his blacksmithing, hung a pre-painted sign out front that read GONE ON LAW BUSINESS—BACK SOON, then directed Lone back here to his office.

Leaning back in his chair, fingers laced over his flat stomach, Pribitt now said in response to Lone's remark about Swain's grave, "Boy howdy. You really didn't like that character, did you?"

"Not even a little bit," Lone confirmed. "I never laid eyes on him but, like I told you, he did great harm to a close friend of mine. A lady up in years. Long story short, he slick-talked her out of her life's savin's and property and did it in a clever enough way so that the law wasn't able to do anything about it."

"But you figured you could."

"Sometimes the law can be twisted around so that common sense gets crowded plumb out of the picture. But that don't mean that wrong ain't still wrong and a polecat who hurts others ain't due some hurt in return."

"Hard to disagree with the way you put it," Pribitt said. "I've heard tell how slicksters in bigger towns get away with some mighty bad-smellin' shenanigans. So-called laws that allow that kind of thing would be way over my head. I'm glad things are more bust-head simple hereabouts."

"Let's hope your luck holds and it stays that way."

Pribitt leaned forward and put his elbows on the table. "So what it amounts to is that the money belt this Swain had on him, the one he got killed over, had your friend's savings in it. And now the robbers have it."

"How it shakes out," Lone grated.

"So are you now goin' after them?"

Lone's expression pulled tight. "Not something I've had cause to think on before this. But yeah. Hell yeah, I'd be inclined to take after 'em. If anybody has a notion who they are."

"Matter of fact they do. A pretty good notion, it turns out." Pribitt shuffled through the papers on his desk and came up with one that he held out to Lone. "A U.S. Marshal came through a couple weeks back. He heard about the stage robbery, was carryin' a pack of those dodgers with him. The hombre pictured there escaped from a prison down Denver way where he was waitin' trial and pretty certain to be hung. This Marshal... Charley Bourbon his name is. Ain't that a corker? On top of that, he's a Negra. Black as a fresh polished pair of Sunday-go-to-meetin' shoes. Anyway, Marshal Bourbon has been on the trail of that escaped bird and he had a hunch him and his old gang, same ones figured to have helped bust him out, might've been responsible for our stage robbery. Lo and behold, when he showed that dodger to the driver and the other passengers who was part of the holdup, everyone agreed he was the ring leader."

Lone studied the face staring back at him from the Wanted poster he'd been handed. It was that of a gent in his middle to late forties, with even facial features some might call handsome. He had curiously gentle-looking eyes but a wide, full-lipped mouth that looked capable of taking on a cruel twist. Hatless in the picture, his hair was full and dark with thick, curly sideburns. A twenty-thousand-dollar reward was being offered for bringing him in, dead or alive.

Lone read aloud from other wording under the picture. "Fenton Eccles. Charged with numerous counts of assault, murder, rape, robbery, and arson all across Kansas, Nebraska, and Colorado. He was a real busy boy who believed in cuttin' a wide swath with his meanness, wasn't he?"

Pribitt replied, "Uh-huh. And now that he's busted loose again, it appears he ain't done yet. Although, accordin' to the witnesses from the stage—and sorta backed up by you—the amount in that money belt when they opened it was awful excitin' to Eccles and his men. Marshal Bourbon had concern it might even be enough to allow 'em to go to ground, lay real low for a spell. Meanin' it'd be a whole lot harder for anybody to track 'em if they wasn't on the move needin' to pull more jobs."

Lone frowned. "You mentioned witnesses from the stage—the driver and other passengers, you said before. How many did that add up to?"

"Just three. The driver and two other passengers besides Swain, a man and woman travelin' together." Pribitt's forehead puckered sorrowfully before he added, "There was a shotgun guard, too, ol' Mossy Bergman. Those robbin' dogs shot him right off the bat, never gave him a chance. They shot one of the horses right away, too, to make certain sure the stage got halted. No way of knowin' how much more killin' they might've hand in mind—your man Swain made sure of his when he put up such a fuss over them tryin' to take his money belt. What-all more might've happened got thankfully interrupted by an army surveyin' crew who was workin' in the hills nearby comin' round to check when they heard the shootin'."

"But they had no luck chasin' after the gang, eh?"

Pribitt made a face. "I don't think they gave it much of a try. They mostly stopped to help the folks on the coach."

"So there were three left alive. And this U.S. Marshal, when he came through, got a chance to question all three?"

"Uh-huh. Luck had it that Bud Howland, the driver who'd been pullin' the reins that day, came through on a run while Bourbon was here. And a-course the other two been here all along."

"The other two... The man and woman, you mean? You sayin' they live here in town?" Lone asked.

Pribitt shook his head. "Oh, no. No, nothing like that. I guess I forgot to mention that the man got caught by a stray bullet when Eccles opened up on Swain. The wound didn't look too bad at first but then there was some kind of complication. Our town doc didn't advise the fella, his name is Bayne by the way, should move on 'til he was full healed. Last I heard, that time was pretty near."

"Where are Bayne and the woman stayin'?"

Pribitt jabbed a thumb. "Finnegan's. Just up the street on the left."

CHAPTER SIXTEEN

Lone walked Ironsides up to Finnegan's saloon and tied him to the hitch rail out front. Business along Bayard's main street as the afternoon waned was modest. A couple horse drawn wagons were rolling along, one in each direction; two horsemen were riding away from the Prairie Palace; in front of the general store, three women with shopping baskets stood chatting; across the street, in front of the bank, a pair of plump men in business suits and bowler hats were engaged in what appeared to be a much more serious conversation.

Lone stepped up on the boardwalk and pushed through the batwings into Finnegan's. It was a standard layout. Sawdust on the floor, bar to the right, billiard table to the left, and round-topped gaming tables scattered elsewhere. There wasn't much of a crowd on hand. The barkeep, a scrawny number with a cigarette hanging out one corner of his mouth and thinning, heavily-oiled hair center-parted atop his head, was leaning on one elbow behind the stick, thumbing through a copy of *Police Gazette*. Two old gents in spectacles were shuffling around the billiard table, sinking balls with a lack of regularity that called into question the quality of the cheaters perched on their noses. At a table near the back was seated a man and woman Lone suspected were who he'd come here to see.

First he went to the bar. The barkeep set aside his magazine and moved to stand across from him. "What can I get you, mister?"

"A glass of beer would hit the spot," Lone responded.

"You bet. We got the best beer in town. Good and cold, too." When he spoke, the man's cigarette bobbed up and down like a tree branch in the wind.

A tall, foamy glass appeared in front of Lone. He put some coins on the bar then took a drink and found it to be as advertised.

"New in town, aren't you?" asked the barkeep.

"Uh-huh. Just passin' through," Lone told him. "Though I am in the market for a bath and a room for the night. Blacksmith down the street said I could find both here."

"He steered you right. We got good, clean rooms and fresh made-up beds for a fair price. And the missus most always has hot water ready on the stove. Say the word, I'll set up a tub and fetch you a couple steaming pails whenever you're ready."

"Won't be until a little later. I'll let you know."

"Whenever you say."

Lone drank some more of his beer then rested his elbows on the bar top and said in a slightly lowered voice, "Tell me. That fella sittin' over at the table with the lady. He go by the name of Bayne?"

"That's right," the barkeep answered. Then, after considering for a moment, he frowned. "Not going to be no trouble, is there?"

Saying, "Don't see why there should be," Lone took the rest of his beer and sauntered in the direction of Bayne and the woman. Reaching their table, he paused and addressed them. "Pardon me, folks. Wonderin' if I might have a few words with you."

Bayne regarded him. He was a lean, hard-looking individual, forty give or take a year. Swarthy complexion, thick black eyebrows over dark, alert eyes. He had on a cream-colored jacket with black-trimmed wide lapels and a matching cream Stetson with a black band. A black string tie was knotted at his throat with a crisp white shirt and patterned silk vest below its dangling tails. His left arm was wrapped in a black cloth sling, leaving his right hand free to deal the hand of solitaire spread on the table before him. The look of him and the deft way he distributed the cards, even one handed, marked him pretty clearly as a gambler by profession.

The woman seated next to him was perhaps six years younger with a finely chiseled face framed by a spill of cornsilk blonde hair. She also regarded Lone, with cool blue eyes. Her rose-tinted mouth gave the impression of being able to express a smirk as quick as a smile; maybe quicker. Attire-wise, she was clad in a long-sleeved white blouse, buttoned to the throat, slightly puffed at the shoulders with a clinging bodice that showed the swell of high, firm breasts.

Responding after a long beat to Lone's inquiry, Bayne drawled, "I guess we could manage a few minutes. You can see we're not engaged in anything terribly important. Take a load off, stranger."

Acknowledging the invite with a nod and a pinch of his hat to the woman, Lone pulled out a chair and sat. "My name's McGantry. Lone McGantry," he said, getting preliminaries out of the way. "You don't know me, of course, but I know you. That is, I know *of* you—you're Emmett Bayne and Miss Rena Matteson. You were passengers on the stage that got held up south of here a while back."

"Unfortunately true."

Lone tipped his head to indicate the sling. "Heard you took a slug. How bad?"

"Tore up some meat and muscle above the elbow. Luckily it didn't damage the actual joint. The local doctor did a good job of patching it up, but apparently there were some lead fragments that went deep and turned to infection. That's what has prolonged my recovery." Bayne paused and eyed Lone more closely. "I appreciate your inquiry after my injury, but I suspect you have something more on your mind?"

"My interest has to do with the other passenger who was ridin' with you—the fella who got shot and killed," Lone affirmed.

"Friend of yours?" asked the woman.

Lone shook his head. "Far from it. He was a lowlife skunk who I won't pretend to have any grief for."

A corner of Bayne's mouth lifted. "He rode with us for only a short ways. In that time, I'll admit he seemed rather preoccupied and not a particularly friendly sort. In the end, though, he—which is to say all of us—met up with four others who proved far less friendly. I assume you talked to Constable Pribitt here in town and he informed you of the gang's identity?"

Lone nodded. Before continuing, his gaze touched

on the whiskey bottle and glass at Bayne's elbow and the coffee cup in a saucer before Rena. "I see you already have drinks," he said. "But can I buy either of you another round or maybe a change of pace?"

"You know, a change of pace don't sound half bad. That beer of yours looks mighty refreshing," allowed Bayne. Then, turning to Rena: "How about you, dear? A refill on your coffee, or maybe something stronger?"

"I'll stick with coffee. I want to be sure and stay alert so as not to miss any of the excitement around here," came the sarcastic reply.

"I heard. I'll have you fixed right up," called the barkeep. "How about you, stranger—another beer?"

"Sure, why not," Lone told him.

That taken care of, Lone got back to his main business. "The fella who got killed went by the name of Swain, Jack Swain. Leastways that's what I know him by. Wouldn't surprise me if he went by other handles at other times. He was a swindler, a flimflammer. My interest in him stems from his fleecin' of a friend, an elderly lady. He bilked her out of property and her whole life savin's."

Bayne's eyes narrowed. "The money belt he was carrying and died over. When the robbers opened it up they found it contained quite a substantial amount, a real jackpot. You saying the contents were what this Swain took from your friend?"

"Most all of it, I expect. Like I said, he glommed on to her whole life's savin'."

Rena said, "And you were after Swain? Are you some sort of lawman or bounty hunter?"

Lone's answer was delayed by the bartender showing up with the requested beers and a coffee refill.

When he turned and left, Lone said, "No, I don't carry a badge of any kind, nor am I a bounty hunter. But I was damn sure huntin' Swain. Strictly as a personal matter."

"Sir Galahad rides," remarked Rena, again with the sarcasm.

Lone decided it wouldn't take spending very much time around her before she might flat piss a body off.

"What about an actual lawman, the badge-toting kind?" Bayne wanted to know. "We had a U.S. Marshal come through here recently inquiring about the Eccles gang who did the robbing and killing. But he mentioned nothing about Swain. If he was the thieving scoundrel you claim, shouldn't he have had warrants on him as well?"

"If it was up to me he would," chuffed Lone. "But, like I explained, he's a flimflammer, a manipulator. He slick-talked my friend into signin' some papers that left him in the clear as far as any action the law could take. But wrong is wrong, and I didn't see what he did as something that oughta be let go so easy."

"I've heard about such schemers taking advantage of the vulnerable," Bayne said somberly. "I'm sorry to hear your friend fell victim to such. At least she's fortunate to have you in her corner. But, in a not so fortunate turn, Swain's demise leaves you pretty much at a dead end, doesn't it?"

"As far as holdin' Swain to account, yeah," Lone admitted bitterly. "But there's still the matter of my friend's money."

"You can't be serious," exclaimed Rena. "You don't mean you're thinking about switching to going after the Eccles gang in order to try and get the money back from *them*, are you?"

"And if you are," said Bayne, "what did you think we could provide that might be of any help?"

Lone drained his first beer, set the empty glass down and heaved a sigh. "That I ain't rightly sure. I'm sorta graspin' at straws here, havin' only recently learned about Swain bein' killed and then where the money he took ended up next. You folks were there. You saw the Eccles gang, heard whatever they had to say. I hoped maybe... Hell, I don't know what I hoped." He shoved back his chair irritably and stood up. "Sorry I bothered you and wasted all our time."

CHAPTER SEVENTEEN

DESPITE HIS FRUSTRATION—OR MAYBE BECAUSE OF IT, since he needed somewhere to settle and sort out his thoughts—Lone went ahead and booked a room for the night at Finnegan's. By the time he had stabled Ironsides, eaten a meal at the local cafe, and soaked for a good long while in a tub of hot, sudsy water, darkness had descended over Bayard.

He carried his rifle and saddlebags up to the room and sat down on the edge of the bed without bothering to light a lamp. The room was shot by sharp shadows and a few slices of illumination reaching in from out in the street. But it wasn't like he needed light to think by.

Christ, it seemed like thinking was about all he'd been doing lately. Grinding everything to a fine dust only to have it turn to mud or get blown away by some change of events that came like a hard gust of wind. The ache over Velda was a constant; yet he knew he would hold her in his memory and heart forever, and that's all he could do. The situation with Ma, though, was something current and, in a manner of speaking, still alive.

Though a difficult task to start with and now made even more so by the killing of Jack Swain, Lone wasn't ready to give up on trying to regain at least part of what had been taken from her. And yet, along with the added difficulty, also came the possibility of a chance at the reward being offered for Fenton Eccles. That alone would go a long way toward recouping Ma's loss.

But how to go about re-focusing on pursuit of an outlaw gang on the run all the way from Colorado? Where to start looking, what was even a logical next step?

Lone got up, walked over to the window and parted the curtains to look down on the street. It appeared cold and empty. The day had never warmed very much to begin with and the evening air had begun turning chill as soon as the sun went down. As he watched, he saw a dust devil stir briefly and then a tumbleweed go skipping down between the rows of buildings.

In his time of drifting from one pursuit to another, he'd often thought of himself as sort of a human tumbleweed. But he'd seldom felt more aimless than he did at the moment.

Turning away from the window, Lone walked back and stood beside the bed. He didn't feel like sitting down again, and certainly not lying down. He was restless both physically and mentally.

He could hear the sounds of activity from the saloon below. Not overly loud, not anything that would have disturbed him if he'd been ready to sleep. But discernible all the same.

He considered going down there for a while. Befitting his name, for most of his adult life he'd generally been considered a loner. Solitude not only went with scouting and hunting and trapping, but it also was something he'd tended to prefer. After spending time with Velda, however—and especially since losing her—he had noticed a change. Being alone now felt empty in a way it never used to.

If he went down and had a couple of beers, maybe a shot or two to go with them, it might make him more ready for sleep when he returned. Hell, maybe the billiard table would be available and he could knock around some pool balls for a while. Hadn't done that in a long time. And it wasn't like he was apt to do any worse than the pair of codgers from this afternoon...

Before he knew it, Lone had himself convinced and he was heading out of the room.

———

IT CAME as no surprise that the barroom was considerably busier than it had been earlier. Twenty or so customers were on hand, Lone judged, appearing to be a fairly even mix of townsmen and cowboys from surrounding ranches. A handful were bellied up to the bar, the rest occupied the various tables either playing cards or just chewing the fat. A plump, pretty, red-haired barmaid wove in and out of the tables, fetching drinks as requested.

Since the billiard table was in use, leaving that as no option for now, Lone found a spot at the bar and rested his elbows. Before doing so, he paused to take note that the gambler Bayne was still seated where he'd been before only now engaged in a poker game with three other men. Rena Matteson once again sat next to him. While Bayne remained clad in his cream and black attire, Rena had changed to a clinging wine-colored dress that left her shoulders bare and plunged low enough in front to reveal a head-turning display of cleavage.

The slick-haired bartender, who Lone had learned was not named Finnegan at all but rather Chauncy, appeared on the other side of the stick. "Evening, Mr. McGantry. Everything okay with your bath and room?"

"All fine," Lone told him.

"Can I get you a drink? Another beer?"

"Sounds good. And a shot of rye to go with it."

After downing the shot, Lone turned around and leaned back against the bar with his beer in one fist. Sipping leisurely, he watched the two cowpokes playing pool. They were pretty good, good enough to dissuade him from going over and challenging for next game. He was too far out of practice. He could accept getting beat, but he didn't want to look like a complete fool doing it. So he continued to watch, hoping one or the other of the players would sink the eight ball and then the pair might move on to something else. If he had the table to himself for a while he could brush up on his technique...or maybe one of the bespectacled codgers from this afternoon would reappear and present somebody he'd have a chance against even in his rusty condition.

Lone had just ordered his second beer and was still waiting for access to the billiard table when a harshly raised voice signaled a hint of trouble and drew the quick attention of most men in the room. Lone's head turned with the others, eyes sweeping to lock on the source of the raised voice.

It turned out to be one of the men sitting at the table with Bayne—make that, someone who *had* been sitting with Bayne. The speaker was on his feet now, his chair suddenly getting shoved back to the point of nearly tipping over as the hombre thrust to a standing position. He was an average-sized specimen, wiry, tousle-haired, dressed in the standard garb of a ranch hand. From his angle, Lone couldn't see his face to judge how old the man was, but he gave the impression of not carrying too many years. In any case, he was poised rigid with anger, feet planted wide and hands curled claw-like at his sides. His ire seemed aimed directly at Bayne and, as he spat out more words, what was eating him became clear.

"I've had it with you, mister. I'm callin' you on your bullshit! Nobody sits there and wins and wins and wins, not night after night the way you been doin'... Not if everything is on the level!"

Bayne sat very still and eyed the cowboy calmly. Beside him, Rena appeared totally disinterested in what was going on. Looking closer, Lone could see that the gambler had a nice stack of bills already in front of him and was paused with his good arm extended, ready to rake in the latest pot. Everyone else had gone very quiet throughout the smoky barroom so that when Bayne replied, even though he spoke low, he could be heard plenty clear. "Mister Rooney, I suggest you choose very carefully the next words that come out of that hole in your face. Because it almost sounds like you're accusing me of cheating—and that would offend me greatly."

The flintiness of Bayne's tone held Rooney in check for a moment. But only just a moment. "Damn it, what's a body supposed to think? You just laid down the second full boat in the past hour. And how many straights and flushes before that? Huh?"

Chauncy the barkeep hurried down to the end of the bar and called over to the troubled table, "Now everybody take it easy before this gets out of hand! Rooney, you know I run a clean, honest place. I've been watching Mr. Bayne play cards in here for a lot more nights than you've come to town. I ain't never seen no sign of any funny business on his part, and neither has anybody else."

"That's because everybody else is too gutless to say anything. Well I ain't!" Rooney proclaimed. "You don't mind havin' this card sharp in here, Chauncy, 'cause you ain't the one losin' money to him. Hell, he's even good for business, ain't he? Him and the free titty show his girlfriend puts on with those dresses she parades around half in and half out of!"

The soft scrape of Bayne's chair sliding slowly back was like a warning whisper.

But whatever might have happened next was interrupted by another sound—the distinctive *thump* of an object being placed heavily on a wooden surface. Eyes swept again and this time landed on the sawed-off shotgun Chauncy had produced and was resting across the top of the bar, its twin muzzles aimed in the direction of the Bayne-Rooney table. As everyone in the blast path, especially the table's other occupants (except for Rena, who remained coolly indifferent), quickly scattered, Chauncy growled, "I *said* for everybody to take it easy. Rooney, you run your mouth just like you play cards—too damn reckless. That's why you lose more often than you win, and that's been going on long before Bayne ever showed up here. Mr. Bayne, I understand how you—"

That's when the next interruption occurred. This

one came from two cowboys who were taking up space at the bar between Lone's position and Chauncy. Up until now they'd been conversing quietly over their drinks and warranted no particular attention. But suddenly the one closest to Chauncy thrust out one hand to knock the sawed-off's barrel upward as he reached with the other to yank the weapon away. He succeeded in gaining control of the gun, wrenching it out of the barkeep's grasp, but in the process one of the barrels got triggered. The blast roared like thunder in the crowded room. The twelve-gauge load tore loose a large oval section of the ceiling and sent a cloud of plaster and wood slivers raining down on customers who threw their arms over their heads and yelped in alarm.

In the midst of this, the second cowboy clambered up onto a bar stool and then skimmed agilely over the top of the bar, rushing to grab hold of scrawny Chauncy. Shaking him roughly, he hollered loud enough to be heard through the ear-ringing of the shotgun blast. "No, you *don't* understand, you little runt! If you did, you'd've seen before this how what Rooney claims is true—how a bunch of us ranch hands have been feelin' the same but, like he said, were too gutless to speak up. So now he's done took the cork out of the bottle and it's time for that damn card sharp to face what comes out!"

"That's right," chimed in the one now holding the sawed-off. He waved it in a choppy, menacing arc before adding, "So you go ahead, Rooney, and finish makin' your play. Me and Jesse will make sure nobody interferes."

Afterward, Lone wouldn't have been able to tell you why he did it. He'd spent a big chunk of his life making sure to not stick his nose into other folks' business. There'd been a few exceptions, but mostly he'd managed to keep it out. In this case, though, Chauncy had been nothing but friendly to him; and though Bayne hadn't provided anything useful, Lone for some reason still felt a kind of cockeyed connection to him due to his encounter with Swain. Neither reason held much logic, but that's what it came down to all the same.

The only thing Lone knew for sure was that all of a sudden he had his Colt in his fist and was aiming at the hombre with the shotgun. Right on the heels of the latter saying "make sure nobody interferes," Lone grated, "You could be wrong about that, bub."

As expected, the shotgunner didn't show enough smarts when it came to his reaction. Thinking the big gun gave him the edge, he started to swing it toward Lone. The Colt barked instantly in response, throwing flame and lead. The slug tore the double-barrel out of the man's stinging hands and sent it skidding across the sawdusted floor.

Unfortunately for him, the cowboy behind the bar didn't demonstrate much in the way of smarts either. Even seeing what befell his partner, he still thought he had a chance against Lone's already drawn gun. Maybe he was the hotshot pistolero of his ranch crew or some such. Whatever the case, he shoved Chauncy away and spun to face Lone, grabbing for the six-shooter on his hip. Lone's Colt spoke again and this time the bullet it spat crashed into the shoulder of the cowboy's gun arm. Now he spun back the other way, howling in pain as he toppled against the shelves of glasses and liquor bottles.

All of this took less than half a minute. But it offered

enough of a distraction so that, in spite of the ill luck suffered by his two supporters, the hot-headed Rooney decided to go ahead with his play against Bayne. Curling his bottom lip into a sneer even as his fingers curled around the grips of his shooting iron, he declared, "This is one pot *I'm* gonna win, you sonofabitch!"

But he was wrong. Again. His gun wasn't even half way out of its leather before Bayne's free hand darted inside the folds of his sling and flashed out holding an over-under derringer that he extended toward Rooney. One of the barrels popped and Rooney's gun hand was knocked away, throwing a spray of blood. The sore loser sank to his knees, doubling forward, hugging the wounded hand to his chest and keening in pain.

Just like that it was over. Everybody stayed still and quiet (except the injured Rooney) for a long beat. Curls of powder smoke lifted and blended in with the cigar and cigarette haze already hanging in the air.

That was the scene Constable Pribitt burst in on, brandishing his long-barreled Remington. "What in blazes is goin' on here?" he demanded to know.

Squaring his shoulders in an act of regaining composure, Chauncy answered him. "Everything's under control now, Lyle. Thanks to the quick reactions of McGantry and Bayne. It was that doggone hothead Rooney who started it. He ain't worth shit at playing cards, never has been. So somewhere along the way it appears him and these other two Bar 7 idiots formed a crybaby club to blame their recent poker losses on Bayne, accusing him of cheating. They got the drop on me and was crowding Bayne mighty tight when McGantry stepped in."

Pribitt scowled at Lone.

The former scout made a show of holstering his Colt and said, "Sorry for the gunplay, Constable. But things started poppin' and the odds were a site too lopsided for my taste. Not that there was time anyway, but I don't look favorably on bendin' my gun barrel over some fool's rock skull the way you like to do. Might affect my aim the next time I go to use it and end up causin' me serious regret."

From where he remained calmly sitting behind his table, Bayne spoke up. "I share McGantry's sentiment for mistreating a good gun on a thick but otherwise empty skull. Furthermore, the weapon available to me in this instance"—he held up his derringer—"would hardly have made a very effective club."

"Okay, you both had your say," Pribitt chuffed. He took a minute to crane his neck in order to get a look at the man sprawled behind the bar and then cut a gaze over to where Rooney was still on his knees groaning before asking, "So how bad a shape did your non-clubbin' methods leave these two in?"

"Not as bad as they deserve," Chauncy replied. "They'll both live but neither of 'em will be in any shape to go grabbin' for a hogleg any time soon."

"How about this one?" Pribitt wanted to know, aiming a glare at the third cowboy, the one who'd grabbed the shotgun and now stood meekly holding his still stinging hands clasped together in front of him.

The fellow answered for himself, saying, "I—I'm okay. My hands kinda burn and ache but they'll straighten up. Jeeze, I'm awful sorry I took part in this, Mr.—I mean, *Constable*. I don't know what come over me to—"

"Shut up," Pribitt snapped. "Get that gun belt of yours shucked off. Then turn around and put those poor achin' hands flat on the bar and keep 'em there until I tell you otherwise. I see you lift 'em even a red hair's worth, it'll give me all the excuse I need to deliver a noggin thump like I'm itchin' bad to do no matter how much other folks look down their noses at it!"

That said, the constable wheeled around and locked his eyes on a saloon customer standing over near the front door. "Herman, hightail it up the street and fetch Doc Wilkins," he ordered. "After he patches up these two jackasses, he'll have to tell me if I need to keep 'em in the drunk tank to heal for a spell, or send their sorry asses packin' back to the ranch. Get a move on!"

CHAPTER EIGHTEEN

After things tamed down in the saloon, Lone slipped away and returned to his room. Once again he didn't bother lighting the lantern. He felt ready for sleep, or at least ready to lay down and rest. Toward that end, he kicked off his boots and shrugged out of his buckskin vest, stretched out on the bed. The mattress was soft, the bedspread fresh-smelling. Oh yeah, here was a good place to spend the next few hours...

A knock on the door, however, meant a delay for getting started on that. Lone sat up, swung his feet to the floor. His right hand came to rest on the grips of his Colt, thumb automatically flipping free the keeper thong.

"Who is it?" he called.

"Emmett Bayne," came a familiar voice.

Lone rose, took time to light the wall lantern, went and opened the door. Bayne stood in the soft glow out in the hallway, Rena Matteson pressed close behind him.

A corner of his mouth lifting, the gambler said,

"Hope you'll pardon the intrusion. This time we're the ones wondering if we might have a few words."

"'Course." Lone ushered them in and closed the door. Since the room had only one sitting chair, Lone pointed Rena into that while he and Bayne stood.

"First things first," announced Bayne, still wearing his half smile. "And that is to express my gratitude for your intervention on my behalf earlier. In all the hubbub that followed, I didn't get a chance to say so downstairs."

Lone shrugged. "Like I told the constable, I didn't like the lopsided odds. What was more, the way that one fool was waving around the sawed-off he grabbed, there were more folks at risk than just you."

"Indeed. I'd already had some experience with young Rooney so wasn't especially surprised by trouble coming from him," said Bayne. "But those other two horning in presented a concern I wasn't prepared for."

"Thankfully Galahad was there to horn in on them," Rena remarked.

Lone let that one pass. To Bayne he said, "Speakin' of bein' prepared, you were mighty handy with that derringer when it came time. But you seem to've lost your, er, holster." He gestured to indicate how the gambler's left arm was no longer wrapped in a sling. "What happened?"

"I took the liberty of cornering Dr. Wilkins downstairs, after he'd finished treating the men we shot," Bayne explained, "and convinced him to finally lift his restrictions on me. So the wing is still a little stiff and sore, but it's going to take using it some"—he raised and lowered the arm as if to demonstrate—"in order to work it the rest of the way out."

"That's good." Lone grinned. "But where you gonna keep your derringer now?"

"Don't worry, I've had that little pea shooter with me for a long time and always manage to have it where it's never far out of reach," Bayne assured him. Then, matching Lone's grin and opening the left side of his jacket to reveal an ivory-handled Colt Lightning nestled in an underarm holster, he added, "Besides, I also keep its big brother close by."

Lone nodded. "Smart."

"Just for the record, to prevent this little show and tell session on firepower from getting too one-sided," Rena spoke up, "let it be known that I happen to carry some of my own." So saying, she lifted her skirt to show a nickel-plated Sharps pepperbox secured in a garter holster.

"And displaying that much leg to get at it makes it all the more formidable," Bayne commented.

Letting the folds of her skirt fall back down, Rena said, "I fear we're making Galahad blush."

"In case you got a knife or maybe a stick of dynamite strapped to the other leg, feel free to show it too. Won't bother me none," Lone told her. "If I appear to be blushin', could be because I'm feelin' a little silly for stickin' my nose in after all. Hell, heavy as you two were armed I don't guess the odds weren't as lopsided as I thought. I could have stayed out of it and finished drinkin' my beer before it went flat."

"That's bullshit and you know it," argued Bayne. "Those two at the bar were flat out more than we could have handled. I don't go out of my way to act beholden to anybody I don't believe deserves it."

Lone eyed the gambler for a long count. "Okay. You

came by to say you're obliged and I appreciate you goin' to the trouble. Why do I now get the feelin' there's something more behind this visit?"

Rena arched a brow. "Galahad is not only brave and strong, he is also quite perceptive."

Lone gave her a look. "In case you'd like to know, that Galahad shit could get old in a hurry."

"Take it easy you two," said Bayne. Addressing just Lone, his mouth twisted wryly as he pleaded, "Don't mind Rena, she doesn't mean anything by it. She makes those little remarks as a way to fight boredom."

"And after three plus weeks in this dust mote of a town, the battle has reached epic proportions," Rena lamented from her chair.

"Well, I'm real sorry for your battle weariness," Lone said. "But I ain't no part of the town or what stuck you in it. So your fight ain't with me."

Bayne held up an index finger. "Ah. You almost touched on our reason for stopping by. But fighting each other is the last thing we have in mind. In fact, what we came to propose is just the opposite. We're here to suggest joining forces."

"Join forces to do what?" Lone wanted to know.

"To do what you already mean to attempt on your own—run down the Fenton Eccles gang."

———

IT TOOK the better part of an hour before Lone came around to believing the gambler not only wasn't joking but that there might actually be some merit in what he was proposing.

"The key goes back to some things Rena and I

recalled after you spoke with us earlier today," Bayne stated. "And also some of the things that U.S. Marshal said when was here."

"More implied than said," Rena interjected. "But it's all of a whole."

"You originally asked us about overhearing anything the gang might have said during the robbery," Bayne went on. "We never gave you an answer at the time but, after considering it more, we did recall something that might be meaningful. In fact, we shared it with Marshal Bourbon and his response is something else that could be useful.

"Once everybody saw how much Swain's money belt contained, one of Eccles' men crowed words to the effect of it being enough to buy themselves their very own corner of Wyoming. When we told this to Bourbon, he muttered how it 'fit' with something more, though never said what. What he did mention, though, was that a member of the gang allegedly had relatives in the Deadwood area. Speculating that their take from the money belt might cause the gang to temporarily 'go to ground'—his words—now that they could afford to hold off on any more robberies for a while, Bourbon seemed to think this relative might be a source for helping them hide out. That inclined him to head for Deadwood when he left here."

"Makes sense," Lone allowed.

It was common enough for family members to conceal the whereabouts of criminal relatives from the law. In fact, once before Lone had been involved in exactly such a matter and it had also been in the Deadwood area. But that was nothing he felt the need to bring up now.

"So," Bayne continued, "Rena and I thought that following in the footsteps of Bourbon might be a good start for anyone else pursuing the Eccles gang from this point. Let's face it, picking up the trail of a black U.S. Marshal going around openly asking questions is bound to be a hell of a lot easier than rooting out a gang who has gone into hiding."

"Yeah, picking up his trail shouldn't be hard," Lone agreed. "Be best if he ain't too long moved on and to know if he turned up something useful while he was there."

"Naturally. If we could cherry pick, all of that would be ideal." Bayne paused and exchanged looks with Rena. Then, cutting his gaze back to Lone he said, "But once we get up around Deadwood, that's where Rena and I can start to be of benefit. You see, you're a scout and tracker in the classic sense of following physical sign. But the Deadwood area is where we circulated on the gambling scene for a good long spell. Where we first met, as a matter of fact."

"You can decide who—if either of us—can lay claim to the winning hand out of that deal," quipped Rena.

Like he'd advised Lone to do, Bayne paid no attention to the remark. Continuing, he said, "A professional gambler learns quickly that, if you want to survive in the long run, you have to go with how the cards are running. If they turn cold in one place, you move on to where they're running hotter. That's what took us away from Deadwood for a while. So we made the circuit—Cheyenne, Laramie, eventually Denver. Hit a few decent streaks, but none that stuck all that tight. So we finally decided it was time to head back and see if things had turned around in Deadwood."

"Which is what put you on the stage that got hit by Eccles and his bunch," Lone concluded.

Bayne made a sour face. "Regrettably, yes. That's established. The robbery included, by the way, all the money Rena and I were carrying. We haven't advertised it a lot and it was an amount certainly meager by comparison to what they got off Swain. But it was nevertheless the poke we hoped to build on once we reached our destination."

"I didn't think about that before," said Lone, "but I guess it stands to reason the robbers would've cleaned out everybody. Sorry for the tough break."

"It could have been worse," Bayne replied, even though his sour expression remained in place. "The bleeding from my inadvertent wound followed by the unexpectedly large haul from Swain excited the pack of curly wolves to the point of distraction. And then, of course, there was the sight of that army surveying crew coming down the road. The gang had already taken my wallet and Rena's purse by then, but they didn't have time to dig any deeper. That meant they didn't grab our weapons and they missed the emergency roll of bills I keep in a secret belt slot—another old gambler's trick, beyond just a hideaway derringer."

"Something else they didn't get to," said Rena, a strained tone suddenly noticeable in her voice, "was what they might have had in store for me if those soldiers hadn't come along."

"God yes. I don't even want to think about that," Bayne muttered.

For the first time, Rena's shell of haughty sarcasm having slipped momentarily, Lone sensed there might actually be a softer, more vulnerable side to her that she for some reason fought hard to hide. "Guess out of all the bad luck that hit your coach that day," he said, "at least some good broke in your favor."

"And none more than those curs being chased off before..." Bayne let his words trail off. Then: "But enough about such a dreadful prospect. The other favorable break, being left with my emergency stash, is what sustained Rena and I for our stay here in Bayard. That and my winnings at the poker table—which, for the record, I never cheated to attain. Plus, if I'd wanted, I could have plucked clean every five-thumbed cowboy who sat across from me. Hell, I folded nearly as many winning hands as I laid down, merely to build back a portion of our poke without causing too much of a stir."

"Yeah, and how did that work out in the end?" said Rena with a tartness that signaled she was back in her shell again. "But now that you've assuaged your ego and made your testimony about being clear of any cheating accusations, don't you think we should get back to what we came here to discuss?"

"You were indicatin' as to how the Deadwood area was where you two might be of particular benefit when it came to closin' in on Marshal Bourbon and maybe even the Eccles gang," Lone offered as a reminder.

"Uh-huh. The thing is," Bayne explained, "Rena and I know a whole network of people up there—other gamblers, saloon owners, bartenders, bouncers, dance hall girls, and so forth—folks who operate on what you might call the fringe of things. None of them corrupt or overtly illegal for the most part, but hardly what anybody would call pillars of the community either. Yet they nevertheless see and hear and know plenty about what's going on in and around said community."

"I get the picture."

"So they may talk freely among themselves, but tend to be mighty tight-lipped around outsiders."

"Especially an outsider wearin' a badge and askin' a lot of questions."

"You got it."

Lone twisted his mouth wryly. "And that'd probably hold true even for a tall, handsome stranger without a badge but still with his own mouthful of questions."

Rena couldn't resist a sly smile. "Not everyone is quick to recognize and appreciate the noble Galahad virtues in a person."

"I can't tell," said Bayne, scowling, "if you two are still pecking at each other, or beginning to flirt right under my nose."

"Don't worry, darling," Rena assured him. "You're the high roller I have my claws sunk in. We're after stolen property and bounty money, remember—not the Holy Grail."

Lone lifted his brows questioningly. "Bounty money?"

"Come on," said Bayne. "If Pribitt showed you the Wanted poster on Eccles, you certainly saw the substantial bounty being offered on him. Don't tell me you still had in mind to go after him *just* for whatever you could recover of your friend's pilfered savings?"

"Can't say it didn't cross my mind how that bounty money might fill some gaps," Lone admitted.

"What's more, even though Pribitt only has a paper on Eccles himself, it stands to reason there's got to be money offered on some of the rest of the bunch, too, don't it?" Bayne grimaced. "Remember, Rena and I looked that cold-eyed crew straight on, each and every one. They're hardcases to the core, and it's a sure bet the rest wasn't biding their time attending Sunday school while Eccles was behind bars."

"So," Lone pouched his lips, considering, "if we throw in together and succeed, then you figure we'll work out a split of the reward money. That it?"

Bayne looked like butter wouldn't melt in his mouth. "Isn't that the way a partnership works?"

CHAPTER NINETEEN

FENTON ECCLES EXHALED A PLUME OF SMOKE FROM HIS freshly lighted cigar and examined the three grizzled faces staring back at him through the bluish haze. "Boys," he said, clenching the cigar between a row of even, white teeth, "it's time for us to make some choices about when and where we head from here."

The statement caused Luther Purdy to cock his head to one side and his narrow, bony face to take on a puzzled look. "I thunk we had that all decided, Fen," he said. "Cuttin' a swath across the top of Wyomin' and cleanin' out all those cowtown banks sittin' fat with cattlemen's money—ain't that what we had in mind?" Purdy was a lean, angular six footer with an unruly thatch of straw-colored hair and a twangy voice heavy with a Tennessee accent.

"True enough," allowed Eccles. "But, like you said, it's something we *had* in mind. And I ain't saying it's not still a possibility. But I heard some things in prison that also put another notion in my head, one I sorta had on the back burner until just recently."

"Like what?" asked Amarillo Ames. "And why ain't you brought it up before this?" Ames was thick-bodied, pushing fifty, making him the oldest member of the gang with much of the hard living behind those years evident on his broad, battered face and in brooding eyes that seemed always a bit narrowed, as if suspicious about something.

"Didn't bring it up before," Eccles explained patiently, "because the time wasn't right. That's what kept it a back burner notion."

"So what changed?" This question came from Bo Lasky, the remaining and youngest member of the group, a boyishly handsome twenty-year-old with eyes nearly as deep a blue as Eccles'. Only a cruel, sullen twist to his mouth and the brace of black-handled Colts slung low on his narrow hips, worn for the cross-draw, kept him from looking wholly out of place amidst the others.

Eccles puffed another cloud of smoke then calmly tipped his head to indicate the bulging set of saddlebags that rested on a bedroll in the corner of the room. "What changed," he answered, "is that unexpectedly handsome take we got from what we figured would be a meager stagecoach haul. Same change that allows us to be laying low here for a spell instead of staying on the run and pulling other piss-ant jobs until we got in position for those bigger ones."

The "here" the gang leader was referring to was an old, weathered, one-room trapper's cabin tucked away in the rocky, forested hills between Deadwood and Lead, on the western fringes of South Dakota's Black Hills. On one hand, it made rugged conditions for men with thousands of dollars at their disposal; on the other, it served as a welcome haven from pursuit brought on by how those dollars were attained (not to mention previous past deeds). Supplies furnished by Luther's cousin—a freighter for the surrounding mining companies who had also guided them to the remote, little-known cabin—had provided plenty of sustenance and shelter for the ten days they'd already been present. And more was available if needed. In truth, all except maybe for young Lasky, had hidden out for longer periods under a hell of a lot worse conditions.

"You see," Eccles continued, "the other notion that got put in my head in prison was always something I reckoned to go after. But I figured I owed it to you fellas, after all the scrimping you had to do while I was behind bars and the hard work you put into helping bust me out, to first put together a string of the kind of jobs we best know how to do aimed at building a good-sized pot to repay you for your loyalty."

Ames scowled, his eyes narrowing even more than usual. "When you say 'the kind of jobs we best know how to do'... What's so different about this other notion you keep talking about?"

Eccles stood up from the rough-hewn wooden table where he'd been seated with the others and began to pace. His boots thumped heavily on the hard-packed earth floor and he trailed a plume of smoke as he walked. "This other thing ain't no kind of hold-up, see. It ain't robbing no train or stagecoach or bank or anything like that. What it is... Well, it amounts to a treasure hunt."

The three men remaining at the table exchanged

uncertain looks. Eccles stopped pacing and turned to see what their reactions were.

Meeting his expectant stare, Luther said, "You mean a treasure hunt for money. Right?"

"Money?" Eccles echoed. He waving his cigar expansively. "No, I mean a hunt for treasure *worth* money! More money than all of us put together could ever imagine if we added up the take from every single bank we even *thought* about robbing! Riches beyond belief. A whole goddamn kingdom's worth of riches and wealth."

"What the hell's in that cigar you're smoking, Fen?" growled Ames. "You're talking crazier than a 'Rappyho witch doctor after puffing a whole bush of loco weed!"

Eccles heaved a sigh, returned to the table and sat down again. "I can understand how you feel that way, 'Rillo," he conceded. "Hell, I did myself at first. But I kept listening. I didn't have much choice since I was sharing a cell with an old geezer who wouldn't shut up about it. He was a lunger on the verge of dying, I was certain in everybody's eyes to soon be stepping through a trap door with a noose around my neck. He figured it was safe to tell me about stuff he'd been holding bottled up for years. It was only after he croaked as expected that I decided to make a trip to the library and do some reading up on what he'd been yammering about. I soon wished I would have."

"Wait a minute," Lasky interrupted. "You saying they got a library in that prison?"

"Sure do. Great big one." Eccles chuffed. "Ain't that something? They pen you up behind iron and stone and then, until you rot or they haul you off to stretch your neck, they give you the means to read about and learn about all the things you're locked away from. Stories tell how there've been some men penned up long enough to learn how to be lawyers and doctors and who knows what-all else."

"Bah," Ames scoffed. "You'd have to lock me up a helluva long time before I'd ever resort to passing time with my nose stuck in a bunch of musty old books."

Luther sighed somewhat wistfully. "I think I probably would. If I knew how to read, that is."

"That's all interesting as hell," said Lasky, a touch of youthful impatience edging into his tone, "but we still ain't heard what this big money notion is that the old man's yammering planted in Fen's head."

Eccles leaned closer and rested his forearms on the tabletop. "Okay, let's start with this. Any of you ragtag polecats ever hear of the Seven Cities of Gold?"

There were a couple long beats of bewildered silence. Until, to Eccles' surprise, a scowling Ames said, "That's some south of the border bullcrap, ain't it? A moldy old bean-eater legend about a heap of conquistador gold that went off course and supposedly ended up north of the Rio Grande. When the iron helmet boys finally got tired of packing it around, they buried it in seven scattered spots and went back home. Whatever their intentions were about coming to reclaim it, for some reason they never did. Ever since then—and likely yet to this day, I expect—fools have been scratching and digging all over Texas, Arizona, New Mexico, and God knows where else to try and find some sign of it. Jesus, I remember hearing stories about that from way back when I was a kid."

Lasky looked at Eccles. "Is that what you're talking about? Is that what your big notion has to do with?"

The gang boss smiled slyly. "What it's got to do with,

yeah. 'Rillo has some of the details twisted around—not his fault, just the way he was told, I reckon—but he laid out the bare bones of it. The seven deposits of treasure, known as the Seven Cities of Gold or sometimes just generally as *El Dorado*, were made up of more than only gold. Silver bars, too, along with jewelry, precious stones, and all sorts of valuable trinkets were in the mix. It was the wealth gathered over many years by a tribe of South American natives called Aztecs."

"Tribe? You mean like Injuns?" asked Luther.

"Uh-huh. But don't picture 'em as the kind we know about from around here," Eccles said. "This bunch, in addition to mining gold and silver and turning it into rich trinkets and such, built whole cities and even a palace for their king, a he-bull by the name of Montezuma."

"Montezuma. Yeah, I remember hearing that name," Ames commented.

"Anyway," Eccles continued, "when the conquistadors came around, led by an hombre named Cortes, they right away wanted to glom on to all this wealth and take it back to their own king in Spain. Ol' Montezuma tried to be reasonable at first, but he wasn't about to just hand over all his wealth. So Cortes left and went back home to get reinforcements. Montezuma knew that when he returned with more men and guns and cannons, the Aztecs and their simple weapons would stand no chance against 'em. That's when he set in motion the plan to gather up all the gold and wealth and scatter it north to hide it from the Spaniards."

"But it sounds like nobody ended up with it. How did that happen?" Luther wanted to know.

"That's a good question," Eccles replied. "Cortes and his boys came back loaded for bear, like expected. Got all piss burned over Montezuma's trick, and pretty much wiped out him and his whole tribe. While they was at it, the jackasses wiped out any person or record of where the treasure stashes got hid. All that was three, four hundred years ago, remember. Like 'Rillo said at the start, folks been hunting to find some part of the treasure ever since."

"So that's the notion the old man's yammering planted in your head?" said Lasky, still impatient. "You think you know where one of those stashes might be?"

"I think I got some pretty damn good clues to follow, yes," stated Eccles.

Ames' brows pinched even tighter together. "Up around here somewhere, you saying?"

"Less than a week's ride."

"Damn!" Ames exclaimed. "All this time everybody's been figuring those stashes were spread across the Southwest. Why would Montezuma's boys lug 'em clear the hell up this far? What makes you or your yammering old man think that?"

"If they lugged 'em all the way to Texas or New Mexico, what's another few hundred miles?" argued Eccles. "Hell, maybe there's some up in Canada for all I know. But what I do know—or have come to believe, anyway—is that there's some of that treasure buried not far from here and I mean to make a try for it."

"So what was all that talk at the start about makin' choices and maybe first still cuttin' a bank-robbin' swath across Wyoming?" said Luther. "Why would we take time for that if this big treasure is so close by?"

Eccles sighed. "I thought I explained that. Ain't no treasure hunt that's a sure thing. Well, robbing a bank or whatever is no sure thing neither—but, unless you get gunned down in the attempt, at least you know you're gonna ride away with *some* money. And before we lucked out with the surprising take from that stage holdup we were scraping so close to the bottom, money-wise, I didn't see any way but to go for some surer paying jobs. Only now things are different—giving us an opportunity to make the choices I mentioned."

Eccles paused to drop his cigar stub and grind it out under his boot heel, then once again scanned the faces of his men before continuing. "There's enough money in those saddlebags over yonder for anybody who wants to take his split and cut out to go off somewhere and get on pretty comfortable—nothing stupidly extravagant, mind you, but *comfortable*—for quite a spell. With that nigger U.S. Marshal who Luther's cousin Myron told us about yesterday, the law dog sniffing to pick up our trail in Deadwood, I figure it's time for us to be on the move regardless. I heard talk about Charley Bourbon in the pen. He's a stubborn bulldog responsible for putting plenty of unlucky devils behind those bars."

"According to Myron, that marshal is doing his sniffing all on his own. Just one man," said Lasky. "I don't see where one badge toter can be that big a threat. But if you think he is, why don't a couple of us—me and Ames, say—just drop back and get shed of him? Myron said he's only showing around papers on you, he wouldn't recognize any of the rest of us until it was too late."

Eccles wrinkled his nose like he'd been hit by a bad

smell. "Oh yeah, that's a swell idea. Everybody knows you gun down one U.S. Marshal you draw a shitload more quicker'n cockroaches to cornmeal. I already got every piss-ant sheriff and town marshal and money-grubbing bounty hunter in four or five different states—everybody short of the women's temperance league—after my ass. Do I need a regiment of revenge-hungry federal marshals, too? Just like I didn't want to bait the army by tangling with their crew of surveyors who showed up to interrupt our stage holdup the other day."

"Okay. You made your point," Lasky responded.

"Besides," Eccles added, "just because Bourbon is only flashing dodgers on me don't mean he ain't got the rest of your mugs planted in his memory. I'm telling you, that black boy is damned sharp!"

"I *said* you made your point," Lasky ground out through clenched teeth.

"What about you, Fen?" asked Luther. "If we divvy up what's in those saddlebags and make dust outta here, you aimin' to go somewhere and take it easy for a spell, too?"

Eccles gave him a look. "Ain't I made it plain what I'm hankering to do, Luth? I'm going after that treasure. You're all welcome to pitch in with me. I hope you do. It'd be the same split as always, only the take could be bigger than anything we've ever imagined. But, no matter how strong I personally believe in it, I realize it could still prove a big waste of time, maybe come with some danger, and end up nothing more than a deep reach into an empty pocket."

This time when Eccles paused, he gave the others a long count to gaze back at him. Their expressions looked heavy with thought but none had anything to say.

Finally, he spoke again. "Okay, I guess I threw a lot at you. Go ahead and chew on it some. But make up your minds by the time we turn in tonight. Come tomorrow morning, I plan on riding out."

CHAPTER TWENTY

LONE HAD FORGOTTEN HOW BUSY DEADWOOD WAS AT ALL hours of the day and night. A throng always seemed present in the downtown area. The number of business structures packed into the heart of the gulch, lining the main street, didn't appear to have increased all that much since his last visit here over a year ago. Probably, Lone reckoned, because there was such limited space to build more. He did, however, note that several of the businesses had been revised taller and gaudier.

The main driver for all of this was the big mining operations in the surrounding hills that continued to find veins of coveted yellow ore. So the laborers who worked the mines poured into town on their days off and showed up rowdy, thirsty, and horny. While the mine bosses made their money from what got dug out of the ground, the town businessmen made theirs from those who did the digging. And on the fringes were the hustlers and schemers who looked to skim off their share of easier pickings.

Lone's exposure to these goings on the last time he

was here had largely been limited, due to the fact he'd spent most of his time on the outskirts working with a detachment of soldiers to corner a pack of murderous scum who had robbed an army payroll and prior to that had killed Lone's best friend, one-legged old mountain man Peg O'Malley. When the gang, led by a scar-faced devil called Scorch Bannon, decided to make a fight of it and all paid with their lives, Lone's involvement in the matter was finished.

But that had still left a bit of personal business that kept him around a couple more days. This was centered around a young woman by the name of Maggie, a brassy, sassy saloon singer who had accompanied Lone on his trip to Deadwood. She'd wangled his protection and escort services in exchange for providing information on locating Bannon's gang. Her information had proven out, but unfortunately she became seriously ill by the end of their cross country journey; rugged trail conditions aggravating a physical frailty carried over from childhood, was the doctor's diagnosis. Pneumonia had resulted and Lone ended up attending her funeral before finally departing the territory.

When the prospect of returning to Deadwood arose, this time in pursuit of Fenton Eccles and his crew, thoughts of Maggie had naturally begun running through Lone's mind. That was why, this first morning back after arriving by stage the previous evening, he decided a visit to her grave was in order. He had time to kill and it was inevitable he would be paying his respects at some point, so he saw no need to wait. Though not generally given to sentimental gestures, he even stopped at a downtown shop and picked up some flowers.

The morning was chill and gloomy under a sooty gray sky, setting a suitable mood for a cemetery visit. Still, the emptiness and quiet of the place was a welcome change from the town's hubbub.

As he placed the flowers in front of Maggie's stone marker, wishing there'd been a touch of sunlight to bring out their bright colors, Lone remembered helping Maggie's friend Bea arrange for the stone right after the funeral service. He couldn't hold back a wry smile at the thought of what Maggie might say about him bringing her flowers now. She was a tough-acting, outspoken type not much given to sentimental displays herself. Though inwardly, he was willing to bet, she would be pleased by the bouquet. Last time he was here, stopping on his ride out of town, he'd left a pack of cigarillos leaned up against her temporary marker in recognition of her smoking habit when she'd been alive. *That*, he told himself with a widening smile, he definitely knew would please her.

Straightening up after placing the flowers, Lone just stood there for a while, gazing down at Maggie's grave, letting the still silence of the setting wrap around him.

Included in his thoughts, of course, was the memory of the last grave marker he had stood beside—Velda's. Not that she was ever far from his thoughts under any circumstance, all waking moments and often in his slumber. When he'd first considered coming to pay his respects to Maggie, Lone had experienced a brief, curious sense of guilt. As if he was somehow disrespecting or being unfaithful to Velda. But the feeling soon passed. He knew what his motives were and if she was in some way looking on or had any awareness, he knew that Velda would fully understand. It wasn't like he hadn't told her all about Maggie. How a mutual attraction had developed between them, sure, but other obligations at the time had prevented it from going any farther. And then Maggie's unexpected and tragic death had added a bittersweet aftermath that deepened the memory he carried of her.

Unexpected and tragic death... The phrase repeated through Lone's mind.

Was there any other kind? Sure as hell not around him, it seemed. And was he destined to always be the lone survivor? Was that a blessing or a curse?

Willing himself not to let this sudden wash of melancholy drag him too deep, Lone seized on the determination that no matter how painful it was to have lost someone close—Peg O'Malley, Maggie, Velda (the deepest wound of all)—having had them in his life for however long he'd been allowed was definitely more blessing than curse. And being a survivor must mean there was more left for him to do—like now, tracking down whoever he needed to and doing whatever it took to retrieve at least a portion of what had been taken from Ma so she could regain a measure of the standing and dignity she damn well deserved.

But what of the rage beast that continued to lay dormant somewhere inside him? Only temporarily, he was convinced. When might it stir again? How could doing something right and proper, like squaring things for Ma, fit with the blind fury the beast would bring forth when it woke?

Lone left the cemetery feeling a little sadder and more restlessly troubled. Yet secure in the belief that coming here had still been the right thing.

BY THE TIME he got back to town, Lone was resolved and re-focused once more on the job at hand. Trouble was, right at the moment there wasn't a hell of a lot he could do to shoulder any of the load.

Bayne and Rena had arrived with him the previous evening on the stage from Bayard. At Bayne's suggestion, Lone had agreed that, once in Deadwood, he would initially part ways with the pair as if he had no connection to them other than having shared a coach ride. Since he and Rena had been away for several months, the gambler explained, fitting back in with their network of acquaintances and getting some worthwhile answers to their planned inquiries might not go so smoothly in case any suspicions arose over them having a big, hard-looking stranger tagging along as a new associate. So that left Lone just hanging fire on the periphery of things until Bayne and Rena hopefully turned up a lead to the alleged relative of one of Eccles' men who then could be leaned on for information about the gang's whereabouts. Lone was willing to hold back and play this waiting game for a while, but if something promising didn't break pretty quick he'd have to start looking for some alternative way to close in on the polecats who now had Ma's (and his) money.

The walk back from the cemetery under a charcoal sky looking steadily more bloated with the threat of rain chilled Lone enough so that he decided to stop for some coffee at the restaurant of the hotel where he'd booked a room. He had breakfasted there earlier and found both the food and the service very satisfactory.

The place, obviously and deservedly quite popular

at the height of the breakfast rush, was far less crowded now. Which suited Lone just fine. The same plump, cheerful waitress who had served him before was still on duty. After seating him at a table near the front window, she brought him a carafe of steaming hot coffee and, though not requested, a plate of fresh biscuits with a cup of homemade strawberry jam. She also placed a rolled up newspaper at his elbow for him to peruse if desired.

"Shame your friendliness and efficiency can't be bottled," Lone told her. "You brighten even a gloomy mornin' like this one."

The waitress beamed a smile. "That's sweet of you to say, but I'm afraid I can't ward off the gloominess out there good enough to stop it from turning to rain before very long."

True to the waitress's forecast, raindrops began dotting the restaurant's front window as Lone was finishing up his coffee and biscuits. It was only a light drizzle at first but the still-bloated sky showed every indication of it building to something more. So far the activity out on the street didn't appear to be diminished much, though two or three bumbershoots could be seen popping open and some folks were donning rain gear.

These sights caused Lone to reflect on his own rain slicker, which was in the livery barn where he'd boarded Ironsides (after the big gray had trotted into town at the end of a tether hitched behind the stage Lone was aboard). Lone had taken his saddlebags and rifle to his room but had left his larger soogan roll, with the slicker wrapped inside, to be stalled with the gray. He didn't see an immediate likelihood he'd be going out in this inclement weather but, by the same token, there was no telling how long the rain would last or what else might arise. So, to be safe, he decided he'd go ahead and fetch the slicker before the rain got heavier. It wasn't like he didn't have time on his hands, and going to the livery would also provide a chance to check on Ironsides to make sure he was being cared for okay.

Leaving a generous tip for the waitress, Lone flipped up his collar and stepped back outside. There was no wind so the drizzle was coming straight down. But the drops were cold and biting. Lone noted more of the folks moving up and down the boardwalks had begun scurrying a bit faster to reach their destinations.

The livery barn he wanted—a modest-sized setup called *O'Feeney's*—was a block up the street, set back a ways on the opposite side. He would have the cover of storefront awnings for most of the way until he had to cross over. He headed off at a standard pace, weaving in and out of others traversing the same stretch of boardwalk as him.

When Lone reached the point where he chose to cross the street, the rain had begun to fall a bit heavier. That, and the need to avoid the wagon and saddle horse traffic paying him little heed warranted a quickened step to keep from getting either drenched or trampled. Maybe both.

Arriving at the barn, he found that the wide, rolling front door had been pulled mostly closed, leaving an opening about six feet in width. Lone stepped through. The cavernous interior of the high-ceilinged barn, generally dim the deeper in you went, was even dimmer this morning due to the overcast sky without. A pair of lighted lanterns were hanging just inside the door, but there didn't appear to be anyone around.

Lone shook the rain off his hat and called out. "O'Feeney? Hey, anybody here?"

There was no response, no sound except for some hoof-scraping and blowing from horses farther down in the long row of stalls. Lone was getting ready to call out again when there was movement in the shadows off to his left. A moment later a man he'd never seen before stepped into view. He was holding a six-gun at waist level—aimed straight at Lone.

"Yeah, there's somebody here," the man said. "Unlucky for you, it's somebody you're gonna be sorry you ran into."

Lone's eyes touched on the gun then lifted to the man's face. He was an ugly cuss made even more so by the pattern of shadows cutting across his face. Unshaven, razor slash of a mouth, mean eyes under bristly dark brows.

"If this a holdup," Lone grated, "I ain't the only one with bad luck. The pickin's you'll get off me are gonna be almighty slim."

"To hell with that. We got more important business goin' on," Mean Eyes told him.

"That's right," said a second voice from behind Lone. "Too bad you put yourself in the middle by not bein' smart enough, as the old sayin' goes, to stay in out of the rain."

Mean Eyes gave his gun a faint side to side wag. "Shuck your gun belt, real slow, and then keep your hands in plain sight. Don't try nothing funny and you might make it out of this without catchin' a bullet."

CHAPTER TWENTY-ONE

LONE SLOWLY UNBUCKLED HIS GUN BELT AND LET IT DROP. He had to figure the unseen owner of the second voice had a gun too, so he saw no kind of opening to try anything "funny." Not yet, anyway. But what the hell was this that he'd walked in on? There was still no sign of O'Feeney, the liveryman, so was it simply a robbery-in-progress? For money—or maybe to steal some of the horses?

Before any kind of answer presented itself, a third voice came into play. Starting from outside, it finished, somewhat breathlessly, as a third man barged in through the front door opening. He was a lean, gawky, young-looking character wearing a soggy hat and a dripping coat with the collar flipped up. "Bourbon's comin' across the street now," he panted. "He's hot-footin' it pretty good on account of the rain comin' down harder!"

"Shit!" swore the unseen man behind Lone. "Okay, we all still know our plan. Stringbean, go ahead and take your position. Royster, get that nosy bastard out of the way—shove him into the tack room and keep him quiet. You'll have to work out of that doorway then, I'll be over on this side. Everybody get a move on!"

Lone's mind raced. Maybe he'd just gotten some answers after all. "Bourbon" was hardly a common name for somebody. That could only mean the man coming across the street—the person these three had such an urgent "plan" for—had to be U.S. Marshal Charley Bourbon. Did that mean his awaiting ambushers were part of the Eccles gang he was known to be on the trail of? Unfortunately, Lone had never heard the names or descriptions of any of the others except Eccles himself. Hell, he could even be the unseen hombre.

While these thoughts and questions tumbled through Lone's head, he was being herded at gunpoint toward a door on the wall near where one if the lanterns was hanging. This evidently led to what the unseen man had identified as the tack room.

"Open it. Hurry up and get on through," ordered Mean Face, now referred to as being named Royster.

Lone still had no choice but to obey. When he pushed open the door, a spill of light thrown by the lantern on the outside revealed a man—O'Feeney, the liveryman—lying on the floor of the narrow room. At first Lone thought he was dead. But a closer look showed a bloody gash just above his left ear, suggesting he'd only been clubbed alongside the head.

Lone suddenly sensed that's what was in store for him, too. What was more, the realization hit him that the *last* thing the ambushers would want to do at this juncture was shoot him. The report of a gun would warn the approaching marshal and risk queering everything the trio had in place.

There was the opening Lone had been waiting for!

With only seconds to take advantage of it, he stopped short and bent suddenly forward at the waist. In the same instant, he pivoted hard to his right and slashed back and slightly upward with the point of his elbow. As anticipated, Royster was crowded close behind him with his gun arm partially raised, getting ready to bash Lone over the head with the barrel of his shooting iron. This positioned the ambusher almost perfectly for Lone's elbow to be driven into his exposed ribs. The impact of the blow produced a loud crunch of bone and gristle caving in, mixed with a strangled cry of pain and the gush of air being pounded out of lungs.

Lone straightened up and thrust back against Royster as he was starting to fold to one side. Getting his right shoulder in under Royster's armpit as his gun arm was starting to drop, Lone continued his pivot and reached to grasp the wrist of the descending arm in his left hand. This gave him leverage to jerk his would-be attacker around and slam him viciously against the side wall of the cramped space. The wall held a variety of bridles and so forth hanging on protruding metal bolts. One of these bolts stabbed deep between Royster's shoulder blades, another into his lower back. He again cried out in pain but Lone cut him short with a right cross that knocked him cold and jolted him free from the bolts, leaving him to crumple to the floor.

From outside the door, across the shadowy width of the barn, the unseen man hissed frantically, "What the hell's going on over there?"

Lone snatched up Royster's dropped gun and moved

to the open doorway in a single long stride. Only after reaching out and around to smash the hanging lantern and remove its now unwanted illumination did he call back with an answer to the hissed inquiry: "Me and your man Royster just made a big change to your plan, that's what goin' on!" Then, simultaneously triggering a pair of rounds toward Mr. Unseen's estimated position, he hollered even louder, "Ambush, Marshal Bourbon! Ambush! Duck for cover!"

Knowing that his muzzle flashes would have clearly marked him, even though he'd killed the lantern, Lone shoved out of the tack room doorway. While there'd still been light to see, he had made note of how his gun belt remained lying on the ground where he'd dropped it about ten feet straight out from the door. Running forward in a crouch, free hand reaching low, his bearings were accurate and he was able to make a blind scoop of the rig's familiar heft. Clutching it to his chest, Lone then darted left and pitched himself into a pool of dense shadows at the mouth of the nearest horse stall.

As expected, Mr. Unseen, enraged at his ambush having been wrecked, wasted no time pouring lead back at where he'd seen Lone's muzzle flashes. "Damn you, you meddling sonofabitch!" he bellowed. Then, hearing the sounds of Lone scrambling to a new position, he blasted more wild rounds up the middle of the barn bay.

This action promptly brought out a wail of protest from Stringbean, the young ambusher who'd earlier been sent to take up a position off in that direction. "Hey, Hardbark! What are you doin'— Why in hell you shootin' my way?"

"It's that goddamn stranger! Didn't you hear him?

He warned the marshal and turned our whole setup to shit!"

"What about Royster?"

"He must be dead. That's why you gotta watch out! The stranger broke out of the tack room and is moving up the stalls on that side. Puts him somewhere between us. I shot at him but—"

"You shot at me but nothing!" Lone jeered. His gun belt was buckled back on and he'd listened to enough. "If your whole bunch shoots as lousy as you, hell, I guess that marshal was never in much danger to begin with." He hoped the taunt would draw more fire toward the sound of his voice...and it took just an instant for him to get his wish! Not only did Mr. Unseen open up again but Stringbean joined in as well.

An instant after calling from one side of his stall, Lone pitched to his stomach and rolled to the opposite side. The stall's width limited very much in the way of maneuverability and the incoming rounds came whistling uncomfortably close above his head, whacking and hammering against boards and upright posts. Wood slivers and dust rained down on him, but otherwise he stayed unscathed. And he gained the rest of what he'd been hoping for—a double set of muzzle flashes to shoot back at.

With his own Colt in his right fist and Royster's hogleg in his left, Lone cut loose with a blistering return volley. He wasn't certain, but he *thought* he might have heard a yip of pain (or maybe just alarm) from where he'd sent some lead aimed at Mr. Unseen—who Stringbean had called "Hardbark." Nor did he spare Stringbean also getting some heat sent his way, but Lone sensed he didn't come very close to the younger, sprier target.

Next order of business quickly became Lone shifting to a new position due to having revealed his current one via the muzzle flashes of the shots he'd just poured from there. His eyes had begun adjusting to the gloom of the barn's deeper interior. After all, in spite of the rain and overcast sky outside, it was still daytime. A couple side windows farther down and enough chinks in the weathered walls through which bands of pale gray seeped allowed Lone to be able to make out murky shapes and a few blurred details.

Having burned through all the bullets in Royster's gun, he discarded it. Then, spotting where he wanted to make it to next, he rose up and broke into another crouched-over run. Slugs from both Stringbean and Hardbark (signaling the latter unfortunately hadn't been seriously hit before, in spite of the yip Lone heard) again hammered the stall behind him.

Lone ran past the next stall in line and then threw himself in behind a stack of grain sacks piled in front of the one after that. He pressed tight against the stuffed, burlap-encased lumps and took a few seconds for his practiced fingers to nimbly replace the spent cartridges in his Colt.

Not too far away, but on the other side of the barn bay, it turned out that Stringbean also had cartridges on his mind. "This has gone to hell in a hand basket!" he called. "I didn't bring enough cartridges to fight no damn war. I say we cut our losses and get out of here!"

After a slim pause, Hardbark responded grudgingly, "Reckon you're right, kid. Damn it all! Go ahead and hightail it out the back, I'll catch up. Shoot anybody you see who ain't me— That nigger marshal is still out there somewhere, remember."

"Maybe even closer than you think!" This new voice—deep and commanding—came from the front doorway everybody's attention had been drawn away from. Stepping through the opening as he spoke was a tall man in a wide-brimmed hat and long, flowing coat. He was holding a Henry repeating rifle at waist level and it immediately took its turn at making a statement. Three times the rifle roared, spitting flame and lead as fast as the man could jack home fresh rounds. The shots were grouped in a fairly tight pattern around where Lone had seen the gun flashes of Hardbark's most recent attempts to plant some lead in him. This time when Hardbark emitted a loud screech followed by the thumping sound of a body falling heavily to the ground, there was no doubt he'd stopped at least one of the rifleman's slugs.

Stringbean saw and heard all of this, too, and it propelled him even more urgently to take his own "cut and run" advice. He sprang out into the center aisle that stretched down the length of the barn bay and began racing toward the far end as fast as his long legs could take him.

Lone extended his gun arm and steadied it atop the highest of the solidly-packed feed bags. He took aim. Even in the murkiness, he could make out Stringbean and his flailing arms and pumping legs okay. Lone fired twice in rapid succession. Stringbean's pumping legs faltered, staggered, then folded under him. His forward momentum carried his long body ahead another few feet before it finally fell and skidded to a stop.

Lone straightened up behind the feed bags, turned

his head to look back at the man in the front doorway. Marshal Charley Bourbon.

He was surprised to find the Henry now aimed at him.

The dark face above the rifle muzzle was regarding him with a somewhat apologetic expression as the marshal said, "I got a pretty good hunch I'm gonna owe you a big 'much obliged' once this is all sorted out. But this job has taught me to be suspicious and extra careful. So, until I'm sure, I'll have to ask you to put your Colt back in its holster and then stand right there with your hands in plain sight on top of those bags."

CHAPTER TWENTY-TWO

"MY HISTORY WITH HOMER 'HARDBARK' WILLIS AND DEX Royster goes back to the days when they was runnin' with a nasty piece of business by the name of Squint Calloway down through Kansas and some into Colorado," Charley Bourbon was explaining. "I finally trimmed the wick of ol' Squint and most of his bunch near a year ago. But Hardbark and Royster got away. I chased 'em some, but got called off and sent on other jobs. They was pretty small potatoes outta the rest anyway. Surprisin', though, how they ended up this far north. After I cut down Squint, I had 'em pegged for strikin' south into the Territories, maybe even as far as Mexico."

Seated on a corner of his desk, Sam Blaylock, the town marshal of Deadwood, made a sour face. More than two hours had passed since the attempted ambush in O'Feeney's livery barn. It was nearly noon, and still raining outside. An undertaker had taken charge of the dead bodies, and a doctor was administering to the wounded. The gaggle of gawkers who'd flocked to the scene, even in the rain, had been dispersed and one of Blaylock's deputies was assigned to keep them away and temporarily watch over the livery. In the meantime, Marshal Blaylock had called this meeting at the jail building to get a final summary on how the incident had occurred.

As far as the current expression on the lawman's face, it occurred to Lone upon considering it that, on none of the handful of occasions he'd been around Blaylock previously had he ever seen him wear anything but a grim look of some sort. Having his job in a rowdy place like Deadwood was probably good cause for that. Still, the stocky, handlebar-mustached fellow, along with a crew of tough deputies, kept a lid on things almost as securely as the bowler hat that seemed permanently clamped atop his head.

"Blamed sorry I can't add anything on those three being hereabouts," Blaylock grumbled. "Don't know when they showed up or how they been occupying themselves. We get so much riff-raff coming and going that, unless they get involved in some kind of trouble— which the really bad ones generally do sooner or later —I can't keep track. I don't remember ever seeing no papers on these ones, though, I'm pretty sure of that."

"No, you likely wouldn't have. Not up this way," said Bourbon from where he was slouched in a straight-backed wooden chair, puffing on a carved ivory pipe. "Like I said, they was pretty small potatoes. I don't know that a whole lot of paper got sent out on 'em anyway, not after Calloway and the rest got took down... As far as the young one Hardbark called Stringbean, I got no idea where he came from or when he started ridin' with 'em. And he's for sure past fillin' us in on anything now—him nor Hardbark either."

Even sitting down, Bourbon made quite an imposing figure. His six-three height was packed onto a broad-shouldered, solid-looking frame. His bold-featured face, the color of strong-brewed coffee, was dominated by alert, penetrating eyes. A few flecks of gray in his neatly trimmed goatee indicated he'd accumulated some years, probably piled toward the high end of forty. And if the physical impact of the man wasn't enough, there was the black, tooled leather gun belt strapped around his waist with a brace of Colt .45s holstered on each hip.

Lone—the only other person present in Blaylock's office, also seated in a wooden chair hitched up before the marshal's desk—spoke in response to Bourbon's mention of the pair who'd been shot dead in the livery barn. "What about Royster, what's his condition?" he wanted to know. "And also, how's O'Feeney, the livery-man, doing?"

"Last word from the doc was that they'll both be okay," Blaylock reported. "O'Feeney's got a cracked skull and expected to be seeing double for a while. But he's a tough Irishman and you know how iron-headed they can be. As for Royster"—and here the lawman cast a somewhat baleful look at Lone—"he's got a busted jaw, busted ribs, and a couple of what the doc called 'odd puncture wounds' in his back. He'll pull through okay, but he'll be one sore, miserable cuss for a while. All at considerable expense to the city, mind you, while the no-account is healing. Pine boxes and wooden markers for the other two, combined, will be a fraction of what Royster's gonna cost."

"I'll keep that in mind should I ever get in another such tussle. Next time I'll make sure the bridle hanger bolts get stuck in deeper," Lone said dryly. "If you think of it, when O'Feeney gets healed up, you might want to suggest for him to install longer bolts."

Bourbon got a chuckle out of Lone's reply. Blaylock clearly failed to see much humor in it.

"Since I *did* make the mistake of leavin' Royster alive," Lone went on, "maybe you can get some use out of it by questionin' the homely rat and findin' out why him and the other two were so bent on ambushin' a federal marshal."

"That's a real good idea," Blaylock came back. "I'll get right on it—just as soon as his jaw is unwired and he's able to talk."

"Hey, take it easy, fellas. We're all on the same side, remember?" drawled Bourbon. "Far as gettin' any information out of Royster, I don't reckon it's worth a whole lot of effort. I figure him and Hardbark, whatever their reasons for bein' up this way, spotted me hangin' around and just naturally reasoned I must be on the hunt for them. Their kind wouldn't necessarily recognize what skimpy pickin's they was and not worth the bother for me. So, to their puny brains, the only thing for it was to ambush me and get me off their backsides once and for all."

"To their way of thinking, I guess that makes sense," allowed Blaylock. "But how did they lure you to that stable where they had their ambush all set up?"

Bourbon shrugged. "Simple. They sent that Stringbean fella, who they knew I wouldn't recognize, to fetch me with a made-up story. He found me at a cafe where I was hunkered over a pot of coffee, waitin' out the rain, and told me he was sent by O'Feeney. Said my horse that was boarded at the stable was actin' off its feed and O'Feeney wanted me to come have a look so's I could have a say on what to do."

"Can't get much more innocent sounding than that," said Blaylock.

"It was slick enough for me to swallow with nary a suspicion," Bourbon admitted ruefully, through a puff of pipe smoke. "So I finished my coffee and headed on over, rain or no. I was right there, ready to walk smack into their trap, when McGantry's hollerin' and shootin' on the inside warned me away just in time."

The marshal pressed his lips tight together and nodded. "Yeah, I got to give McGantry that much. Pitching in on your behalf ain't the first time he's popped up in our neck of the woods and helped spoil the plans of some bad hombres. Not too awful far back he was scouting for some soldier boys who had the Scorch Bannon gang cornered up in the hills just north of here, a place called Wolverine Wash. McGantry managed to skinny down a cliff in back of the culprits, then from there brought about an end to the stand-off *and* to Scorch's bunch."

Bourbon's eyebrows lifted. "I'll be dogged. I remember hearin' about that at the time. Scorch and his boys had glommed on to an army payroll, wasn't that how it went? Yeah. I don't recall hearin' the name McGantry, but I do remember a lot of talk about recoverin' that payroll."

"To be honest," Lone said, "the payroll part wasn't as important to me as the matter of settlin' a personal score with Bannon's pack of curly wolves."

"Uh-huh. You mentioned that at the time, though

you never really went into much detail." Blaylock paused, his forehead puckering with an abrupt and worrisome thought. "Say...you ain't back looking to settle some new score, are you?"

Lone had been wondering, ever since taking a hand to prevent the ambush attempt on Marshal Bourbon, how he would answer the question bound to come up of what he was doing in town. Now the moment had arrived and he was still undecided.

But with it put directly to him, he had to say something. So he opened his mouth to respond and the damnedest thing happened. The truth fell out. "As a matter of fact," he said, "I sorta am. That is, I'm on the trail of some varmints who've taken possession of something I aim to get back. If I'm able to catch up with 'em and they ain't willin' to hand it over peaceably—which will likely be the case—then I reckon we'll have to commence settlin' it some harder way."

"This a bounty job you've taken on?" asked Blaylock.

"Wasn't no part of it when I started out. Though it's since come to light there *is* a bounty involved. Mighty big one, in fact. 'Spect Marshal Bourbon can speak to that more than me"—here Lone cut a sidelong glance over at the federal lawman—"on account of he's been foggin' the trail of Fenton Eccles even longer than I have."

CHAPTER TWENTY-THREE

"IT'S MIGHTY GRATIFYING THAT YOU FELLAS ARE ALL willing to ride with me after that Aztec treasure. And you blame well know how bad I've been itching to get after it... But not so bad I'm willing to strike out in the middle of this cold-ass rain."

So stated Fenton Eccles as once again paced back and forth within the confines of the old trapper's cabin, streaming smoke from the cigar clamped between his teeth. Outside the rain was coming down straight and steady, making a long, low, continuous hissing sound on the cabin's roof. A roof that, after years of withstanding such rains—and many harder ones, not to mention wind and snow and blistering sun—no longer offered shelter without a few chinks.

"Hell, any more leaks come pissing down on us in here, we might as well go on out in the thick of it," lamented Bo Lasky after shifting his chair and coffee cup to a new spot at the rough-cut table to avoid a fresh dribble of rainwater that had begun plopping into his cup.

"Go ahead if you want," Amarillo Ames told him. "Number one, it'd leave more dry spots for the rest of us to move to. And number two, it'd give us a break from your constant bellyaching. Jesus, how can you worry so much about a little rain pissing on you when *piss*—and moan—is all you ever do."

"Aw, go to hell," Lasky sneered in return. "If anybody was concerned by the rain, I'd think it would be you... The threat of getting wet might seem too close to taking a bath. And, from the smell of you, that must be something that near scares you to death."

"Knock it off, you two," said Eccles. "For a couple of hombres with a cut of for-certain money laying over there in those saddlebags and a kingdom's riches waitin' just down the trail, why be so goddamned irritable about a little rain? That treasure has been there in the shadow of Devil's Tower for hundreds of years. One more day's delay ain't gonna give it cause to suddenly up and disappear now."

Ames eased up a bit and even managed a crooked smile. "But that don't mean it ain't gonna up and disappear from its musty ol' hidey hole pretty soon—smack into our hands."

Eccles grinned, too. "Damn right."

Luther Purdy, who'd been standing over by a window, gazing out quietly and drinking coffee, abruptly turned around and said to Eccles, "What did you mean about it waitin' in the shadow of the devil, Fen?"

Eccles' grin was quickly replaced by an annoyed grimace. He willed it away almost as fast as it appeared but the truth behind it—annoyance with *himself*—stabbed deeper than he let on. The mention of Devil's

Tower was a slip-up he hadn't meant to share with the others just yet. But now that it was out of the bag, he didn't have much choice but to discuss it some.

Lasky added to forcing his hand by saying, "What I heard was 'shadow of the Devil's Tower'... Wasn't that it, Fen? You mean that big ol' mound thing over in Wyoming?"

"What mound thing? What devil?" Ames wanted to know.

Eccles took the cigar out of his mouth and heaved a sigh. "Yeah, I said Devil's Tower. I thought I mentioned before. And yeah, it's that high butte—or mound, if you want to call it that—over in Wyoming."

"And that's where the treasure is?" asked Luther.

"It's a *marker* to where the treasure is," insisted Eccles, wanting to reinforce the idea there were still details only he knew. "But once we get that far, we'll be powerful close."

"Long as we don't have to do no diggin' into that hellamighty big slab of rock," declared Lasky. "That'd be a chore might make for leaving it there another hundred years."

Luther's eyes widened. "Is it really that big? You've seen it?"

"Can't say I ever got right up to it. But I got a good look from a distance," Lasky said. "Hell, they claim it's a thousand feet high so you can't hardly help but see it, even from a long way off. A big slab of bare gray rock. Sorta makes you think of a giant tombstone."

Ames made a sour face. "Jesus. All this talk of the devil and giant tombstones and the like... A body was to think on it too much, wouldn't be hard to conjure up the notion of bad omens. Maybe there's good reason that treasure ain't ever been found. Maybe it deserves to be left alone."

"No, it deserves is to be found alright—by *us*," crowed Lasky. "Any spooks try to interfere, I'll stick one of those silver bars up its ass. Ain't that what the old legends say about getting rid of ghouls and werewolves and whatever? You ram a chunk of silver in 'em and they're done for."

Ignoring the younger man's bravado, a stern-faced Eccles said, "When you got your look at the tower, what direction was it from?"

Lasky looked puzzled. "What do you mean?"

"I mean were you west of it, east of it—which way?"

"Oh. Uh, south I guess... No, actually more south-west... Can I ask what difference it makes?"

"Having never been out that way myself," Eccles explained, "I'm just trying to picture the layout for our approach. From what I understand, the terrain around the tower varies quite a bit. We'll be coming in from the northeast, which I'm told is pretty rugged country. Not so rugged we can't travel over it, but I'm wondering if we'll still be able to spot the tower okay."

"Oh, hell yeah. Like I said, we get anywhere close I don't see how we can miss it," Lasky stated confidently. "Down where I was it was mostly rolling, grassy hills. A few trees, not much else. I guess I remember seeing some cliffs to the north, on past the mound. But nothing that would come close to blocking the sight of it. Rises over everything else like a big, fat thumb poking up."

"Why don't they call it the Devil's Thumb then?" grumbled Ames.

"How the hell do I know?" Lasky replied irritably.

"Look, here's an idea of what I saw—you ponder on it and decide however you want to think of it for yourself."

So saying, Lasky grabbed the pencil and sheet of brown butcher's paper they used to keep score for the games of pinochle they'd been playing to kill time. He pulled it to a dry spot on the table, turned it over to its blank back side and began sketching a rough image of how he remembered the landmark under discussion—a chunky rectangle stood on end, flared out at the base, flat at the top. On the sides of the flared base he scribbled what was supposed to be some trees and then added several ragged vertical lines to the face of the rectangle.

"There," he announced when done, tossing down the pencil. "That's the way it looked to me. Anybody can call it whatever suits you."

"Hey that ain't half bad," said Eccles, sounding genuinely impressed. "Matches pretty damn good against the pictures I saw in that prison library."

"Ask me, I say it does look like a tombstone," murmured Luther.

"Like Lasky said, anybody can call it whatever suits him. Butte, mound, tombstone, thumb—don't matter a damn." Eccles leaned over and thumped a forefinger down on the sketch. "But what does matter, what I see when I look at it, is the gateway to gold and riches that will have us living like kings for the rest of our days!"

CHAPTER TWENTY-FOUR

LONE SPENT THE BALANCE OF THE DAY EVADING THE RAIN and sampling the variety of diversions to be found along Deadwood's main drag. For starters, after finishing up with Marshal Blaylock, he and Charley Bourbon enjoyed a leisurely lunch together. Bourbon picked up the tab, as part of demonstrating his "much obliged" sentiment for Lone's intervention at the livery barn. Once Lone had explained the history of the contents in the money belt that Fenton Eccles' bunch stole off Jack Swain and how he intended to continue his own pursuit of the gang (without mentioning the involvement of Bayne and Rena), the former scout was surprised that Bourbon didn't raise a strong objection. Instead, all the federal man said was, "I can't fault you for feelin' the way you do, and I won't try to stop you. Not that I could anyway—you bein' the type I read you to be—short of trumpin' up some charge to chill you behind bars for a spell. But I don't feel the need for that. I'll add this, though: Don't get in my way, and don't withhold anything you might run across that'd amount to suppressin' evidence in a federal case. You was to do something like that, it'd piss me off personally and I *would* do my best to throw your lily white ass in the clink."

With that settled between them, they'd parted and Lone had gone in search of ways to kill time. At the Birdcage Saloon & Dance Hall he spent the better part of an hour watching a chorus line of immodest, pretty young ladies display lots of shapely legs and derrieres in a series of high-kicking dance routines. A ways down the street, at the Grand Duke Theater, he perched on a hard slab bench and watched a troupe of performers with thick Slavic accents presenting scenes from the writings of Shakespeare. One such scene involved a sword fight staged with silver-painted wooden laths that clacked together with ridiculous hollowness made even worse by the missed timing of some off stage presence trying to provide more realistic sounding steel on steel strikes. The scene ended abruptly and inadvertently when one of the swordsmen—a portly gent stuffed like a sausage into a pair of lime green tights and evidently requiring the help of a substantial amount of vodka to go through with publicly parading himself in such a manner—fell off the edge of the stage. This by far drew a longer, louder round of applause than any of the other performances Lone stuck around for. Stopping next, just for a chuckle, at a tent with a sign out front that read MADAME OUIJA'S VISIONS FOR THE FUTURE, Lone got what he was looking for when told by a crone wearing a filmy veil that did little to conceal a single gold tooth poking out from between thin, bloodless lips that he would soon be going on an ocean voyage and to ensure his safety from the sea demons who lurked in the depths he needed to buy a charm from Madame Ouija's gift shop. He paid fifty cents for the charm and then, back out on the street, hung it around the neck of a soggy, stray dog slinking along under the boardwalk awnings and wished the pooch "bon voyage." Finally, a short time later, true salvation came in the form of a drab, narrow building squeezed in between a gaudy hurdy gurdy palace and an equally gaudy four-story hotel. The flaking paint of the lettering on the smeared glass of the narrow building's front window read PECK'S BILLIARD HALL and Lone was immediately drawn in.

Once inside, things got even more to his liking when he saw that he had the joint all to himself. Just him, half a dozen empty tables well-spaced down the length of the room, and the proprietor. The latter was a legless Civil War vet (having lost his "pins" to a cannon ball, he would later explain) occupying a wooden wheelchair. He had narrow, bony shoulders, a sunken chest, washed out once-blue eyes, and liver spots dotting the bald dome of his head; but when he pushed a rack of balls across the counter top to Lone, his forearms rippled with long, stringy muscles acquired from propelling himself around in the chair.

Lone took the rack, chose a cue stick from the selection lining the wall, then went to the second table from the front and began knocking around the colorful balls. It was warm in the long, high-ceilinged room, the air stale and heavy with the leftover odor of cigar and cigarette smoke. Nice and quiet, though, except for the click of the cue ball striking against the others. The click of balls striking, but seldom the thump of any falling into pockets as intended. Jesus, Lone thought to himself,

I'm even rustier than I thought. This made him even more grateful to have the place to himself, so nobody else was around to see just *how* rusty.

Or so he thought.

After about a half hour of failing to sharpen his skills any discernible degree, he got some attention from the proprietor who up until then had appeared to be showing bored indifference. Abruptly, the man came around the end of his service counter and rolled up to Lone's table. "My name's Ambrose Peck," he announced. "I been runnin' this joint for near ten years and I think you might be the worst pool player I've seen in all that time. You shoot pool about as good as I dance the Irish jig."

Lone lifted his eyebrows, not exactly appreciating the unsolicited assessment. But, at the same time, he hardly had the grounds to dispute it. In the end, he grinned and said, "Am I so bad you're kickin' me out?"

"Do I look like I can afford to kick out a payin' customer?" Peck replied. "But, if you're interested, *maybe* I can give you a few pointers that'd keep you from looking a little less like a blind man swattin' flies."

So, for the next two plus hours, that's how it went. Peck took a cue for himself and rolled this way and that way around the table, making impressive shots to demonstrate the legitimacy of his skills while instructing Lone on everything from shot trajectories, to how to position the cue tip for different ball reaction, to how hard or soft to make certain strokes. Lone's skill did improve some under the tutelage but, most of all, it was a pleasant way to pass time and to see the old vet getting animated, showing off a bit and seeming to enjoy himself as well.

When other customers began filtering in, Peck had to excuse himself to go take care of their needs. Before quitting Lone, he looked up at the tall stranger and said, "You ain't ever gonna be no pool shark, son, not if I spent from now to Christmas working with you. But I got a hunch you got other skills—like with that smoke wagon riding on your hip. And by the heat I see smoldering deep in your eyes, I got me another hunch there's some sorry sonofabuck due one day soon for a scorchin'. Just remember, there's a time to stroke soft and a time to ram your stick plenty damn hard."

Lone grinned. "I'll be sure to remember that, old timer."

CHAPTER TWENTY-FIVE

When Lone emerged from Peck's, he found the rain had stopped. The sky remained overcast, though a paler shade of gray now that it had released its load of precipitation. The clouds were still thick enough, however, to shorten the afternoon and hasten the descent of evening's deepening shadows.

Lone wasn't ready for supper this early, yet he was tired of roaming the street especially with the crowd building back up now that it was no longer raining. He decided he would return to his hotel room for a stretch of alone time before heading out again to get a meal. In the course of checking out different establishments earlier he had poked his head in a few gambling joints, thinking he might see Bayne and Rena at one of the tables, plying their trade and working their network of contacts for information. There'd been no sign of either of them. But, like Bayne had said, it was going to take time for them to get re-established. Meanwhile, Lone told himself, he needed to be patient.

As it turned out, not for much longer.

They were waiting for him in his hotel room. The lingering aroma of Rena's perfume out in the hallway was his first signal; the fact the door was no longer locked, the way he was certain he'd left it, was the second. Those two things added up to enough reason for Lone to draw his Colt and stand off-center of the doorway when he gave the door a sudden push wide open.

Bayne was on his feet, had been pacing by the look of it—until the door slapping open stopped him short and brought his head whipping around. Rena was in the room's thinly upholstered reading chair, appearing bored and mildly disinterested—even after the door slapped open. She was wearing another revealing, off-the-shoulder dress, this one emerald green in color. Bayne had changed to a tobacco brown jacket with black trim, the same cream hat.

Lone went on into the room, heeling the door shut behind him.

"Jesus Christ, man," exclaimed Bayne. Then, his eyes dropping to the gun in Lone's fist, he blurted, "What the hell!"

"Yeah, you tell me what the hell," Lone said. "What the hell are you two doin' bustin' in my room?"

"Oh, for God's sake." Rena gave an exasperated eye roll. "No one 'busted in' anywhere. We're friends with the desk clerk. We explained we're also friends of yours and asked if we could wait here rather in the lobby for you to return. So he let us in. Simple as that."

"So since we *are* friends—or partners, at least," added Bayne, regaining some composure, "how about you put that damn gun away?"

Scowling, Lone holstered his Colt. Then he growled,

"If you wanted to have a pow-wow, all you had to do was send word when and where."

Now Bayne worked up a scowl of his own. "Maybe we would have—if you hadn't already been so busy 'pow-wowing' with every damn lawman in the territory."

"You're talkin' about Charley Bourbon, I take it."

"Him, and the town marshal, too. From all reports," Bayne said, "you spent enough time with the two of them that I'm surprised to see you don't have a deputy's badge pinned on you by now."

"You better back up a corn row or two, mister," Lone grated. "Who and for how long I spend time with is my business. I didn't go nosin' around about this 'network' of yours that you're minglin' amongst, did I?"

"You knew about that right up front. What you didn't bother letting us know was that you planned on buddying up with star packers."

"It wasn't no *plan*, you suspicious ass. The only reason I got tangled up with Bourbon was on account of me walkin' into the middle of an ambush bein' set for him. Some lead got throwed around, two men ended up dead and another busted up some. As you ought to figure, the local marshal took an interest in a thing like that and, since I was part of it, I naturally got hauled in for questionin'. Luckily, since I'd saved Bourbon's hide and town marshal Blaylock knew me from a past time when I'd been on hand to put an end to some other bad hombres, I came out of it okay."

"You seem to have a knack," Bayne remarked dryly, "for shooting your way to the attention of local lawmen."

"How about, leastways in this case, shootin' my way

into their good graces?" Lone suggested with a crooked grin. "After all, I'm Galahad, remember—pure of heart and deed."

This drew a sudden, short laugh, almost as if in spite of herself, from Rena. "Touché, you big lug," she said. Then laughed a little bit more.

The moment was enough to break the tension that had formed between Lone and Bayne. The latter heaved a sigh and made an open-palmed gesture with both hands. "Okay. You're right. I guess I overreacted to something I didn't have the full story on. But even though you're in their good graces, as you put it, doesn't their added awareness of you also add to the risk of them catching wind what we're up to?"

"So what if it does? We're not doin' anything illegal."

"Not illegal maybe, but I can't imagine a U.S. Marshal caring much for any bunch of civilians crowding the same trail he's fogging." Bayne frowned. "Damn. I didn't expect him to still be here. I figured he would have moved on, one way or the other, by now."

"He might have if he wasn't so stubborn in his belief about the Eccles gang havin' gone to ground—and stickin'—somewhere close around here. He's still tryin' to root out the name of the relative he figures is hidin' 'em. Or at least knows where they're at."

"He told you this?"

"He did... And I gave him to know, explainin' about Jack Swain and the rest, how I got my own interest in Eccles and his bunch."

This widened the eyes of both Bayne and Rena.

"You admitted that?" Bayne questioned.

"I just said so, didn't I? I left your names out of it, if that's what you're worried about," Lone told him. "But stop and think. With Bourbon still here pokin' for a thread of a lead on Eccles, what chance have we got, even with your secretive network of folks who know all the dirt on things, of doin' any serious pokin' of our own without Bourbon hearin' about it? You think he'd be any less pissed off came to sharin' his hunt if he figured it was with a bunch of sneaks, as represented by me if I hadn't leveled with him and Blaylock when they wanted to know what I was doin' in town?"

"If you're so sure that leveling with them was the right thing, why *didn't* you mention us to him?" challenged Rena.

"Number one, because I wanted to give you a say before I did," Lone replied. "Number two, because I hadn't gotten a full read on Bourbon at that point. I know Blaylock to be a straight shooter, wasn't so sure right off about Bourbon."

Bayne eyed him. "But now you are?"

Lone gave a firm nod. "Yeah, I am. Matter of fact, I'll go so far as to say I think we should try workin' together with him on chasin' down Eccles the rest of the way."

"You've got to be kidding," said Rena.

But Bayne, though still frowning, appeared to at least be giving the notion some thought. "Even if we were willing to go at it that way, what makes you think Bourbon would be agreeable?"

"Partly a hunch, partly the fact he didn't get his back up over the idea of me continuin' with my own reasons for goin' after the gang," Lone answered. "His only warnin' was to not get in his way and not to hide anything to purposely swerve him."

"That doesn't sound unreasonable."

"What I thought."

"But that was talking to *you*," Rena pointed out. "Bourbon has reason to be personally beholden to you and, like you said, you've also had past favorable dealings with Marshal Blaylock... All that is a lot different than being willing to throw in with a gambler and his woman."

Now wavering back the other way, Bayne said, "Makes a valid point."

"Maybe so. But I think Charley Bourbon is more open-minded than that," Lone argued. "Don't forget, he's a black man. Even with the badge he wears, I expect he's run into plenty of folks not willin' to throw in with him. Representin' that badge, way I read him, is a mighty important thing. And so is takin' down Fenton Eccles' bunch. Ain't like he don't figure he can do it on his own—hell, that's the way he's used to operatin'. But neither do I see him turnin' down some backin' up was it offered to him."

"You seem to have read an awful lot from spending such a short amount of time with the man," remarked Bayne.

Lone shrugged. "Sometimes that's how it works... Look, he ain't no threat to claimin' the reward money, if that's what you're worried about. A federal marshal can't claim rewards... And that badge of his could come in handy if we was standin' behind it with him. Even if your sources cough up a name of somebody related to one of the gang, for instance, how can we be sure they'll cooperate and tell us anything?"

"Come on," Bayne sneered. "I can think of ways. And don't tell me a former scout and Indian fighter don't know a few as well."

"Yeah, I know more than a few," allowed Lone. "And

I wouldn't hesitate puttin' 'em to use if I had to. But something like that could end up siccin' Bourbon on our asses as hard as on Eccles. That ain't something I particularly want or need. Not when there's a better way right at hand."

"Meaning employing Bourbon and his badge to get the information out of the relative, if and when said person is ever identified."

There was a hint of something in Bayne's tone, a smugness, that Lone didn't miss. He regarded the gambler flinty-eyed. "You got something you ain't made it around to tellin' me yet?"

Bayne and Rena exchanged glances. When Bayne's eyes came back to Lone, he said, "Yes, as a matter of fact there is. Why we came looking for you in the first place. You see, our contacts paid off even quicker than we dared hope. We found out the name of a man who's related, a cousin, to one of the members of the Eccles gang."

CHAPTER TWENTY-SIX

"Doggone embarrassin', that's what it is," grumbled Charley Bourbon. "I been a week watchin', listenin', and proddin' but comin' up empty as a pocket with a hole in it. But you two waltz in and in less than twenty-four hours got the name I been tryin' to root out."

"We came up with *a* name," amended Emmett Bayne. "Whether or not he turns out to be the right one and how useful this Dickerson is willing to be...well, Marshal, we figure you're the professional best suited to get the most out of him."

Listening to this, Lone cringed a little yet at the same time had to hand it to Bayne for the smooth-talking, highly respectful (damn near fawning) demeanor he'd adopted. This from a gent who only an hour or so ago didn't want anything to do with the U.S. Marshal. Lone just hoped that, now since he'd had a change of mind, the card man didn't try to lay it on too thick. Lone had a hunch Bourbon possessed a pretty good bullshit detector and would balk in a hurry if it got set off.

Puffing on his carved ivory pipe, Bourbon

responded, "I'm grateful you came to me with this, Mr. Bayne...as well as you, Miss Matteson. And McGantry. It could be a big step toward takin' Fenton Eccles back into custody. And also dealin' with the scoundrels he's surrounded himself with—the very same who busted him out of the pen and then have been ridin' with him on this tear that included the stagecoach robbery affectin' each of you in some way."

This discussion was taking place in a private back room of the Miner's Haven saloon. It had been selected as a discreet meeting location for the sake of Marshal Bourbon. Arrangements for the space were made by Bayne, calling in a favor owed him and Rena by the proprietor for the business they had brought him at the gaming tables out front. Once the room was secured, Lone had gone to fetch the marshal with a promise of having access to some very worthwhile information.

That having been delivered, the issue at hand now was what was being sought in return.

Puffing another cloud of pipe smoke, Marshal Bourbon went on to address this very thing, saying, "Which brings us to what you're lookin' to get out of bringin' me the name of this Myron Dickerson—a cousin to Luther Purdy. If it pans out, if he spills a lead to where his cousin and the rest of the gang can be found, then you want in on the apprehension of 'em. For personal payback and also a crack at the handsome reward ridin' on takin' 'em down. That what I'm to understand?"

"Rena and I make no pretense otherwise," Bayne said somewhat stiffly. "True, we lost some money in the holdup. But that alone wouldn't have caused us to go seeking payback. Frankly, we were thankful to have eluded any worse harm." He paused to cast a meaningful glance over at Rena. Then he continued, "But when we *did* learn about the reward and then McGantry showed up with both the skills and the intent to pursue the robbers...well, that was the point we decided we had something to contribute if we joined him in his pursuit and made a try for a share of that reward money."

"And we've made our contribution, just like we predicted we could," Rena spoke up. "So now we're hoping you'll let us join *you* in the continued pursuit."

Bourbon's eyes cut to Lone, as if expecting him to say something.

"You all know my main driver in this. I'm out to retrieve the money was cheated out of a lady back in North Platte." Lone shrugged. "But if I can beef that up with a cut of the reward money—hell, I'm neither too dumb nor too proud to pass it up."

Bourbon frowned. "That 'not too dumb' part might be arguable comes to the lot of us. Why else would we be sittin' here wantin' to get after runnin' down a pack of murderin', rabid-dog criminals? Money, yeah. But they's a hell of a lot easier ways to make money."

They were seated at a round, felt-topped table where private high-stakes poker games were regularly played in marathon sessions. Bayne, with Rena at his side, had participated in more than a few of these, so he knew the room well. There was a small but well-stocked bar against one wall and from it he had earlier brought to the table glasses and a couple bottles of top-shelf whiskey, some wine for Rena. The gambler, his lady, and Lone had been sipping their drinks measuredly. Not so Bourbon. Almost as if trying to live up to his name, he had already put a serious dent in one of the whiskey bottles and now, at the close of his rather bleak statement, he reached to pour another refill.

"You run down curly wolves on a regular basis," Lone pointed out. "And a U.S. Marshal's pay not only ain't easy money but it ain't even big money. Sure as hell not for what you have to do to earn it."

"See?" Bourbon came back. "I told you a claim to not bein' dumb was arguable."

"So why do it then?" asked Rena.

Bourbon paused with his freshly filled glass raised part way to his mouth. He stared down into the amber liquid for a long beat before saying, "Because I'm good at it. And because doin' it matters."

He threw down the drink and for another long beat nobody said anything.

Until Bourbon spoke again. "Look, I don't blame you folks—or anybody—for wantin' to go after these big rewards that get offered. Don't think there ain't been times when I considered chuckin' my badge and grabbin' some of the fatter ones for myself. But that's another story, one that always ended the same—me not doin' it. Thing is, though, reward or not, I long ago learned to know and accept and deal with the risks of huntin' down rabid human dogs. Had to, or I wouldn't've lasted as long as I have. Not to brag by sayin' so too many times, but I'm pretty doggone good at it."

He paused again, letting his gaze sweep over the three faces staring back at him. Then: "Reckon you folks are gonna make a try for the Eccles reward whether I'm agreeable to it or not. And I guess you got the right, long as you stay out of my way. Thing you might want to consider, though, is that if the information you've given me on this Dickerson fella pans out and I'm able to use it to corral the gang—then that might be enough just in itself to earn you a piece of the reward without takin' no further risk."

"There are a couple pretty big 'ifs' in there," said Bayne. "And neither am I crazy about that 'piece of the reward' part."

Bourbon took the pipe from his mouth and his lips curved in a thin smile. "Your greed is showing, Mr. Bayne."

"Nothing new about that," Bayne replied. "I already admitted as much."

Growing weary of all this talking and skirting around the edges, Lone said with some brittleness in his tone, "How about we cut to it, Bourbon. We came to you with what we believe to be a solid lead and a proposition. Now you could take that name and go it alone and, I suppose, use your badge to try and block us out. But I didn't make you as that kind of horse's ass, and I sold Bayne and Rena on my belief you'd be reasonable. Sure, you can head out to 'front those polecats all on your own like you've done plenty of times before—but what's the sense in that when you've got added guns right here ready and willin' to back your play?"

"*Your* gun I'd welcome backin' me any time. I've seen you use it and even have to admit to it playin' a part in savin' my hide." Here the marshal's gaze shifted from Lone and settled once again on Bayne. "As for you, I expect whatever you're packin' in that shoulder rig under your fancy coat—and probably a derringer somewhere to go with it—has served you well enough in poker table disputes. But that don't mean either them or you will measure up in a rough country shootout with the likes of the Eccles gang."

Bayne's eyes narrowed menacingly. "Under different circumstances and if not for that badge you're wearing, sir, I might take strong enough offense at your words to *show* you what I'm capable of with these weapons!"

"If you're so capable with 'em, why didn't you put up more of a fight when the gang robbed the stagecoach you were ridin' in?"

Bayne thrust to his feet, nearly upsetting the chair he'd been sitting in. "That's too much, damn you! You may question my skill, but if you're accusing me of cowardice—"

Rena cut him short by grabbing his sleeve and insisting, "Emmett! Stop it!"

Bourbon leaned back in his chair, puffing on his pipe as it hung from one corner of a crooked smile. "Relax, gamblin' man. The coach was blocked by a dead horse, the shotgun guard was immediately killed, and you was trapped inside with no maneuverability and the safety of your woman to consider if you'd done anything to draw fire from the pack that had you surrounded, outnumbered, and outgunned. Only a damn fool would've tried to put up a fight in that situation."

"Then why did you say such a cruel thing?" Rena demanded to know.

Bourbon took the pipe from his mouth and made a gesture with it. "Wanted to see if your man had enough fire instead of just greed in him. He'll do, by the way."

"That was still a damned cruel way to find out!"

"In case you didn't get the message from your encounter with 'em, the Eccles bunch can be a hell of a lot crueler." Bourbon pulled out a silver pocket watch on a chain, checked the time, put it back. Standing up, he announced, "It's gettin' late. The freight company where Dickerson works is in the town of Lead, about an hour and a half's ride from here. If we want to catch him before he gets loaded up and gone on a haul, we'll need to get there early. There's a bridge over a small creek on the west edge of town. Meet me there at first light. Come ready to ride hard and, in case we don't pin down the gang all that quick or easy, bring gear and rations for at least three days on the trail."

With that, Bourbon strode to the rear exit door where he paused for a final time. Looking back, he pinched his hat and said to Rena, "Ma'am." Then, nodding to Lone and Bayne, he added, "Thanks for the information and the whiskey, gents. See you in the mornin'."

CHAPTER TWENTY-SEVEN

LONE WAS THE FIRST ONE TO ARRIVE AT THE CREEK BRIDGE next morning. The sky was clear, sprinkled with some fading, leftover stars and a slice of moon ahead of daybreak. The air was chill and still damp from the previous day's rain. Thin layers of fog hung over the water.

He reined up Ironsides at the east end of the bridge and swept his eyes in a slow scan of the area. Away from the lights of Deadwood, his vision had adjusted to the gloom and he could make out shapes fairly well. Nothing moved, nor did his ears detect any nearby sound save for the soft whisper of the creek's meager current. Vague street noises drifted from the town behind him, somewhere among them a barking dog.

Lone kneed Ironsides forward across the short, rail less, wagon-wide wooden bridge. His hooves clumped hollowly on the weathered planks. On the other side, Lone again stopped to scan and listen intently. When he was satisfied he and the gray were the only ones present, he swung Ironsides into a stand of birch trees and held him there. He sat his saddle, motionless, silently waiting.

Having already made up his mind on accepting his recently acquired partners, Lone had no reason to be freshly suspicious of any of them. But taking added caution whenever possible had proven a wise habit over the years. And sometimes you just might learn something by observing a person's approach when they didn't know they were being watched.

His thoughts drifted in the murky quiet. Much as they had all night. The hotel room bed was comfortable, he'd rested his body but deep slumber evaded him. He thought of Velda naturally; and Ma. Told himself again what a shame it was they'd never met, how certain he was they would have hit it off. He thought, too, about the joint venture he was about to strike out on. How different it had become from the way he'd set out alone (familiar territory) with a singular goal. Now the goal was bigger (though it still contained his original one at its core) and he was no longer on his own. But Bayne and Rena had already proven to be of worth, and there was no doubt about Charley Bourbon's mettle. The lingering question of the rage beast still contained deep inside, contained but waiting—for something, he knew not what the trigger might be—tried to surface but Lone held it at bay for now... Finally, an odd, deeply personal thought kept winding its way in and out of the others. It stemmed from the reward money, the bounty, that had now become part of what they were setting out after. Bounty hunting, Velda's former trade. Something he had expressed reluctance in pursuing full time with her on occasions when they had discussed how they might build their future together. Reluctance then, yet here he was involved in that very thing. Only to ensure a righting of Ma's misfortune, he told himself. And that held water. Mostly. Yet doing it still left a pang of curious guilt, much as he'd felt when visiting Maggie's grave...

The next rider to show up at the creek bridge was Charley Bourbon. He came on a tall black gelding, sitting a silver-trimmed black saddle. He, too, paused at the east end of the bridge, but only briefly before continuing on across. Once on the other side, he checked down in the center of the trail. After another brief pause he took out his pipe and struck a match on his belt buckle.

"Was I an Injun," Lone said lazily from the shadows of the birch stand, "you'd be dead about six times over."

The abrupt, unseen voice clearly gave the marshal a start. He nearly dropped the just fired match. But recovering quickly and not wanting to display any overreaction, he went ahead and unhurriedly touched flame to the pipe bowl. Only after he'd worked up a couple good puffs of smoke did he reply, "You're a damn sneaky rascal, McGantry, I'll give you that. Might be you'll come in handy more ways than just with your gun."

"Never can tell," allowed Lone, heeling Ironsides out of the shadows and pulling up alongside Bourbon.

The latter blew out his match. "Where's the gambler?"

"You said first light, he's still got time," Lone answered. "Ain't likely he won't show—not with a cut of that reward money at stake."

"Yeah, there's that. Reckon a high maintenance gal like that blonde of his," Bourbon mused, "makes it important for him to stay in the chips."

Lone chuffed. "If you've noticed the natty way Bayne keeps himself decked out, I'd say he sets pretty high maintenance on himself, too."

"I like deckin' out sorta on the natty side myself," Bourbon admitted. "I look at it as remindin' folks I'm a black man of distinction and the days of my kind bein' nothin' but cotton pickers or houseboys—leastways not all of us—is over."

Grinning, Lone said, "No, I don't think very many folks would take a look at you and feel inclined to ask you go fetch 'em a mint julep or any such."

"Fetch 'em a rap up alongside the head is what it'd get 'em," Bourbon declared. "But goin' back to a high maintenance woman, that's something I never could see. Too much work and worry for the same as you can get out'n a plain gal, says I. You find one ain't so plain she's frightenin' to wake up next to of a mornin', treat her right and get pleasured in return...that's the way. Another thing about that kind, you don't have to worry so much about some horndog comin' 'round to steal her away. And if one does, well, no big investment means no big loss. See what I mean? You just move on and find another."

"Marshal, you are a philosopher and a connoisseur of the ladies all rolled into one," said Lone. "I'm surprised you ain't got a whole harem just followin' you around."

Bourbon chuckled. "Who says I don't have me a harem? Travelin' man like me, I just got 'em dispersed around in different towns is all. Always got one waitin', wherever I show up."

"Speakin' of showin' up," said Lone with a nod toward the trail leading out from town, "looks like the rest of our crew is comin' now. And speakin' of high maintenance gals, it appears Bayne ain't by himself."

Sure enough, the pale gray of pre-dawn now spreading across the sky clearly showed two riders approaching—Bayne on a deep-chested bay, Rena on a sleek paint. Both were dressed for the trail. Bayne had on a short-waisted corduroy jacket and striped pants stuffed into boots polished to a high sheen; his Colt Lightning was now holstered openly on his left hip, butt forward for the cross draw. Rena was clad in a split riding skirt, also corduroy, and a leather jacket; her hair was piled up and encased in a narrow-brimmed, flat-crowned Stetson.

Taking all this in as the pair clomped across the wooden bridge, Bourbon groaned aloud and said only partly under his breath, "Oh no. No, this ain't gonna happen."

When Bayne and Rena reined up they were met with a waiting scowl from the marshal, aimed square at Rena. "I hope you're only here to see your man off," he said to her, "'cause you surely can't believe you're gonna ride along on this gallop with us."

"I surely do," she countered without hesitation.

Bourbon shook his head firmly. "Then best set about changin' your mind, and be quick about it."

"I have no intention of changing my mind, quickly or otherwise," Rena stated with equal firmness.

"Look, this has the makin's of turnin' into a rugged undertakin', even for a man," Bourbon argued. "No way it's a fit thing for a woman to be part of."

"But I *am* a part of it," Rena insisted. "I have as big a stake as any of the rest of you, and I mean to stay with it all the way."

Bourbon swung his scowl to Bayne. "Damn it, man! Can't you control your woman?"

A desperate looking Bayne, clearly reluctant to be caught in the middle of this, opened his mouth to try and offer something. But Rena didn't give him the chance. Branding the marshal with her own blazing scowl, she said, "*Control* me? On what grounds—that he somehow *owns* me like a damn horse or mule or something? I would've expected you to have heard the news by now that the days of people owning other people is over!"

Bourbon was clearly taken aback by this outburst. He suddenly appeared about as lost for words as Bayne had looked a minute earlier.

But Rena still wasn't finished. "For your information, Marshal," she continued, "I can ride a horse as good or better than most men I've met. I can shoot accurately, too, if I need to. You see, I was born and raised on a north Wyoming ranch less than two hundred miles from here. Oh, it wasn't a big, prosperous ranch with plenty of hired hands and a thriving herd. No, it was the muscle-straining, bone-breaking dream of a stubborn man who, as he reminded his family frequently, had no let-up or give-up in him. So he drove us, his family, as hard as he drove himself. All of us kids started doing simple chores as soon as we could walk, and it escalated steadily from there. I could ride and rope proficiently by the time I was ten.

"Bad luck, bad weather, bad decisions...none of it was enough to stop my father as long as he had one lousy cow and one blade of grass to try and keep building on. Not even working my poor mother and two oldest brothers to death was enough. It finally took the old bastard dying himself before he let go. Even then, my two remaining brothers and a sister tried to stick with it." Here Rena's eyes took on a fiery brightness that seemed especially intense in the lingering gloom. "But not me. I was out of there the same afternoon his funeral service was over, and I've never looked back. So now I like pretty clothes and jewelry and a lifestyle that means eating in restaurants and calling for room service instead of sweating over a hot stove to get a meal. But that doesn't mean I don't still have the skills and grit to go on this little 'gallop' of yours, Marshal. Now you said you wanted to get an early start, so what are we waiting for?"

If he hadn't needed to keep his pipe stem clenched between his teeth, Charley Bourbon might have been left hang-jawed. But he wasn't. Not quite. On the other hand, neither did he have a prompt reply.

Leaving it up to Lone to say, "I think the lady has made her point. In more ways than one. So since Lead and the freight outfit we want to reach is thataway"—a thumb jab over his shoulder—"how about we point our tails the opposite direction and ride?"

CHAPTER TWENTY-EIGHT

EVEN THOUGH THE TRAIL WAS MUDDY FROM THE PREVIOUS day's rain, they made good time reaching Lead. The way was well cleared and cut fairly level through the rugged terrain. And in places where there were slopes and gullies, the ground was sandy enough to still provide the horses adequate purchase.

Though having begun as settlements at roughly the same time, Lead had neither the size nor boisterous reputation of Deadwood. But the surrounding hills and low mountains had plenty of the same rich ore, which meant busy mining operations at work up in those reaches requiring a steady stream of supplies, tools, equipment, and various other goods getting hauled to them. That's where outfits like the Price Brothers Freight Company came in. And the Price Brothers operation was where one Myron Dickerson, cousin to Eccles gang member Luther Purdy, was employed.

Lone, Bourbon, Bayne, and Rena sat their horses on the east edge of the clearing occupied by the freight terminal. The town of Lead lay a short ways farther, deeper down in the valley. The sun was well up in a clear sky now, warm on the backs of the four riders as the studied the layout before them. There were two large warehouses at the center, a barn and corral for the pulling mules off to one side. Seven heavy duty, high-wheeled wagons were in evidence; two were sitting idle at the moment, two others were having their contents offloaded into storage, three were being loaded in preparation for making deliveries. Twelve to fifteen men were moving about in all of this, busy performing related chores.

"Good sized operation. Bigger than I expected," remarked Bourbon as he scanned the scene.

"That a problem?" asked Bayne.

"Not necessarily. Might make it a little trickier to pluck our man out is all. But if he's in there, we'll get him."

Lone said, "In case he might be part of one of those wagons bein' loaded up, we oughta go in and find out before they roll. Don't you reckon?"

"Yup, that's exactly what I think. Why I wanted to get here early," Bourbon replied. "Only thing I'm debatin' is if I should go in alone or if we all ride in."

"What difference does it make?" Bayne wanted to know.

"Maybe none. Maybe plenty. For one thing," explained the marshal, "all of us ridin' in together will for sure get noticed quicker. Especially with Miss Rena bein' one of us. Gettin' noticed quicker will mean wonderin' what we're up to quicker. If somebody in that gaggle of workers has something worrisome naggin' at him, something he feels guilty over and don't want nobody to know about—somebody like our Mr. Dickerson, who as far as we know is a regular sort with the bad luck of havin' an owlhoot for a cousin—he might all of a sudden decide to make himself scarce for a while so's not to get cornered into answerin' questions he don't want to face."

"But how's that different than if you go in alone, flash your badge, and start asking directly for Dickerson? Seems to me that might make him bolt even quicker," said Rena. Then, with a slightly impish grin, she added, "And, in case you don't realize it, Marshal, you hardly make an *un*-noticeable entry even without flashing your badge."

Bourbon chuckled. "As is often exactly how I want it. But trust me, pretty lady, with a crew of men like the ones at work out there in that clearin', wouldn't nobody take no never mind of me compared to you."

"Well, *somebody's* got to go," Bayne grumbled irritably. "Let's make up our minds and get to it."

"I vote the marshal goes in on his own," said Lone. "He can hold off flashin' his badge until he locates the yard boss. Let him be the one to point out Dickerson. Meanwhile, us three can hang back and keep our eyes peeled. Even though we don't have a description of Dickerson yet, we can watch for any sign in case somebody acts dodgy or tries to rabbit."

"I like the sound of that. There's our plan," declared Bourbon.

And so that's how it went. The marshal went ahead and sought out the yard boss, a barrel-chested individual who stood with his fists planted on his hips and his head on a swivel, eyeing the activity taking place on all sides for any sign of slackers. While he and Bourbon talked, Lone and the others who remained on the edge of the clearing also scanned the work crew, though looking for a miscue of a different kind. None of those under scrutiny did anything out of line from either perspective.

It didn't take long before Bourbon came galloping back to the others. Beads of sweat dotted his broad fore-head from being out in the direct sun. His expression was impassive as he checked down his mount in to the shade of the trees on the fringe of the clearing.

"Well? Any luck?" asked Bayne.

Pulling out an oversized hanky and mopping his face, the marshal said, "Yeah, this is the place Dickerson works right enough. In fact, the yard boss, a fella name of Otto—who impressed me as a hard number who wouldn't go out of his way to say anything particularly kind about his own mother—seems to think kinda highly of our boy Myron. Top hand, he called him, and said he'd hate to lose him if he was to rate endin' up behind bars."

"So he won't cooperate then?"

"No, he cooperated. Otto's hardness for obeyin' his rules on the job site," Bourbon explained, "carries over to respectin' and obeyin' public law as well."

"If that's the case, where's Dickerson? Why didn't Otto hand him over?"

Bourbon grunted. "Cause he ain't here *to* hand over. He's off on a special haul, headin' up a three-wagon train that rolled out before daybreak. Headed for a high, remote mining camp called the Sally Longlegs Dig."

Rena arched a brow. "How charming. Have Sally's legs led the way to a strike of any significance?"

"Sounds like. They're callin' for more and heavier

diggin' equipment. That's what's on the haul Dickerson is ramroddin' up to 'em," Bourbon said.

Now Lone got in on the questioning. "When is Dickerson due back?"

"Maybe tonight. Maybe. But late, at best. The mine is quite a ways up and the trail, according to Otto, is an especially rugged one." Bourbon made a sour face. "With the recent rain, it might even be worse due to some new wash-outs or landslides. In other words, it could very likely be tomorrow before those wagons make it back."

"Damn." Lone spat. "I don't know what anybody else thinks, but I don't much favor just holdin' here waitin' for 'em. Twiddlin' our thumbs the rest of the day and tonight, probably into tomorrow. Even if they got a two-and-a-half, three-hour head start on us, our horses oughta be able to catch up with heavily-loaded wagons climbing a rugged trail by noon or not much later."

Bourbon nodded. "I don't disagree with any of that. So yeah, we'll be goin' after those wagons—and for more reasons than just the ones Lone laid out."

"What's that supposed to mean?" asked a scowling Bayne.

Bourbon put away his hanky and took out his pipe. "Seems there's been an increasin' amount of trouble hereabouts gettin' payroll money up to some of the minin' camps. Robbers been pickin' it off before it ever makes it. So the mine owners and banks been tryin' different things to get the payrolls through. Beefin' up the guards, makin' dummy runs to throw off the robbers, usin' roundabout trails, so on and so forth." The marshal paused to strike a match and fire up his pipe before continuing. "One of their latest attempts is a little trick involvin' the very freight haul our boy Myron is headin' up. Part of the load, you see—a secret to most, but not Myron—is a fat overdue payroll for the Sally Longlegs crew."

Lone gave a low whistle. "Whee-oo. Talk about bad timing and plantin' a mighty powerful seed of temptation in a body. No matter how much of a 'top hand' Dickerson might be, havin' even a shirt-tail connection to the Eccles bunch and havin' 'em right here handy at the same time he's got the inside track on a money haul. How can that *not* add up to some wrong thoughts clawin' to take hold?"

"Pretty much what jumped to my mind. And Otto's," Bourbon revealed. "But, not wantin' to be in too big a hurry to create panic amongst his higher-ups over what *might* happen, and havin' me and my badge standin' right there in front of him, Otto got even more cooperative and was downright eager to turn it all over to me. That is, me and the posse of deputies I happened to mention I had waitin' over here in the trees."

Rena lifted her brows. "So now we're deputies?"

"Strictly the unofficial kind," Bourbon assured her. "Way I saw it, y'all have been that right from the start."

"Why didn't you say so when you were trying to dissuade me from coming along?" Rena challenged. "The hypocrisy might actually have been enough to turn me back."

Bourbon grinned. "I doubt it. Besides, Deputy Miss Rena has a nice ring, don't it?"

"Never mind the jokes," said Bayne, still scowling. "Let me get this straight. You saying, Marshal, that you think Eccles and his men have been the ones staging these payroll robberies?"

"Don't see how," Bourbon replied. "The payroll grabs started before Eccles' bunch ever got here. But that don't mean they wouldn't be interested in a piece of the action if Cousin Myron saw fit to give 'em a heads up on this special haul of his."

"Now there's the makin's for a real whoop-de-doo of a party." Lone's mouth curved in a crooked grin. "What if Eccles' boys get lured in by the cousin and the regular robbers have somehow caught wind of this special haul too? Was they to bump into one another part way up, that rugged trail to the minin' camp could get mighty crowded and turn a whole lot more rugged."

"That's an ugly picture to paint," said Bourbon, his own grin lost in a cloud of smoke. "Even uglier if we was to get caught in the middle of it."

"All the more reason then to catch up with those wagons and make ourselves and that payroll secure from anybody and everybody who comes around with wrong intentions," declared Lone. "And, in the process, get our hands on Dickerson, who we came after in the first place."

"Say," said Bayne. "If we were to get a crack at the payroll robbers—you know, the ones who've been operating for a while now—you think there's any reward money being offered for them?"

Rena gave him a look. "Good God, Emmett. Don't you think you'd better concentrate on dealing with the first thing in front of us before you worry about grabbing for the next pot of money?"

The gambler's face darkened. "That's rich, coming from you. You never seemed to mind me raking in pots before, not when you were counting on getting your share."

Bourbon didn't hesitate to pounce on that. "That's enough of that, you two. The both of you had *better* be concentratin' on what's right in front of us, or you can stay the hell here and wait for me and McGantry to get back. This 'gallop' just took on maybe bein' even tougher and meaner than we figured at the start. No time now for squabblin' in the ranks."

Bayne glared a moment longer at Rena, then cut his eyes to Bourbon. "Nobody's squabbling, Marshal. Just point us up the trail those wagons took and let's not lose any more time."

CHAPTER TWENTY-NINE

Yard boss Otto had informed Bourbon that the trail he was sending them on was referred to by the wagon crews who regularly traveled it as Hacksaw Highway. It didn't take long to see how the name was arrived at, nor to find out where it got its reputation for ruggedness. It was a twisty ascent up between bare, jagged rock walls that narrowed in some places to where Lone found it hard to picture freight wagons being able to fit through. What was more, in some of these pinch points the sides were worn or broken away in such a manner that it left sharp ridges stabbing inward, like passing between saw blades formed out of rock.

The incline, at least in the early going, was at a modest angle and the footing was a sand-gravel mix that gave the horses good purchase. Their biggest challenge was to keep from stumbling in the deep ruts gouged into the still damp ground from the recent passage of heavily loaded wagons.

After a mile or so, the ground hardened and became packed with flat slabs of stone. Had these been still wet from the rain they could have proven treacherously slippery for shod hooves. But the sun was high enough and hot enough by now to have baked them dry.

When they'd been climbing for more than an hour, Bourbon called a brief rest halt. He'd been setting an aggressive pace. The horses were beginning to lather and the riders were sweating freely. Canteens were tipped high and their contents taken in deep gulps. After the horses had cooled some, Lone and Bourbon left their saddles and watered the animals from their hats.

"Might be a good time, Lone," the marshal said, "for you to strike on ahead for a ways and do some of the scouting that's your strong suit. I doubt we're very close to the wagons yet, but it won't hurt to make sure. We don't want to run up on 'em too sudden."

"I been thinkin' the same thing," Lone agreed. "I also been thinkin' about our back trail. We need to keep an eye peeled in that direction, too. This ground's dry enough now with enough loose dirt to kick up dust from horses comin' in any kind of hurry."

"Who'd be hurrying up behind us?" Rena asked. "I thought that yard boss said he'd leave the handling of this to Marshal Bourbon."

"I don't mean anybody comin' from behind to help us," said Lone. "But think about it. If there *are* any robbers gonna make a try for the payroll up ahead—be it Eccles' bunch or whoever—then they either have to already be in place, waitin', or they'll have to come along and close in from the rear same as we're doin'."

"There's that ugly picture again. Us caught in the middle," groaned Bayne. "And in case nobody's noticed, there aren't very damn many off-ramps on this Hacksaw Highway."

"That cuts both ways. Ain't no off-ramps for anybody we want to close in on neither," Lone told him.

Bourbon nodded approvingly. "Lone's right. As long as we stay sharp and stay prepared, we got the bulge. We know the possibilities we need to watch for, none of them have any clue about us."

"Okay, that sounds somewhat encouraging. But it would sound even better if we got moving again," said Rena. "All of a sudden just holding in one spot makes me feel real uncomfortable."

Lone grinned. "That's good. Feelin' uncomfortable keeps a body sharp. You'll have time to feel comfortable when this is all over and you're countin' your reward money."

———

FORTY MINUTES LATER, Lone was back from his forward scout.

Bourbon could tell right away by the look on his face that he'd encountered something not to his liking. "What did you run into?"

Lone pushed back the brim of his hat, sleeved sweat from his forehead. "Ran into something we thought was lacking up hereabouts—an off-ramp," he answered. "Or, in the case of how it got recently used, an *on* ramp. A brush-choked slash down the side of the mountain, even twistier and narrower than what we're followin'. No way a wagon could ever begin to use it. But a man on horseback who was determined enough and willin' to lose some hide scraped off himself and his animal could. And *six* of 'em, ridin' in single file, did just that. They broke up onto this trail not too far ahead of when I reached the spot, then swung on after the wagons."

"Robbers aiming for the payroll?" Bayne said.

"Hard to figure it as anything else," growled Bourbon.

"But six... There's only four in the Eccles gang," Rena pointed out.

"That we know of," replied Bayne. "They could have taken on a couple more men between now and when they robbed our stagecoach."

"Could have," Bourbon allowed. "But Fenton Eccles has always been choosy about addin' to his crew. And bein' on the run with a tall price on his head, now hardly seems the time for him to relax that practice."

"Strikes me that whoever came up that slash had to've had some familiarity with the territory," said Lone. "That pretty much rules out Eccles. Ask me, I'd say those six are most likely the same skunks been doin' the other payroll hits."

Bourbon set his jaw. "I float my stick the same. But comes down to it, it really don't matter. Whoever they are, we need to go get in the way of 'em grabbin' that payroll. And just incidentally, if they *ain't* Eccles' men, then something else for us to get in the way of is our boy Myron bein' shot full of holes defendin' his haul!"

CHAPTER THIRTY

"Is that gunfire we're hearin' up ahead?"

This was the question immediately posed by an anxious looking Marshal Bourbon upon Lone's return from his second forward reconnoiter. After taking time to tie leather pouches around Ironsides' feet in order to mute the iron on stone ring of the gray's shod hooves, Lone had once again forged ahead of the rest for the purpose of rapidly closing the gap on the six riders whose presence he'd discovered previously. This measure was meant to appraise more certainly what the six were up to and to have this information ready so when the others caught up they could make plans accordingly.

The result of Lone's appraisal had now been signaled ahead of him needing to give voice to a report. Still, as he reined up Ironsides before Bourbon, Bayne, and Rena, he went ahead and confirmed what they'd already discerned for themselves. "Yeah, that's gunfire right enough. Those six riders caught up with freight wagons and didn't waste any time tearin' into 'em."

"How far?" Bourbon asked.

"Little over a mile."

"What's the situation?"

"Ain't pretty. But it could be worse. From what I saw, it appears the wagons got halted by a rockslide. Most of the crew must have been out clearin' the trail when the six showed up. Luckily, the teamsters were smart enough to have left a couple men stationed at the rear of the train while the rest were workin' on the 'slide. Elsewise the robbers would have swarmed over the temporarily abandoned wagons like bees over spilled molasses."

"Accordin' to Otto, the middle wagon was canopied for a reason. It's the one with the payroll strongbox," Bourbon explained. "They also put a pair of extra shotgun guards under that canopy. Expect they're the ones who dropped back to cover the rear."

"Whoever it was, they did a good job of stoppin' the swarm." Lone's mouth pulled into a grimace. "But the robbers still took a pretty heavy toll on the crew members caught out in the open before they could scramble back to the cover of their wagons. I saw two or three sprawled dead. No tellin' how many wounded. They're all pinned down now, under the wagons and behind dead mules, puttin' up a fight to continue holdin' the robbers off."

"Any of the robbers get cut down?" asked Bayne.

Lone shook his head. "Not that I could tell. When their initial attack got turned back, they quit their horses and took to the rocks. High and low, workin' forward to flank the wagons. That way they can shoot and move, duck and re-position. With the teamsters pinned in place tryin' to protect their loads, they're in a bad way. Damn near sittin' ducks."

"Then it's up to us to give 'em some relief," growled Bourbon.

"We've got a little bit of luck to help us get started," Lone said, wheeling Ironsides back around to face the way they'd just come. "The gunfire will drown out our hoofbeats, so we can ride like hell to make it there. Then, just before we reach the stretch where the wagons are stalled, there's a juke in the trail that'll let us get damn near on top of everything with little risk of bein' spotted."

"Don't just tell us about it—show us," Bourbon told him. "Come on, everybody knock on it!"

So, with Lone in the lead, that's exactly what they did. Up the rugged, jagged trail they pounded, urging their mounts hard, kicking up stones and dust, scraping the sawtooth sides on occasion, but with barely a flinch so intent were they on the task they'd chosen for themselves. The trail grew steeper, rockier. And the gun blasts became sharper and louder as they drew nearer.

Finally, reaching a spot where the trail suddenly veered off a short distance ahead, Lone raised his arm to signal a halt. They reined up in the midst of a half dozen other saddled horses—the mounts left behind by the robbers, rein-tied to rock outcrops and scant growths of bramble.

Skinning down off Ironsides and pulling his Yellowboy from its scabbard, Lone told the others, "Secure your animals, grab your long guns. Then move up behind me and keep your heads low."

Without looking back, trusting the others were doing as instructed, Lone moved forward in a half crouch, aiming for a vertical slab of rock that marked the inside corner of the veer-off. The gunfire just ahead seemed to have turned somewhat more sporadic, the reports still crashingly loud and then reverberating through the surrounding hills.

Reaching the corner of the veer-off, Lone dropped to one knee and peered cautiously around. The others crowded in close behind and got their first look at the layout of stalled wagons and attackers. It was as Lone had described. The three wagons were pulled up close together, the lead one just short of a heap of trail-blocking rubble and drying mud that marked a rain-loosened breakaway from the higher ground to the right of the trail. Over half of the animals in the four-mule pulling teams were dropped in their traces, shot dead either purposely or inadvertently. Some of the team-sters were hunkered down behind these carcasses, using them as breastworks to return fire on the robbers; other men were squirmed in under the wagons, shooting back from there. The robbers, as Lone had reported, were doing their shooting from shifting points as they moved through the rocks on either side of the trail. To the right was a raggedly notched and creased wall rising several hundred feet at a sixty-degree angle; to the left was a stretch that extended away almost flat—except for spine-like upthrusts and sharp intermittent cuts—for about thirty yards before falling off sharply into bramble and a fringe of trees farther below.

As Lone and the others watched, they could see two of the robbers picking their way slowly through the high notches on the right, stopping to shoot down and then ducking out of sight to adjust their positions before shooting again. In the spiny rocks to the left, another polecat was doing the same. Directly ahead of the observers, up close to the rear wagon, two of the robbers had taken up stationary positions behind large boulders, and were pouring lead steadily from there. That left one of the six attackers unaccounted for, at least for the moment. It would be nice to think he'd caught a bullet and was lying dead, but Lone believed it more likely he was on the move in the rocks somewhere and they just weren't seeing him right now.

Whispering over his shoulder, Lone said, "Well, there's how it shapes up, Marshal. How do you want to play it?"

Bourbon scowled in thought. "You saw it first and have had more time to chew on it. You got any ideas?"

Indeed Lone did. He said, "For starters, I'm thinkin' I could take to the high rocks and pretty quick work my way behind and above the two hombres already squirmin' around up there. I figure I can take out one before they even have a clue I'm in the neighborhood. Second one might be a little trickier, but I'll get him, too. From there I should have a pretty good vantage point for maybe helpin' with anything else that's left."

"As far as what's left," Bourbon said with a wry twist to his mouth, "you wouldn't mind too much, would you, if the rest of us thinned them a little bit?"

Lone grinned. "'Spose not. What have you got in mind?"

The marshal looked at Bayne. "Reckon you could do some crawlin' through those lower rocks on the other side of the trail? Maybe sneak up and stomp on the rattle of that snake slitherin' over that way?"

Now it was the gambler who twisted his mouth

wryly. "Not exactly a chair at a gaming table, where I do my best work. But I can damn sure give it a try."

Lone reached to the small of his back and withdrew from his belt the short-barreled Colt Lightning he had tucked there earlier for extra backup. He held this out to Bayne, saying, "Here, take this instead of the long gun I told you to grab. You're gonna be workin' close to your target, too close for a rifle clunkin' around in those spiky rocks. This Colt ain't as fancy as yours, but otherwise it's a good match and will give you added firepower if you need it. Just keep yourself in one piece so I get it back."

Bayne showed a thin smile. "I'll try to remember that. Thanks."

Looking back to Bourbon, Lone said, "I'm guessin' you figure you and Miss Rena will work from down here on the flat?"

"I'm a few years past my rock claimin' prime so yeah, that's my plan," replied the marshal. Then, to Rena, "You got any hard reservations about shootin' at men from the rear?"

"Men, maybe," Rena answered. "But if you mean the vermin up ahead who cold-bloodedly cut down those teamsters, not to mention a bunch of stupid, innocent animals. No, I have no compunction at all about opening up on the likes of them."

Bourbon's brows pinched together. "Ain't for sure what 'compunction' means—but I think that's the answer I wanted. Let's get to it."

Lone stepped over to a ragged, weather-worn trough running up the slope of the high rocks and said, "Give me and Bayne a little bit to work partly into position before you open up. And everybody keep a third eye peeled for that last owlhoot still unaccounted for."

"Keep an eye peeled for Myron Dickerson too," Bourbon reminded everybody. "We need him alive remember. Otto said he's tall and lanky, wearin' bib overalls and a short-billed, red leather cap."

"Shouldn' be too hard to pick outta the crowd," Lone remarked. "See y'all later when the powder smoke clears..."

CHAPTER THIRTY-ONE

IN A MATTER OF MINUTES, LONE WAS DRIPPING SWEAT. The sun was near its noon zenith overhead, hammering down hard and making the bare rock shoulders of the trough Lone was climbing within almost too hot to touch. It was a bit cooler in the rain- and wind-scoured recess where he was finding enough irregularities to plant his hands and feet, but the angle was nevertheless steep and challenging. Maintaining a grip on his Yellowboy only made it more difficult. Despite his advice to Bayne to go with handguns for his situation, Lone's intent to fire on his targets from a higher and greater distance made the added reach and punch of a rifle essential for what he had in mind.

He had just reached the height he judged to be sufficient and was shifting out of the trough and beginning to work forward over the stingingly hot rocks on a course parallel to the trail when Bourbon and Rena triggered their opening volley. Lone held in place, flattening himself to drink in a long look at how things were playing out below. Until his cohorts opened up and joined the fray, it appeared not too much had changed. The teamsters were still pinned down, finding it difficult to eke out a chance to fire back with any effectiveness while the more mobile robbers continued to pour lead from both sides and the rear, relentlessly chipping away at the wagon crew's cover, their nerves, and eventually more of their lives.

But the salvo from Bourbon and Rena suddenly threw the proverbial bucket into the buttermilk. The two riflemen firing on the rear of the wagon column from behind large boulders were their most obvious targets and it was this pair they set their sights on.

The beefy owlhoot on the left side of the trail jerked rigid and spun halfway around when Bourbon's first bullet hit him. His mouth twisted in anger and pain, spitting a curse as he blindly hip-fired in retaliation. Two more slugs pounded into him, driving him back hard against his former refuge and leaving a scarlet smear as he slid down its face and crumpled into a lifeless heap.

On the opposite side, the other rifleman, a stick-limbed, spidery looking number, took a shoulder hit that propelled him forward against the boulder he'd been squatted behind. Instead of turning to shoot back or dart to one side, he dropped to his hands and knees, abandoning his rifle, and scurried around one end of his boulder then darted into an impossibly narrow crack on the back side. Rena's bullets chased him, cracking and ricocheting off the rock but failing to score another hit on the man himself. "Damn!" she cursed.

Moments later, however, the attack by her and Bourbon created a benefit beyond just the damage they'd inflicted directly. Ahead and slightly lower down from where Lone was halted, one of the robbers who'd been raining hell on the wagons from the high rocks showed enough concern over what just happened to temporarily reveal himself—not to those in the wagons, but to the unknown presence of Lone behind and above him.

"Klieber! Spinny!" the man called. "What's goin' on down there? What the hell just happened?"

A trembling, high-pitched voice called back from within the boulder crack where the spidery little runt had disappeared. "I think Klieber's dead! I'm hit, too! Watch out! Somebody got in behind—"

Bourbon and Rena didn't let him finish. Even though recognizing they couldn't score a hit on the runt, the decided they could at least shut him up and did so by peppering his boulder with a flurry of crashing, cracking lead. It not only worked to silence the runt but it enraged the shooter in the high rocks to the point of him being even more careless.

"You sonsabitches!" he bellowed swinging his rifle barrel away from where he'd most recently fired down on the middle of the wagon column and now aiming it back toward Bourbon and Rena at the rear. This resulted in exposing even more of himself to Lone.

It was a longer shot than Lone had planned to take, but his confidence in his marksmanship was strong enough and the target was too clear to pass up. He planted his elbows, steadied the already chambered Yellowboy, and stroked the trigger well ahead of the hothead centering his aim on Bourbon and Rena. The rifle bucked against Lone's shoulder, sending an echoing boom through the rocks and a .44 caliber slug tearing through the throat of his target. The man was knocked out of his shooting perch and pitched over the side, emitting a short, gargling scream before smacking to a sudden stop on a hard slab and going silent forever.

Now the scene was thrown into all new turmoil. In what amounted to almost a single fell swoop, the attacking force of would-be robbers had been cut in half (maybe more, if the unaccounted for sixth man was already shot and either wounded or lying dead in some unseen spot). And the teamsters were jarred into realizing some assistance had shown up and they were no longer at the disadvantage that had seemed nearly hopeless mere moments ago.

In fact, the two known remaining robbers were the ones suddenly at the big disadvantage. Both in number and positioning. The one out in the flatter area who had been dodging and firing from the cover of the staggered, spiky rocks strewn there found himself the worst off. Now, with the rain of lead from behind and above diminished to just one high shooter, the teamsters spread out behind wagon wheels and dead mules were on a level plane with this hombre and had openings to pour out some lead of their own. Not hesitating to do so, they quickly made it hot for the slithering snake—sending bullets to strike in between and ricochet off the rock tips thrusting up all about him. Slugs sang high and low and sliced in from every angle.

Abandoning any continuation of his part in the attempted robbery, the snake turned his attention to trying to escape. Apparently feeling desperate enough to brave the drop-off on the outer edge of the rock-studded flat area if he could make it that far, he aimed his belly-crawling in that direction. But this only succeeded in bringing him within range of Bayne, who announced his presence with a warning shot and a command to halt. The snake's desperation produced a final surge of resistance and he tried to return fire on the gambler. But his attempt faltered when his rifle barrel clunked against one of the rock spikes—the exact reason Lone had advised Bayne not to go with a long gun in that terrain—before he could get it swung around. Bayne had no such trouble with the short-barreled Colt Lightning he used to plant two rapid-fire rounds in the snake.

That left only the second of the riflemen up in the high rocks. He decided to make a fight of it, even with the odds now turned hard against him. He made a pretty good showing for a while, stubbornly ducking in and out of cover, continuing to get off intermittent shots down at the wagons. With Lone's presence no longer a surprise, like it had been to the first high shooter, this cagey varmint managed to keep himself concealed from the former scout, too, even cranking a couple rounds that came uncomfortably close. But in the end it was a futile stand-off. With Lone crowding him from on high and the teamsters now spread out wide and all focused on him between his sporadic shots, it was just a matter of time. It came when Lone slipped in a shot mere inches behind where the rifleman was hunkered, forcing him to shift on instinct, essentially flushing him to where a half dozen guns in the hands of the men below were waiting to blast him in a near simultaneous volley. The rifleman twisted and jerked, doing a grotesque, bullet-riddled dance before curling over the lip of the pocket he'd been hunkered in and falling silently to a ledge farther down.

It was over. What was left, in order of priority, was

gathering up the dead and wounded and getting the latter to medical attention as soon as possible. In addition to the outlaw Spinny, the little runt Rena's bullets had wounded and then chased into the boulder crack, there were three teamsters also with bullet wounds. None were life threatening once the bleeding was stanched but the men still needed to see a doctor pronto. With saddled mounts available back around the veer-off, it was determined the wounded were fit enough to sit a horse and be returned to Lead in that manner.

In addition to the four slain robbers, there were three other teamsters who'd been shot dead. The initial thought was to temporarily leave the seven bodies behind, protectively covered, and pick them up on the way back down after the wagons had been emptied of their cargo. This brought forth strong objection from several surviving teamsters pointing out the disrespect to their dead by expecting them to be left lying next to their killers for even the briefest length of time. This was resolved by making room for the dead teamsters in the canopied payroll wagon and carrying them there until a proper final resting place was reached.

No sooner was this settled when a new dispute arose as a result of the sixth and previously unaccounted for robber stepping forth to surrender. He explained how he'd been assigned to make his way with all haste through the high rocks—ahead of the other two and without revealing himself by shooting down on the wagons—until he reached a position at the rockslide *in front* of the wagon column. From there he would have added yet another point of attack to wear down and cut down the wagon men until they were forced to give up.

Having arrived at his position when things were already starting to fall apart, this hombre—he said his name was Walsh—held off until it became clear his only chance was to be the one who gave up.

This almost backfired on him when the remaining teamsters, the dead and wounded from within their ranks still fresh in mind, expressed a variety of colorful ways to deal with this member of the bunch responsible —everything from lynching him from an elevated wagon tongue, to flinging him from a high point and watching him be bashed to death on the lower rocks, to simply ventilating him full bullet holes.

But it was Charley Bourbon, reminding everybody of his presence and his standing as a lawman—not to mention how him and his "deputies" had just saved their asses—who brought it all under control. "I understand how you feel. And was it strictly up to me, I'd look away and leave him to you," he told the vengeance minded group. But then, rapping a meaty thumb against the badge on his chest, he added, "Only *this* won't let me do that! My job is to take this piece of crud, knowin' full well what he is on account of previously dealin' with too many just like him or worse, and turn him over for proper justice to get served. In his case, him and the other one, the runt who got wounded, it will start with the marshal down in Lead. You boys be a little patient, you can sit in on their trials and most likely see 'em both swing by their necks legal-like."

The latter prospect went a ways toward mollifying some of those out for blood, but there were a few still grumbling for something more immediate when one of their own—a tall, lanky number in bib overalls and a red leather cap—stepped up beside Bourbon and turned to face out at the rest. "The marshal's right," he said. "He's got a job to do and so do we. That rockslide ain't gonna clear itself and those miners up at Sally Longlegs are overdue for their goods. Did we fight and bleed and die protecting our wagons just to turn into the same kind of mongrels who tried to take 'em from us? And when we get back home and have to face the healin' and consolin' and grievin' amongst family and friends, do any of you really want to do it with the unnecessary blood of vengeance on your hands?"

That succeeded in driving the message home. The men turned away, shame-faced now rather than sullen, and began to quietly go about the necessary tasks. The prisoner, Walsh, stood near with his head hung low. One end of a pair of handcuffs was clamped around his left wrist, a short chain's length away the other end was around Bourbon's thick wrist. Lone stood close behind the marshal. A few yards away, Rena and Bayne stood over the wounded men who were seated on the ground awaiting the saddled horses being brought up. Rena held her rifle casually in the crook of one arm, its muzzle only a few inches from Spinny's ear.

The man in the red leather cap, who was of course Myron Dickerson, glanced down at the chain connecting Bourbon and Walsh, then lifted his eyes to meet the marshal's flat gaze. He said, "Grateful as I am you showed up at all, I'm pretty sure it wasn't due to some lucky hunch the robbers were gonna hit us like they did. What I figure more likely is that you really came lookin' to slap another pair of those on me. Am I wrong?"

"You guilty of something I oughta cuff you for?" Bourbon replied.

"I know you been in and around Deadwood of late, showin' a Wanted dodger on Fenton Eccles and askin' about local ties to one of his gang members. Sorry to say that fits me, so I expected it was just a matter of time before you found it out."

The marshal eyed him. "Then why didn't you either run or step forward?"

"Can't rightly say. Guess I kept hopin' you *wouldn't* find out and would just move on. All I'm guilty of is doin' a favor for a relative—partly out of a sense of family obligation, partly out of fear over what might happen to me or my wife and kids if I didn't."

"Your cousin Luther Purdy strike that kind of fear in you, does he?"

"You know better than that. Luther would never harm me or mine." Dickerson's expression hardened. "But he's a bit on the simple-minded side, too simple to understand the full evil of Fen Eccles and the others he's got mixed up with. He don't begin to realize the danger he put me and mine in—danger from Eccles if I didn't cooperate—by bringin' them to me."

"So that's the only reason you cooperated with 'em?"

"Is there a better one?" Dickerson balled his fists. "I know, even if you believe me it don't make no difference, right? Aidin' and abettin' fugitives, ain't them the fancy words for what I did—hidin' 'em out and fetchin' 'em supplies?"

Bourbon cut a sidelong glance over at Lone. Then, bringing his gaze back to Dickerson, he said, "Look, mister, I've heard enough and seen enough to believe you ain't no crook. Not like your simple-minded cousin, for damn sure nothing like Eccles and the others. I saw how you fought to save your wagons, I heard the common sense way you talked down your men a minute ago. Men who clearly respect the hell out of you. I can't make no promises, but if you was willin' to come around and cooperate with the *right* side now—meanin' me and my deputies—by showin' us where the Eccles bunch is hidin' out, I promise to do everything in my power to see the law goes easy on you."

"What about my wife and kids? You promise to protect them in case something goes sour?"

Bourbon's jaw muscles bulged visibly on his dark face. "The best way I can do that is to make sure nothing goes sour and to *nail* Eccles!"

Nobody said anything for a couple long beats. A flood of emotions played across Dickerson' face. Then, finally: "Okay. I'll cooperate all the way. But I got one big favor to ask. Let me finish my job of ram-roddin' this delivery through. It'll only take a few more hours. As soon as the wagons are in the camp and I've handed over the payroll, my men can handle the rest. I'll grab a horse and make dust to join you down below, take you straight to where Eccles is holed up. I swear!"

Bourbon's forehead puckered. "That's a lot to ask. I got to get these wounded and prisoners back down. We can't afford to lose any more time than we already have."

The men who'd been sent to fetch the saddle horses were in sight now, approaching and leading the string of animals.

"Tell you what," Lone said abruptly. "I'll stay with Dickerson. Pitch in to help his short-handed crew and at the same time make sure he don't change his mind and try craw-fishin'. Leave Ironsides and a horse for him. By the time you get back down below and see to your prisoners and the wounded, we'll be on our way and you won't hardly have no wait at all."

"I ain't fixin' to do no craw-fishin'!" Dickerson protested.

"So much the better then," Lone told him.

Bourbon heaved a sigh. "I'm too damned tired to argue down the both of you. I guarantee this, though, if you don't show up like you're supposed to, I'll sure as hell find the energy to *hunt* you down!"

"You just go ahead and get those nags loaded and movin'," Lone told him, "or you might find us ridin' up your backsides before you make the bottom."

CHAPTER THIRTY-TWO

"THEY'VE LIT OUT, NO TWO WAYS ABOUT IT!"

This was the firm assessment of Charley Bourbon, issued in a highly irritated growl as he stood in the middle of the sagging, one-room old trapper's cabin formerly occupied by the Fenton Eccles gang. Also present in the room with him, continuing to poke idly through the left-behind clutter even though it seemed evident there was little chance of anything worthwhile remaining, were Bayne and Rena. In the open front doorway, Myron Dickerson stood looking on with a bewildered expression on his face. Behind him, outside, the long shadows of late afternoon were stretching across the choppy hills and dense trees that surrounded and served to so effectively mask this remote spot.

It was two hours since they'd left the marshal's office in Lead, having fulfilled their obligations there at least for the time being. Led by Dickerson, they'd hastened here in order to arrive before darkness set in. Dark or light, the ultimate goal had been to strike while the iron was hot and corner the Eccles gang where they'd gone to ground. Instead, they were now facing the bitter disappointment of finding their quarry had fled.

"I don't understand," Dickerson said in a dull tone. "I was supposed to bring 'em more supplies day after tomorrow. They never gave no hint of plannin' to leave any time before then. Matter of fact, in his usual threatenin' way, Eccles made sure to remind me I'd better not forget and better be sure to bring plenty to last 'em."

"When was that? When did you last see 'em?" Bourbon wanted to know.

"Four days ago."

Bourbon made a face. "Well, something spooked 'em, caused 'em to rattle their damn hocks between then and now."

Lone entered through the back door, which was little more than a slab of wood hanging crookedly on leather thongs serving as hinges. "Whatever it was," he said, "accordin' to the tracks out back it didn't budge 'em until fairly recently."

"How recent?" said Bourbon.

"Between now and yesterday's rain. Eight to ten hours, I'd say. Probably rode out first thing this mornin'."

"Damn!" the marshal swore. "I hate comin' so close only to turn up empty."

"We ain't altogether empty. We got a fresh trail to follow," Lone said stubbornly.

Bourbon didn't look very encouraged. "Yeah, but a trail to where? And how long will we be able to follow their sign in this rocky, broken damn country?"

"Don't sell me short," Lone was quick to snap back. "Unless we get another hard rain or they stick feathers up their asses and fly, I'll be able to track 'em."

"Okay, I trust you will." The marshal held up a hand, palm out. "Take it easy."

"Whether we're able to follow them or not," said Bayne, "there's still the question of why they took off so unexpectedly. Did somebody discover them here, give them reason to have to leave? Or could it be they perhaps have found out we're so close on their tail?"

"Mighty hard to believe anybody found 'em here," responded Dickerson. "This old shack has been stuck back in these hills for thirty, forty years. Trappin' long since dried up and there was never no sign of gold in any of the gulches or creeks anywhere close, so nobody's got no reason to come around no more. I only know about it on account of my grandpop bringin' me fishin' hereabouts when I was a kid."

"Besides," Lone added, "the only sign anywhere besides ours is that of the horses bein' ridden out by the four owlhoots."

Dickerson's expression pulled long. "And far as 'em thinkin' anybody was on their tail, they knew that, in a general way, right from the get-go. That's why they wanted to lay low and let things die down in the first place. I'll admit, though, that I did mention hearin' how Marshal Bourbon had showed up in Deadwood flashin' that Wanted dodger on Fen."

"Well that's just great," said Bayne, glaring at him. "Why didn't you say so before you led us here on this wild goose chase?"

"That was four days ago. They didn't act like it bothered 'em all that much," Dickerson responded. "Like I said before, they arranged for me to bring 'em more supplies for a longer stay. If mention of the marshal is what spooked 'em, why did they wait until this mornin' to take off?"

"Yeah, that's a valid point," allowed Bourbon.

"Admittin' more," said Dickerson, "when I told 'em about the marshal I was hopin' it *would* make 'em decide to move on sooner. I wanted nothing worse than to get 'em out of my hair and away from my family. If that had worked or if I'd known they took off for any other reason, I would-n't've gone to all the trouble of bringin' you here. I swear."

Bourbon regarded him for a long count before saying, "I've strung with you this far, I guess I believe that part, too. But it sure don't help us nail that bastard Eccles."

"The times you were around 'em," spoke up Lone, addressing Dickerson, "did you overhear 'em say anything about where they might head once they did decide to go on the move?"

Dickerson looked dismayed. "I can't think of anything. Except for my cousin yammerin' like the whole business was a big lark, the rest of 'em were pretty tight-lipped whenever I showed up. Except to bellyache if I brought something that didn't exactly suit what they wanted. But wait a minute, there was a time when the one they called Amarillo or just 'Rillo—"

"That'd be Amarillo Ames," interjected Bourbon.

Dickerson nodded. "Yeah, him. Anyway, this one time, I forget exactly what was said to get a rise out of him, but he gave a big laugh and came back with some-thing along the lines of 'Wait 'til we introduce ourselves to the fine folks of Wyoming and they get to know the pleasure of our company'. Then Eccles gave him the stinkeye and 'Rillo didn't say no more."

Bayne grunted. "Wyoming. That sure don't narrow it down much."

"No, but it fits with some of the blowin' Eccles did when he was in the pen," said Bourbon. "He bragged more than once that when he got out—something he always swore he'd manage, no matter how many others swore he was gonna hang—he'd strike for fresh pickin's in Wyoming, a place he'd never been and nobody knew him."

"He might end up bein' half right, but that's all," Lone grated. "He might make it to Wyoming, only we're gonna be tight on his tail and it just so happens we *do* know him."

"I like your confidence, McGantry," said Bourbon. "I've developed some fair trackin' skills myself. Between the two of us, I'm countin' we *can* stay tight on Eccles' tail. But I've had that view long enough and I'm blasted sick of it. I mean to close the gap on that polecat and get around in front so's I'm lookin' him square in the eye when I slap the cuffs on him."

"What if he digs in his heels and makes a fight of it even after we do close the gap on him?" Bayne wanted to know. "That Wanted paper on him says Dead or Alive, don't it?"

Bourbon gave him the narrow eye. "I'm well aware what the paper I'm serving says, mister."

"Yes. Yes, of course you do," replied the gambler, quick to backtrack. "I certainly never meant to imply otherwise. Besides, I was jumping ahead by even bringing up that matter. I mean, the first order of business remains catching the scoundrel, right? Rena and I have been counting on McGantry's tracking skills all along. And now yours. I just wish they could be aided by some better idea of where that pack might be headed —a better one, that is, than the whole damn state of Wyoming."

From where she stood leaning over the rickety table, examining the papers strewn on top of it, Rena said quietly, "Maybe we do have something."

All eyes cut to her.

Bayne frowned. "What do you mean?"

"I think there might be a clue in the markings here on these papers," Rena replied.

From the doorway, Dickerson said, "Those are just pinochle scores. Eccles was, whatycall, obsessed with playing pinochle. He learned the game in prison and taught the others. That's how they passed the time here, they spent hours and hours playing pinochle. One of the first things Eccles demanded I bring out was a roll of butcher paper and some pencils for the score keepin'."

"That might be," allowed Rena. "But while I may not know a lot about pinochle, I understand enough to know that drawing pictures isn't generally a part of it. That's what I'm talking about here—not the score keeping, but this sketch somebody made."

"What sketch? What are you talking about?"

Now the men all came forward and crowded around the table, leaning in to get a better look at the sketch— the one made by Bo Lasky to give the other gang members an idea of what Devil's Tower looked like—as Rena spread it out and smoothed it flat for all to see.

"So it's a drawing of some mountain or whatever," muttered Bayne. "How is that a clue that narrows our hunt down much more than we already knew? Not like there's a shortage of goddamn mountains in Wyoming."

Frowning, Bourbon said, "No, I think I understand

what Miss Rena is thinkin'. That ain't just any old mountain—I'd say it looks more like a butte, a particular landmark of some sort. If we recognized what it was, it might mean—"

Rena cut him short, saying, "I do. I recognize what that's a likeness of."

"Go ahead. Tell us," encouraged Lone.

"It's called Devil's Tower. You're right, Marshal, it's a butte. It's very tall and distinct, quite widely known I've always thought. I'm surprised none of you ever heard of it."

"Yeah, I heard the name. Never really knew what it looked like, though," said Dickerson.

Lone nodded. "I've heard of it, too, though never got around to ever seein' it. It's over in Wyoming's northeast corner, ain't it? Can't be all that far from here."

Rena's mouth turned down at the corners. "I'm not very good at directions or distances. It's somewhere up in the northern part of the state, yeah. My mother had a sister who lived up that way and we visited her once when I was a little kid. That's when I got to see the Tower and how I'm able to recognize it. It's a pretty memorable thing, I'm surprised none of you aren't more familiar with it. Several of the local Indian tribes even have legends about it. Most of them tell a tale of how some Indian children were once being chased by a giant bear and their desperate prayers to the Great Spirit caused that butte to rise up and lift them to safety on its top. Those marks down the side, and this sketch actually shows it quite good, are gouges and seams where the bear supposedly tried to claw up to them."

"That's all interesting as hell," said Bayne in an annoyed tone. "But what am I missing? Why does some old Injun legend and a half-assed artist's scribbling on a piece of paper matter to what we're interested in?"

"It matters if that scribblin' is where the Eccles gang could be headed for, you wool head," Bourbon told him. "Seems to me somebody must've had a reason for makin' that sketch. If it was just the doodlin' of some daydreamer, maybe a half-assed artist like you said, don't you figure there'd be more sketches layin' around in all these scraps of paper? I don't see any, do you?"

Bayne scowled. "No, I don't. By God. But what I do see, now, is what you're driving at. Yeah, that sketch *could* mean something. It could very well signal where those thieving dogs are headed to next."

"Makin' it sign that even you can track, gambler," said Lone with a sly smile.

Bayne responded with a smile of his own, a rueful one. "Don't get too carried away. You're still the tracker for this outfit, you and the marshal. My tracking is confined to the wilds of a poker table, no further. Our artist friend would have to drop one of those sketches every quarter mile or so for me to stay on his trail—and even then I wouldn't bet on me not possibly missing one."

"You want to talk bets, I'll give you the surest one you could ever make," declared Bourbon. "It's this: You can bet on me not lettin' us quit Eccles' trail until we run him down. And if that means cornerin' the no-good devil at Devil's Tower, maybe that's what they call... damn it, what's the word I'm lookin' for?"

"Poetic justice?" offered Rena.

"Yeah, that's the one. Leastways it'll do. We got a ground trail to follow and now what seems like a clue to where it's gonna lead. I've run down polecats on a lot slimmer than that to start with." Bourbon paused to glare at the faces looking back at him, almost as if challenging one of them to say anything contrary. When no one did, he added, "So take a good gander at these fine, first-class accommodations surroundin' us, children—all except you, Dickerson—'cause here's where we're spendin' the night. Come first light, we'll be settin' off hard on the devil's trail."

"What about me?" asked Dickerson.

That earned him a glare all his own from Bourbon. After letting it burn in good and deep for a beat, the marshal heaved a sigh and said, "Since you're a different critter than I'm used to, I'm gonna have to deal with you different. I'm releasin' you under your own recognizance to go back to your family and job and keep your goddamn nose clean. Report back to the marshal in Lead, tell him I ain't pressin' no charges at this time and I'll send him a wire backin' that up as soon as I get somewhere there's a telegraph."

Dickerson blinked a couple times, looking somewhat stupefied. Then a corner of his mouth lifted in a faint grin. "Thank you, Marshal. I—I will. Keep my nose clean, I mean."

"You damn well better," Bourbon growled. "Was I to pass back through Lead—which I'll make it a point to do—and find out otherwise, it would annoy me considerable. Then *you* would be the next one I'd set out to run down. Trust me, you wouldn't like that...and neither would I. Now beat it before I change my mind!"

CHAPTER THIRTY-THREE

THEY RODE STEADY FOR THE NEXT THREE DAYS, PASSING quickly into Wyoming and continuing on. Each morning started ahead of the sun, only brief and infrequent daytime rest stops were made, and night camps weren't pitched until well into evening. On the first day out, at a town called Red Fork, just across the Wyoming line, they made a quick stop to add to their trail supplies and the rations Bourbon had advised to have ready when they first started out. The stop also gave Bourbon the chance to send his promised wire back to the Lead marshal.

Good to his own promise, Lone was able to continue cutting sign for their quarry with relative ease. It helped of course that they weren't putting any effort into masking their trail. What they *were* doing, he could tell by the span and sharp imprints of their horses' hoofprints, was riding hard toward their destination. The folks of Red Fork, opening up freely to the sight of Bourbon's badge, had provided some welcome information on the distance and clearer direction for locating

Devil's Tower. Though Eccles and his men had swung wide of the town, the course they were on still jibed well with the way indicated for reaching the distinct landmark.

For much of each day, Lone rode apart from the others. He left camp ahead of them in the morning, scouring the landscape in general, paying particular attention to the trail of the gang. He watched for any change in pattern, noting the pace they were able to maintain, judging the time gap between them and his group. Unfortunately, that didn't appear to be shrinking much. He marked his own course clearly, especially over rough terrain and creek crossings, so Bourbon and the others could follow easily and hopefully steady enough to start cutting that gap some.

Overall, the land wasn't too hard to traverse. Some low, choppy hills studded with pine, aspen, and cotton-wood growth, scattered rocky ridges, and flat stretches of short-grass prairie. Weather-wise, it stayed about as good as you could ask for. Warm, sunny days under a clear sky, chill nights painted blue-silver by a fat moon and a canopy of glittering stars.

Considering the more pampered lifestyle they were used to, Lone was somewhat surprised and guardedly impressed by how well Bayne and Rena were holding up to the long hours in the saddle. Not that their faces and stiff movements didn't show a healthy dose of exhaustion at the end of each day, but they nevertheless pitched in and held up their end of night camp duties. Bayne was more prone to signs of impatience and a bit of under-the-breath bellyaching, but Lone reckoned the gambler's raw greed was strong enough to keep him going. Rena actually seemed to take to the hardships of the trail easier and more naturally. Lone remembered her recounting of a hard life growing up on scrub ranch driven by a task master of a father, and he could see where the roots from that had reached down deep and weren't yet pulled all the way loose.

On the second night out, in that lull time after the supper meal was done and the plates and pans all cleaned, except for the pot of strong, simmering coffee hanging over the edge coals of the campfire, Lone returned from checking the horses and found Rena sitting alone beside said fire. She had a blanket draped over shoulders and was holding a cup of coffee between her palms. Bourbon was over on the edge of the clearing, propped up against the trunk of a cottonwood tree, dozing; his pipe, with a lazy curl of smoke rising from the bowl, was cupped loosely in one hand. Bayne, as announced earlier, was off soaking his aching feet in the cool, soothing water of a nearby stream.

Lone hooked an empty cup, poured himself some of the steamy mud and motioned to Rena with the pot. "Need yours topped off?"

She shook her head. "No, thanks. I'm good."

Lone re-hung the pot then asked, "Mind sharin' some of that fire?"

"Not at all." Rena smiled. "Pull up a piece of ground and sit."

Lone did so. After he was settled, he reached into his hip pocket and withdrew the whiskey flask he'd taken earlier from his saddlebags. Holding it up, he said, "If you're open to a suggestion, here's something else you ought not mind. This here's straight up, regular ol' bust-head redeye. Nothing like that top-shelf stock your man Bayne reaches for, or the fancy wine I've seen you sip.

But I guarantee that a splash of this in your coffee will go a long way toward easin' those saddle aches I figure you're feelin' right about now in places you forgot you even had places."

Rena's gaze went from the flask to Lone's face then back to the flask. A corner of her mouth lifted in a fresh smile. "Why Galahad, you are full of surprises," she said. "Not only do you boldly carry hard spirits on your person and clearly have experience partaking of same, but now you are brazenly tempting a fair maiden with such evil elixir."

Her words stirred a sudden memory in Lone. To a time just last year when Velda, after Lone intervened to turn back some pesky renegades who'd been pursuing her, likened herself to a fair maiden rescued by Lone in the guise of her White Knight. It wasn't an unpleasant memory since few involving Velda ever could be (except for the horror of her being shot). In fact, the "fair maiden/white knight" incident was especially far from unpleasant as it marked the occasion of their first embrace.

Still, something about it being brought to mind must have shown on Lone's face because it caused Rena to follow up with, "I'm sorry. Did I say something wrong? I guess I made another 'Galahad' crack, didn't I?"

Lone tried to cover with a quick, sheepish grin. "It's nothing. Guess I got stabbed with a saddle ache of my own. Far as the Galahad thing, reckon I've got used to that. Though you don't actually say it much anymore."

"Probably because you're hardly around to say it *to*," Rena replied. "You gallivant off first thing in the morning and usually don't show back up until evening.

If anything, it seems like the name you work hardest at living up to is 'Lone'."

"Something that got stuck on me as a kid," Lone explained. "Didn't have much say in it, just like I didn't have much say in the roamin' off alone part. Leastways not in the beginnin' when I took up scoutin' for the army at an early age. Scoutin' is just naturally a lonely business. Don't know that I'd go so far as to say I work at it, though, even if it's continued as sort of a habit even after I quit the army." Another unbidden thought passed through his mind: How, with Velda, he'd been more than ready to break the habit of being alone. He made no comment on that, however, instead saying, "I see it as bein' able to take or leave bein' around other people. For me, stretches of solitude don't come as a hardship like it seems to for others."

Rena regarded him. "Marshal Bourbon told Emmett and I the story of you being orphaned as the result of your folks getting killed in an Indian massacre, and how the wives at the army post collectively raised you from an infant."

"Sounds like Charley's capable of talkin' too much," Lone grunted.

"He meant no harm. He admires you."

"Maybe so. But people flappin' their gums too much is what makes it good to get off alone for stretches of time."

Rena continued studying him. "The elderly woman you set out to help, the one who got jilted out of her money... She's one of the fort wives who helped raise you, isn't she?"

Lone returned her gaze with a sharp look. "Did Bourbon tell you that, too?"

"No," Rena said quietly. "I just...sensed it somehow."

Lone took a breath, let it out slowly. "Well, you sensed right. Not that it changes the tale any. Her name is Adeline Sharples. Ma Sharples, most everybody calls her these days, even though she never had any children of her own. I may have been the closest. Yeah, a lot of the fort wives pitched in to look after me, but Ma—and her husband, a crusty old sergeant—were the main ones. He's been dead for quite a few years now. I owe them plenty. Gettin' Ma's money back is the least I can do."

"And you'll do it, too. I'm confident you will," Rena said earnestly.

Lone sat his coffee cup on the ground beside him and unscrewed the cap of his flask. "We kinda got off the subject at hand. Time to get back to it," he proclaimed. "I realize this ain't hardly the kind of room service you're partial to, but it's the best I can offer. I didn't hear you say no before, so if you want a touch of this pain duller, go ahead and hold out your cup."

Rena arched a brow somewhat skeptically, but nevertheless held out her cup. "This isn't one of those kill or cure remedies is it?"

"Ain't never lost a patient," Lone assured her. But after tipping the flask and adding a generous dollop to her coffee, he added in a lowered voice, "Leastways not yet."

Without further hesitation, Rena downed a hearty swallow followed promptly by a second and then eyed Lone somewhat smugly, saying, "I hope you didn't think you invented pain duller whiskey, Galahad."

"If I did," Lone replied, grinning, "I guess I just got a

surprise of my own. Appears you've been 'brazenly tempted' by somebody ahead of me."

"Even my straight-laced old man knew the value of taking a touch—strictly for medicinal purposes, of course—to ease the after effects of a particularly back-straining day's work," Rena said. "And, hard as times usually were for us, he brewed his own corn. If you think this mother's milk of yours is harsh, some of the batches Dad turned out could melt a UP rail section."

"Sounds like you're basin' that on more than just from observin'. I guess that explains tossin' down my bust-head so easy."

"Though I've developed a personal preference for wine, it seems my palate recalls the taste of whiskey with no great revulsion." A bit of a faraway look crept into Rena's eyes. "It wasn't like my father passed the jug around to us kids at the supper table, mind you. But, at the same time, I'm pretty sure he knew we snuck some touches of our own sometimes—to be daring as much as to deal with our aches. A couple times when he could tell my older brothers had gotten into it too heavy, he'd work them extra hard the following day to make sure he sweated it out of them."

"Seen that same thing done by plenty of hard-nosed army sergeants on hungover troopers," Lone said. "Always suspected it was something passed on from an earlier experience of the person dolin' it out."

"Speakin' of dolin' out," said Bourbon, rousted from his nap and pushing up from the tree trunk he'd been propped against, "is that flask there in your hand what I think it is? If so, are you stingy enough so's you didn't intend to dole a touch out to everybody?"

"I was only bein' considerate of the beauty sleep you're so badly in need of," Lone told him.

The marshal huffed. "I get even uglier when I catch a whiff of good whiskey and none gets offered to me."

"In that case, you'd better get over here and have some. There's still coffee left in the pot. Pour a cup and lace it with what's in my flask."

Bourbon stopped in his tracks and frowned mightily. "Son, when I drink coffee, I drink coffee. When I drink whiskey, I drink whiskey."

So saying, he reached for the flask and tipped it up for a long pull. Watching, Lone recalled how the man had copiously downed whiskey at their meeting in the rear gaming room of the Deadwood saloon. It made him glad he had a spare bottle in his saddlebags. It also made him decide not to mention this second bottle too soon, for the sake of leaving some "pain duller" available for the next evening.

CHAPTER THIRTY-FOUR

ECCLES AND HIS MEN SAT THEIR HORSES LOOKING OUT from the crest of a red rock ridge. Due ahead, to the west, the sinking sun hovered just a sliver above the horizon. North, off to the riders' right, a collection of weathered, misshapen buildings filled a shallow, natural bowl scooped out between two sloping shoulders of sparse grass stubbled with ledges of broken, crumbling rock. To their left, looking close though still a deceptive number of miles south, loomed the murky, shadow-cut butte known as Devil's Tower. The sketch drawn by Lasky back at the trapper's cabin made it unmistakable to those gazing on it for the first time.

"Well, boys. There it is," declared Eccles, resting a forearm across his pommel and allowing a hopeful expression to settle over his face. "The marker to wealth like none of us ever dreamed of before."

"Any other time it might not look so inviting. Kinda gloomy and foreboding even," said Amarillo Ames. "But after what you've told us, Fen, it looks downright inviting."

"I ain't saying we're gonna gallop down there and right away trip over a pile of gold bars. Nobody's claiming it's gonna be that easy," cautioned Eccles. "But the treasure is somewhere close. I swear I can *feel* it."

"We gonna ride in closer before we make night camp?" asked Luther.

Eccles took time to fire up a fresh cigar before replying, "Nope. As a matter of fact, for tonight, we're gonna first swing over yonder to the town. Place by the name of Reasoner's Gap."

"Don't look like much. Not from here, anyway," said Ames. "But if it's got a saloon of some kind that would pretty it up a whole bunch."

"And if the saloon had a couple back room gals available, that would make it downright beautiful," crowed Lasky. "I ain't had me a woman in so damn long I'm starting to get cobwebs down around my handle."

Ames grunted. "Uh-huh. The size of your handle is about the right size to interest a little spider. Was mine to go unattended long enough, it'd take an eagle's nest to smother it over."

"Yeah, don't you wish," Lasky shot back.

"I gotta admit, though," sighed Ames, "it's been way too long between romps. Stuck out in that mossy ol' cabin didn't help any, neither, thinkin' about the last real looker any of us saw—that blonde babe we had to leave behind at the stagecoach robbery. The money we grabbed was good, but she sure would've sweetened it all the more."

Lasky's face scrunched in agony. "Ouch! Now you're just doubling the pain. I been trying with all my might *not* to think about that blonde. Just for bringing her up,

I call first dibs on any sweet thing we run across in this town."

"Oh no you don't," Eccles said sharply. "Workin' girls are one thing. Tear up all of them you want. But leave anything else alone. We might be poking around this area for a while, I don't want to do anything to bring the law down on us if we can help it."

"What about you, Fen? Ain't you interested in havin' a woman?" said Luther.

"Well hell yes," growled Eccles. "If this pans out, I plan on havin' me a whole goddamn harem full of women. So I can afford to wait and not settle for no saloon sweeps in the meantime. The gals I line up will be top shelf and classy all the way—make that blonde from the stagecoach look like an army post wash-erwoman."

Ames frowned. "So what *do* you want to get out of going into this town, Fen?"

Eccles puffed cigar smoke around a wide grin. "Why, I'm going in to visit a priest."

————

AMARILLO AMES' assessment of Reasoner's Gap looking like "not much" from a distance turned out to be a little harsh. True, the downtown area, modest in size, was comprised of older buildings, weathered and rather drab looking. But they stood sturdily enough, with their boardwalks swept clean and their display windows washed clear to show off whatever goods were available on the inside.

The Wrangler's Rest saloon was no exception. It had bright red batwing doors and fancy gold lettering proclaiming its name on a broad front window. Eccles and his men tied their horses at the hitch rail and sauntered on in.

It was the middle of the week and still early, so there weren't very many customers in the joint. A lone cowboy was leaning against the bar, halfway down, and two old timers sat playing dominoes at one of four round-topped gaming tables. At the far end of the bar, a toothpick thin bartender stood talking with a bored looking young woman in a spangly dress and a plump man who had a pressed shut accordion dangling above the swell of his gut.

The bartender hurried down to the new arrivals as they bellied up to the bar. "Evenin', gents," he said in a deep bass voice that boomed out in contrast to his spindly build. "What can I get you to drink?"

Eccles ordered for everybody, saying, "Four tall beers, coldest you got. And shots of decent redeye to go with 'em."

"Comin' right up."

While the stick man was preparing the drinks, Ames and Lasky wasted no time leaning out from their spots at the bar and gawking down at the girl in the spangly dress. They managed to keep from actually drooling, but that was about all. The girl was decidedly plain, with bony shoulders under the thin straps of her dress, dull eyes, and pock-marked cheeks not even a thick layer of rice powder could cover up. But she was a female. That alone would have been plenty sufficient for Lasky and Ames. But the fact she neither made any attempt to act coy nor avert her eyes from their hungry stares—clearly signaling she wasn't put off by such attention—made her exactly the right *kind* of woman for their pent-up yearnings.

Once the barkeep had their drinks fanned out in front of them and Eccles had paid, Lasky leaned eagerly forward on the bar top and said, "Hey, mister. That gal down yonder... Any more like her in the back or upstairs?"

"Only got the one. Her name's Mona," the bar man replied. "You waitin' for a formal introduction or something?"

Lasky frowned. "Hell no. I can take care of that for myself."

"*We* can take care of that for ourselves," Ames was quick to interject.

They glared at each other for a beat, then both cut their eyes to Eccles. "How about it, Fen? You in a hurry?" Lasky wanted to know. "We got time to go, er, introduce ourselves?"

"I suppose," the gang leader allowed. "But if I ain't right here when you're done, wait 'til I get back. And remember what I said before about not causing any trouble."

"Well, yeah. Of course, Fen."

"Uh-huh," Eccles said skeptically. "So who's gonna go first?"

"I am!" they answered in unison. Then immediately started arguing.

Eccles put an end to that with a sharp command to knock it off. "That's about what I figured," he said with a disgruntled sigh. Plucking a coin off the bartop, he held it up. "Okay, here's how we'll settle it. I'm gonna flip this. Heads, you go first, Lasky. Tails, it's you, 'Rillo. Whichever way it falls, that's the end of it. No more bickering afterwards. Understood?"

Two sullen nods were his answer.

When the coin landed and tipped in his favor, Lasky let out a triumphant whoop. By then the object of all this attention, Mona, had drifted down from the end of the bar and stood looking on in a hip-shot stance meant to be provocative. A cigarette dangled from one corner of her painted mouth and her expression appeared mildly amused.

Lasky gave her a slap on the rump and said, "You're gonna find out how lucky you are that I'm the winner, darlin'! You ain't gonna have to wait to get your pretty little toes curled like you ain't ever had 'em curled before!"

"We'll see about that," Ames muttered. "You go ahead and get warmed up on the youngster, gal—then I'll show you toe curlin' from a real man."

Mona let smoke drift from her nostrils in another attempt to be provocative as she drawled, "Maybe you should both come with me and we'll all curl our toes together."

"Oh no," Lasky was quick to protest. "I won first dibs fair and square, and that's how it's gonna be. Just let me finish my drink and we'll get down to business."

Mona exhaled some more smoke and let her gaze drift lazily to Eccles. "How about you, General? Ain't you gonna want a turn?"

Eccles replied diplomatically, "Tempting as the offer is, my dear, I have more pressing matters to tend to."

Undeterred, Mona next turned to Luther. "That leaves you, Slim. How about it?"

Luther's narrow face turned a brilliant scarlet and all he could do was stammer, "I...I..."

Mona smiled and reached out to pat his cheek. "That's okay, honey. You take your time decidin'. I'll still be available when you do."

"Not any time soon you won't be," declared Lasky as he thumped his empty glass down on the bar. He reached out to take Mona's hand. "Lead the way, darlin'. I plan on keeping you plenty busy for quite a while!"

———

THE MAN who answered the door to Eccles' knock was middle aged, a bit thick in the torso, with a fleshy, clean-shaven face and iron gray hair combed straight back from a widow's peak centered low on his broad forehead. He had brown eyes that seemed instantly kind and caring, but maybe that was only Eccles' imagination. The fact the man had his shoes off and was wearing a black vest unbuttoned over a white shirt with the sleeves rolled to three-quarter length clearly indicated he was settled in for a relaxing evening and expecting no visitors. Yet he appeared quite unperturbed by the intrusion.

"Mr. Farrow...er, Reverend Farrow?" inquired Eccles.

"Yes, I'm Charles Farrow. Can I help you?"

Eccles removed his hat, as did Luther standing close behind him. "Sorry if we're coming by at a bad time, perhaps interrupting your supper."

"It's alright, my wife and I ate early this evening," Farrow assured him.

"Good. I'm glad for that. My name is Egan, Frank Egan," Eccles lied. Then, gesturing to Luther, he went on.

"My friend and I, along with some others, are passing through town on our way to hopefully find work on one of the big cattle spreads up in Montana. I asked for this brief stopover in Reasoner's Gap so I could take the opportunity to speak with the friend of a friend. The fella I'm looking for used to be known as Padre Pete. But Ferd, the barkeep at the Wrangler's Rest, told me that nowadays he goes by the name of Misner, Peter Misner, and that you'd be the one to help me get in touch with him."

Reverend Farrow frowned thoughtfully. "It's rather unusual for me to get a referral from Ferd. We travel in different circles, as you might imagine. Though he surely would be welcome within my doors"—here the reverend gestured toward the tall and brightly white-washed church building that stood only about twenty yards away from the modest house that was the minister's residence—"any time he wished to enter."

A corner of Eccles' mouth lifted slightly. "As, I suspect, you would be in his...sir."

Farrow looked uncertain for a moment, then he, too, showed a thin smile. "Touché. Though, I assure you, one is far more likely than the other."

Eccles cleared his throat. "Look, Reverend, a fella in your line of work is supposed to believe in forgiveness and redemption and so forth, so I won't beat around the bush. This mutual friend of mine and Pete's—or Misner, if that's more suitable nowadays—was a fella named Borland. He's dead now. Died of tuberculosis. In prison. That's where I knew him."

He paused, watching for a reaction out of Farrow. The reverend simply nodded and said, "Go on."

"So Borland talked a lot about Padre Pe..." Eccles

stopped again and scowled. "I mean no disrespect, but Padre Pete is fixed in my head. That's how I know him, always heard him called. If I keep backing up to call him by the other, this is just gonna take a lot longer."

"Fine. Go ahead," Farrow said again.

"Okay. So Borland told me how Pete was a defrocked priest turned into a drunken derelict who got by swamping out saloons for drinks and a few scraps of food. That's the way Borland got to know him. He was a bad drunk back then, too, I guess. What eventually led him to...well, where I met him. We were cell mates. It was in his final months, as he was getting sicker on his way to dying, that he started talking a lot about Padre Pete. Seems that even in his drunken mumblings, Pete still spoke about God and forgiveness and the Hereafter. Borland remembered that as his time drew near. Found comfort in it, fought hard to embrace it and believe it all."

Farrow's expression showed a touch of dismay. "Unfortunately, that's often the case. When it's too late..." He stopped short, the look of dismay turning into a hard frown. "No. Strike that. It's never too late to embrace the word of God and seek salvation. Forgive me my human frailty of sometimes feeling petty and bitter. Go on with your story, Mr. Egan."

Eccles cleared his throat again then continued. "Well, that's mainly what I wanted to stop by and let the padre know. It's what Borland asked of me. I told him, see, about my plans to head to Montana when I got my release. So he asked me, was I to swing anywhere near Reasoner's Gap, would I look up his old drinking pal and let him know how his words had been remembered and helped bring a tormented soul some comfort toward his end."

Farrow appeared to consider for a long moment. Then: "That's actually a rather inspirational tale. Demonstrating how the word of God can reach through time and the troubled lives of two unfortunates to find a way to ultimately provide hope and comfort. And it's very noble of you, Mr. Egan, to go out of your way to bring that message full circle."

"Don't get too carried away, Reverend," Eccles cautioned. "Attaching the word 'noble' to me is a mighty big stretch."

"I think you're selling yourself short," replied Farrow. "But, as with many things in this life, we shall leave that to a Higher judgment. In the meantime, what we can do here and now is see to the completion of your mission. Allow me to slip my shoes on and I'll take you to Peter. He has living quarters in a room at the back of the church. He earns his way, and does an excellent job of performing his assigned chores, I might add, by keeping the church immaculately clean and also tending the surrounding grounds, including the nearby cemetery. I preach the Baptist gospel, not Catholicism such as Peter was ordained in. I make no attempt to influence him one way or another, not even requiring him to attend our services, but I think merely being within the orbit of Biblical teachings and the guidance of our mutual Lord is good for him. Certainly better than being dragged down farther by the poisonous hand of John Barleycorn."

"Amen!" Luther blurted suddenly.

Eccles gave him a look, but Farrow smiled.

As he started to turn to go inside and fetch his shoes,

the reverend lingered in the doorway a moment longer. He regarded Eccles. "It occurs to me," he said, "to wonder what state your friend found Peter to be in during their time together—other than one of near constant drunkenness, I mean?"

Eccles' brows pinched together. "Not sure I follow you, Reverend."

"The thing is," Farrow explained, "Peter is presently, well, a bit addled is the kindest way I can put it. That's the way I found him when I first moved to town a little over a year ago and assumed the ministry here. It wasn't long after that I took an interest in Peter's plight and eventually got him away from the saloons and set up our current arrangement. His mind was already damaged by that point—from years of alcohol poisoning, no doubt, but also by some other trauma I've yet to understand fully. I'm not sure which came first. But one or the other, or perhaps a combination of both, has left him as you will now find him.

"Usually he is functionally lucid, though often morose, as he was earlier when I took him his supper. But every once in a while, for no discernible reason, he will become particularly agitated and start ranting about evil and demons and the hopelessness of Christ's power over them. Such talk is naturally quite disturbing to hear. It stems, as near as I can tell, from some experience he had while trying to establish a mission when he first came to the territory. That's as close as I've come to pinning down the source of his trauma. I've learned not to press him too hard when he's already agitated in that manner, as it only makes it worse."

"Yeah, it sounds like a tricky thing to try and deal with," Eccles allowed.

"I mention it now," Farrow said, "to prepare you just in case we find his mood has changed from earlier. Though no doubt sad for his old friend's passing, I believe Peter will welcome hearing about how his talk of God and the Lord's word brought succor to Mr. Borland in his time of need. I hope it will be *good* for Peter to hear that. But, as I said, just in case..."

Eccles nodded. "I appreciate the warning, Reverend. But I'll take my chances. I sorta promised Borland, so I want to see this through."

Farrow nodded in return. "Very well. Let me fetch my shoes then I'll take you to Peter."

CHAPTER THIRTY-FIVE

"Man oh man, am I glad to see you!"

This was the hearty greeting Marshal Bourbon received when he came riding down the main street of Reasoner's Gap at the head of Lone, Rena, and Bayne. The greeting sounded from a stoop-shouldered, elderly man who abruptly disengaged himself from a knot of other folks who had been gathered around him in front of a small one story building. Hurrying forward in a somewhat shuffling gait that seemed to favor one leg, the man came straight toward the mounted Bourbon who had to check down his horse in order to avoid a collision. Behind the marshal, Lone and the others also reined up sharply.

"For cryin' out loud, man—watch out!" growled Bourbon.

The greeter finally came to a stop in the middle of the street, but his eyes continued to brim with a combination of anxiety and excitement. "I don't know what brings you up this way, but the sight of that U.S. Marshal's badge you're wearing couldn't come at a better time," the man proclaimed. "We've got ourselves a pickle here, Marshal. A real pickle. And I don't mind admitting I ain't sure how to go about dealing with it."

From where he'd moved up alongside Bourbon, Lone watched the group of people who had been clustered around the excited man start to edge forward in his wake. About twenty or so in number, made up mostly of men but with a handful of women in the mix, they didn't appear to be any sort of threatening mob despite all their faces being set in somber expressions. Returning his gaze to the excited man, Lone noticed for the first time there was a badge of some kind pinned to the chest pocket of his rumpled, loose-fitting shirt.

This was addressed a moment later when the man, continuing to speak directly to Bourbon as he gazed anxiously up at him, said, "My name's Hank Mosher. I'm the town marshal here. I do the best I can, but we don't hardly ever have no serious trouble in our little community. Only now, all at once, it's a different story. A real pickle, like I said."

Bourbon scrutinized Mosher and the knot of grim-faced folks once again forming in behind him. "Could it be," he said, "this pickle that's got you so worked up was caused by four polecats showin' up here recently?"

A responsive murmur passed through the crowd and Marshal Mosher said, "Yes, that's it exactly! Do you know them—are you on their trail?"

"'Spect they're the ones we been followin', yeah," allowed Bourbon. He reached in his jacket pocket, pulled out a folded up copy of the Wanted dodger on Felton Eccles, held it out. "Was that fella one of 'em?"

Mosher took the paper and unfolded it but only glanced at the picture and wording briefly. "Ain't for me to say. I never got a firsthand look at any of the rascals," he muttered. Then, swiveling his head to look around at the pack crowded close, he called out, "Where's Reverend Farrow? Ferd? Who else got a good look at those men?"

There was some shifting of feet and craning of necks before a painfully thin young woman with tired eyes and pock-marked cheeks stepped forward. Even though the early afternoon sun was pouring down plenty of warmth, she had a somewhat tattered shawl wrapped around her shoulders. It drooped below her throat, showing bony ridges of collar bone pressing out against pale skin that looked to have seldom seen daylight.

She said, "Ferd went back to his saloon. Reverend Farrow had something to take care of at the church, said he'd return in a minute. But I can say whether or not whoever's on that dodger matches one of the four—I seen 'em all when they came in the Wrangler's Rest right after they got to town."

Mosher held the paper out to her. "Recognize him, Mona?"

It only took a single downward eye flick. "Yeah. He acted like some kind of boss over the rest. I called him the General. One of the others said his name once, said 'Fen'. Probably short for *Fenton*. Fenton Eccles, like it says there on the paper. For what it's worth, though, none of that matches with what he told the preacher his name was. You can double check with Reverend Farrow when he comes back, but I'm pretty sure I recall him saying the man introduced himself different. Frank Egan, I think it was. And I got a good memory for faces and names."

"Ain't uncommon for a criminal to use an alias," said

Bourbon. Then, after considering a moment, he added, "Kinda odd, though, to go to the trouble for just a quick robbery."

Mosher frowned. "What makes you think he had anything to do with a robbery?"

Bourbon returned his frown. "Because robbin' is what the Eccles gang does. You saying they didn't hit your bank or a store or some such?"

"No, that wasn't what they done at all." Mosher shook his head. "Well, they stole a horse and saddle from the livery stable. I guess that's the same as robbing. But the main thing they done was abduct one of our citizens."

"Abduct?" echoed Lone. "You mean a kidnappin'?"

Mosher looked more anguished than ever. "I ain't sure. That's what makes the whole thing all the more confusing and troubling. A kidnapping usually means a try at getting money for ransom, right? Well, this fella they took is about as ransom-proof as a body could be. He's got no money or wealth of his own, no family, no real friends. Sadly, not much likelihood of anybody caring enough to cough up a price to get him back."

"That's a hell of a thing say," Mona muttered bitterly.

"Now, doggone it," protested Mosher, "I didn't say it wasn't still a bad thing to have happen, did I? And didn't I form up a posse to go searching as soon as we knew it took place?"

"When did it take place?" asked Bourbon. "And was there any kind of ransom note?"

"No, no note. As far as when it all took place, it was some time in the middle of the night when everybody was deep asleep and nobody saw or heard anything."

Mosher removed his battered old hat with one hand and ran the palm of the other back over his completely bald dome. The furrows laddered across his forehead seemed to pile amazingly high up into the dome. "Once we realized what all had happened, I formed a posse to follow the trail of the four men—five now, with the horse they stole carrying Padre Pete we figure—northwest out of town. We lost sign in the rocky ground a few miles out, though, and had to turn back. Some of the men here"—he jabbed a thumb over his shoulder, loosely indicating the group behind him—"rode with me. Don't none of us rate too high as trackers, though. We returned only a short time before you showed up."

"You called the abducted man 'Padre Pete'," said Lone. "You sayin' he's a priest?"

"*Was* a priest," Mosher corrected. "That was a long time back. I don't know the whole story, but for some reason he fell apart. Turned into a drunk, a saloon dreg, and that's when folks went from calling him Father Peter to Padre Pete. Wasn't until a year or so ago that our Baptist minister, Reverend Farrow, took Pete under his wing and got him sort of straightened out. Pete's been living in a room at the rear of Reverend Farrow's church —that's where those skunks snatched him from."

"This whole thing sounds like a tangle that makes less and less sense," growled Bourbon.

Mosher gazed up at him plaintively. "You ain't telling me nothing I don't already know."

"Can I make suggestion?" Lone said to Bourbon.

The lawman gave him a look. "You ain't been shy about makin' 'em up to now. What you got in mind?"

"How about you, Rena, and Bayne take the marshal aside along with anybody who can add anything and squeeze out all the details you can get out of 'em?" Lone said. "While you're doin' that I want to have a look at the trail those skunks left headin' out of town, see if it ain't something I could probably stick with a ways farther. Once I get back, we can piece things together as best we can and decide how we play it from there. Hopefully there'll still be enough daylight left to use for continuin' after 'em."

"Sounds as good a plan as any to maybe untangle some of this and at the same time not let those varmints gain too much more ground on us," Bourbon allowed. "You go ahead, get started. Marshal Mosher, gather up anybody who might be able to tell us anything worthwhile and let's go over this again until we get it boiled down thorough-like."

Mosher clapped his hat back on and nodded agreeably. "Mona, go tell Ferd we need him some more. And somebody go fetch Reverend Farrow, too. He's got more at stake than anybody when it comes to Padre Pete."

Mona paused long enough to reach out as Mosher was getting ready to hand the Wanted dodger back to Bourbon. "Can I have that?" she said.

Bourbon looked puzzled. "Huh?"

"If Eccles is a famous outlaw, well, he'd be the first famous person I ever spent time with," explained Mona. "So that poster would be a kinda souvenir for me."

"What the hell," Bourbon grunted, holding out the paper. "I got other copies, go ahead and keep that one."

CHAPTER THIRTY-SIX

Amarillo Ames looked concerned. "Jeez, Fen, are you sure about this holy Joe? He's loony and getting loonier the more whiskey we poor in him. What makes him so important to finding that Aztec gold?"

"Because he's the key," Eccles insisted. "He's the one who told my old lunger cellmate about it in the first place. He found the treasure once before, he can lead us to it again."

Ames aimed a scowl in the direction of Padre Pete, who sat alone over on the far side of the clearing, cradling a half empty bottle of whiskey in his arms, rocking slowly back and forth as he stared off at the sunset. It seemed the stare of a lost shell of a man. One couldn't judge him by appearance any closer than to guess somewhere between forty and sixty. Stick thin and frail in a jacket at least one size too big, his skin was almost as pale as his wispy white hair. And even his staring eyes, a washed out blue in color, seemed to be fading into the same uniform tint.

By contrast, the cloudless sky and surrounding

terrain were filled with a bright smear of colors ranging from pale rose up high to deepening pools of shadow forming in the low spots of the undulating landscape. Due south of the camp, still several miles off, the hulk of Devil's Tower rose up; cast in a splash of pastels on its west face, cut by a hundred vertical shadows thrust into the deep seams up and down its north-facing side, and throwing a long black blot to the east.

Ames heaved a sigh and said, "I've always trusted your savviness, Fen. I just hope you ain't lost your touch when it comes to this character. He don't look to me like he could lead the way to find a good spot for takin' a piss."

"You just wait 'til tomorrow when we've worked our way in closer to the Tower and it all starts comin' back to him," Eccles said. "That's where he had his dream of building a mission and that's why I been working so hard on stirring that dream back up. Repeatedly telling him how we're here to help make his dream come true. All he has to do is show us the foundation of the mission walls he started to build before, and we'll take it from there. Way he told it to Borland, see—the part I *ain't* reminding him of—is that when he was digging up rocks for those mission walls was when he stumbled across the Aztec gold bars. So if he gets us close enough to where that happened, you damn betcha we'll take it from there!"

Ames still looked skeptical. "It all sounds good when you lay it out like that. But didn't the Baptist sky pilot you talked to say how something about trying to build his mission is what drove the padre loco and turned him into a drunk to begin with? What makes you think he'll be so eager to go back and try again?"

"I'm counting on tapping into what you just said—the shame of defeat, of giving up on his dream, losing his collar and ending up in the gutter. Part of what caused him to fail, according to some of the things he mumbled when the reverend took me to meet him, was nobody sticking with him on getting the mission built. Yet he still babbles about God and what not, so in his head he ain't lost that connection all the way. That's why," Eccles stressed again, "I'm hammering so hard on the notion of us wanting to help him finish building his doggone mission. If I can keep that foremost in his thoughts, I'm hoping his alcohol-soaked befuddlement won't allow him to worry too much about anything else."

Ames eyed Padre Pete some more, watched him tip up the bottle he'd been cradling and then go back to rocking back and forth. "Well, by the look of it, he's sure as hell holding up his end of acting befuddled."

Eccles' expression clouded. "If all else fails, if he ain't willing or able to get himself un-befuddled enough to be helpful the easy way, we'll have to drag the poor dumb bastard in closer to the Tower and gouge some recollection out of him the hard way."

Ames' mouth curved in a thin smile. "Now you're getting back to the basics of how we usually operate."

"Maybe so, but keep in mind there ain't nothing basic about the haul we're going after this time out," Eccles told him.

From where he'd been bent over the nearby campfire, clanging lids and stirring pots, Luther straightened up and called, "Grub's ready, fellas. Just in time, too, on account of I see Lasky ridin' back to join us."

Eccles and Ames swiveled their heads to look north

and saw, as Luther said, the approach of Bo Lasky on horseback. The youngest member of the gang reined up and swung down from his saddle.

"Man, I been smelling coffee and bacon for the past mile and more. I hope you saved me a big plateful, I'm hungry as blazes!"

"You're in luck, we're just gettin' ready to dig in," said Luther.

"Good." Lasky winked at Ames. "I worked up a powerful big appetite last night. For vittles, I mean. I got my other appetite took care of mighty fine. I hope I didn't leave her too tuckered out to still do you some good, 'Rillo."

"Tuckered out?" echoed Ames. "Hell, she was practically fresh as a daisy. Plumb eager, the way she put it, to get her own appetite took proper care of."

"Now don't neither one of you start up with that shit again," Eccles growled. "How did our back trail look, Bo?"

"Clean as a whistle," came the answer. "If any of the sad sacks from that town tried following us at all, I'm betting they didn't stick with it very far. Hell, I doubt we even had to make the diversionary swing out through that rocky stretch. They likely didn't have anybody could've tracked us no matter if we'd headed straight for the Tower. At any rate, there ain't nobody fogging us now. I made sure of that."

Eccles nodded. "Good. We'll still post watch tonight, but I agree we ain't got much to worry about from anybody out of Reasoner's Gap."

Lasky sneered in the direction of Padre Pete. "Look at what we took from 'em. Would you go to much trouble to get back that used up shell of humanity?"

"Matter of fact, I would," Eccles answered. "In a manner of speaking we just did go to a fair amount of trouble, snatching him away like we had to do. I took us to that shithole of a town expecting an easy time of it— providing the sot was still alive, of course—figuring we'd be able to simply drag him out of some gutter where people would be happy to quit having to step over him. But it was worth the extra trouble, regardless. Because, like I reminded 'Rillo just a little while ago, I know what that used up shell is the key to."

Lasky shrugged. "If you say so. But the only key I'm interested in right now is the one to some vittles. How about it, Luther? I'm still hungry as blazes!"

CHAPTER THIRTY-SEVEN

THE NEW DAY DAWNED GLOOMY AND CHILL UNDER A SKY packed with high, slowly churning gray clouds.

"This just keeps getting better and better," lamented Emmett Bayne. "First we pass up the chance for a hot meal and a warm bed back in that town. All for the sake of wasting a handful of hours following what turned out to be a false trail that ended up pointing right back where we were already headed. Then we're forced to endure a cold night camp. And now we wake up to a sky that looks like it's going to pucker up and pour down bucketfuls of rain any minute."

"Don't you ever get tired of bellyachin', gambler?" Lone grated. "Nobody's stoppin' you from callin' it quits and turnin' back any time you want."

"Fat chance of that," Bayne responded. "I didn't come this far to give up now. But you'd like it if I did, wouldn't you? Give you a bigger piece of the pie to take back to your *alleged* old—"

"Mister," Lone cut him short, "you'd better be real

careful what next comes out of that hole under your nose."

"Emmett! That's enough," Rena said in a chiding tone.

"Damn right that's enough, the both of you!" Bourbon barked. "Jesus! Now that we're damn near on top of those polecats, the last thing we need is to start shootin' our own selves in the foot!"

The marshal gave it a beat to make sure his words (and Rena's) had eased the tension between Lone and Bayne. When it appeared that it had, at least for the moment, he locked eyes directly on Bayne and added, "I don't usually make a habit of explainin' myself, not even once, Bayne. Sure as hell not twice. But I'll remind you that the reason we needed to follow what turned out to be a false trail and not waste any time about it was because the Eccles bunch was all of a sudden actin' peculiar and we had to try and figure out why.

"We still ain't sure, but at least they're back on track aimin' at Devil's Tower. And a campfire last night could have been seen for miles, maybe warnin' 'em for the first time we're on their heels. I mean to keep the element of surprise, the one slight edge we got, for as long as I can. So be thankful I allowed this small, smokeless fire for mornin' coffee and—like McGantry said—quit your goddamn bellyachin'!"

As soon as he'd finished, Bourbon swung his gaze to the newcomer sharing their camp this morning. Reverend Charles Farrow was looking back at him, the corners of his mouth lifted slightly in an empathetic smile.

Bourbon's own expression scrunched with discomfort. "Sorry for the hollerin' and coarse language,

Reverend. I'll see to it... No, doggone it, sayin' it that way would flat be a lie. I'll *try* to see to it I don't make a habit of it around you. Sad to say, though, I'll probably slip again 'fore long. I know it's a sorry excuse, but spendin' time regular-like, the way I do, with mostly lowlife human critters...well, keepin' a civil tongue in my head and never takin' the Lord's name in vain are practices that have sorta fallen by the wayside for me."

Farrow's mouth went ahead and curved into a wide, full smile. "All things considered, Marshal, the way you work to keep the frontier scoured of the kind of villains you regularly deal with, in my opinion adds up to atone-ment worthy of off-setting a good deal of bad language. If it makes you feel better to curb your words somewhat in my presence, that's up to you. But I know I'm already being a great imposition by insisting on accompanying you in hopes of finding Peter, so I can't expect still more."

"Even after givin' in to you comin' along," Bourbon said with a sigh, "I was kinda hopin' that after yester-day's ride through that rough country and last night's cold camp, you might've changed your mind about stickin' with it. Reasoner's Gap is straight behind us, you can easy go back. As far as what's ahead... Well, I can pretty much guarantee it's gonna get rougher before it's over. And the chances of gettin' your friend Peter out safely when the bullets start flyin' the way I expect."

"I appreciate your concern, Marshal, but I assure you I understood all of that from the start. In fact," Farrow said, his tone grave, "a chance to extract Peter safely is the main reason I felt it so important for me to come. While the rest of you will likely become engaged in confrontation, my *not* being involved might provide an opening to... well, I don't know exactly. But what I do know is that I've got to try. Seeking to build his mission near the north side of Devil's Tower—in the heart of what some locals call 'the Bad Circle', compounded by his occasional mumblings about an obscure treasure—was the start of everything falling apart for Peter. Who knows, if we *can* get him safely away from these abductors who seem to be forcing him to return there for whatever reason, maybe the experience might somehow jolt him out of the trauma it inflicted the first time... or, God forbid, possibly make it worse."

Bourbon's brows lifted somewhat uncertainly. "Reckon we all got our reasons for ridin' into this, Reverend."

"Speaking of what we're riding into," spoke up Bayne, "I'd like to hear more about this 'Bad Circle' thing. That's something new that sure doesn't sound very inviting. But what about this 'obscure treasure'? That might be a whole other matter."

"Oh, Emmett," Rena said in a dismayed tone.

Before Bayne could snap back at her, Lone cut in to say, "Seems to me we're doin' more gum flappin' than anything else. It's possible to talk while sittin' a saddle, you know. Oughtn't we be gettin' a move on, Marshal?"

"Yes, of course." Bourbon scowled. "Swallow down any coffee you have left, everybody. Then get saddled up. Smother what's left of that fire. Lone, you'll of course ride ahead again. See how close we really are to those varmints, let us know. Looks like we can reach the Tower by evening, but before we close too tight we'll naturally have to have an idea how Eccles' bunch is positioned."

Without reply, Lone went to where an already saddled Ironsides awaited.

As Lone galloped off and the rest of them began preparing their mounts, Bourbon glanced over at Reverend Farrow and said, "As we go along, I'm gonna want to hear more about this 'Bad Circle' business, too..."

CHAPTER THIRTY-EIGHT

THE SKY REMAINED BLOATED WITH DULL GRAY CLOUDS BUT produced no rain. The middle of the day came and passed. Eccles and his men rode through the noon hour without slowing, drawing ever closer to Devil's Tower and feeling a growing sense of excitement that pushed aside any desire to stop until they had reached it.

The one exception within the group who neither sensed nor shared in this anticipation was, of course, Peter Misner. Padre Pete. The confused, dazed state he'd been in ever since the others took him from his room at the rear of the church and then rode him out of town in the middle of the night—all the while bombarding him with talk of re-establishing his mission and fueling him with frequent belts from the bottle of whiskey they'd immediately provided him—had varied hardly any throughout. He just complied quietly, obligingly with whatever instructions given him; whether it be while on horseback or sitting in an out-of-the-way spot when they made camp. Other than frequently tipping up his whiskey bottle or sometimes rocking his torso slowly back and forth, he barely moved and spoke even less.

Until, that was, the realization of his surroundings finally and suddenly hit him. It was as if the sight of the north face of Devil's Tower, a thousand feet high and over a third as wide and only a couple miles ahead, loomed all at once out of his whiskey haze, thrusting itself into his awareness like a predatory beast leaping out directly before him. Peter's reaction came accordingly. He first went rigid in his saddle, then leaned back sharply, pulling on the reins and jerking his mount to a sudden halt. After emitting a startled cry, he began shouting, "No! We must not be here! This is a bad place, an evil place... We must leave before the demons come in the night—the *Lupus Custos*!"

Riding just ahead of Peter, Eccles quickly checked down his own horse and wheeled back around toward the distraught man. The other gang members did likewise and for a minute there was a confused jumble of twisting, snorting horses and cursing men.

"Whoa. Whoa, take it easy, Pad—er, I mean Father Peter," said Eccles, fighting to keep the annoyance out of his voice and make his tone soothing. "Everything's alright, there ain't no problem in us being here."

"Yes there is!" Peter insisted. "This is an evil place. We must flee before darkness settles in!"

"No, no. It's okay this time," Eccles said, moving close up alongside him. "Me and the boys are right here with you, we ain't gonna let anything happen."

Peter's eyes were huge and bright with fear. "You can't stop them. They come from ancient depths—so deep the fires of Hell burn black!"

"Aw, now. There can't really be no place like that,

right?" Eccles smiled reassuringly and reached out to place a comforting hand on Peter's shoulder. At the same time, though, he could sense an uneasy ripple pass through the other men. Ignoring that, he continued speaking gently to Peter, saying, "Besides, we got the Lord on our side, don't we? Ain't that why you wanted to build your mission here in the first place—why we're here now to help you finish it—to bring the word of God to this heathen land?"

"It's too late," Peter said, his voice turning harsh. "This whole area is cursed—the *Aureus Maledictum!*"

"Come on now. You need to calm down." Eccles' patience was slipping; an edge was starting to be evident in his tone. "Here"—he lowered his hand and took the two-thirds empty whiskey bottle, its cork long gone, from the folds of Peter's jacket and waved it under his nose—"you need some of this to help get a grip on yourself."

"No! That's yet another curse!" Peter shouted, slapping the bottle away with such force it was knocked from Eccles' grip and flew back to strike him in the face. The vessel hit crossways on the bridge of the gang leader's nose, crunching cartilage and splashing its stinging contents into both of his eyes.

"Ow! Sonofabitch, I can't see!" Eccles bellowed, twisting away so hard he nearly pitched himself out of the saddle. This caused his horse to lurch to one side and ram a shoulder hard against Lasky's mount. The latter rammed back on reflex, in the process its rump swinging out to smack against Luther's mount, and for a moment there was another jumble of snorting, stomping hayburners. Peter and his horse were no part of this, however—giving the former priest an opening to wheel full around and spur away at a hard gallop.

"My eyes!" Eccles continued to howl. "Somebody give me a canteen, for Chrissakes, so I can rinse this burning goddamn whiskey out of 'em!"

"Here, Fen." Luther thrust the requested canteen into his boss's hands.

As he tipped his head back and began sloshing water over his eyes and the tracks of blood running from his nostrils, Eccles demanded to know, "What the hell's going on? Why do I hear a running horse?"

"It's the padre. He lit a shuck outta here—ridin' away like blazes!"

"Well somebody go get him!" Eccles roared, sputtering water and blood like a geyser. "Run him down—but don't hurt the crazy bastard, we still need him!"

An instant later, Ames and Lasky were pounding off in pursuit.

But Peter had a significant head start of more than twenty yards and was driven by the urgency of needing to escape not only the two riders now giving chase but also the terrifying demons he deeply believed in as well. What was more, the horse the gang had stolen for him proved to be a strong runner who was far fresher than the mounts of Ames and Lasky after the string of long days on the trail they had recently endured.

As the pursuing pair pushed their animals for everything they could get out of them yet failed to diminish the gap between themselves and Peter (if anything, seeing it seem to increase), Lasky pulled one of his guns and began triggering rounds.

"What the hell are you doing?" Ames hollered over

at him as they raced on, stirrup to stirrup. "Eccles said not to hurt him!"

"I ain't shooting to hit him—I'm trying to scare him into stopping!" Lasky hollered back.

"All you're doing is spooking his goddamn horse into running faster! Knock it the hell off!"

———

FAINTLY YET UNMISTAKABLY, Lone heard the sound of distant gunshots. And men shouting.

He checked down Ironsides and held very still in his saddle. Listening intently. The shooting and shouting stopped. But then, almost immediately, he could make out a new sound. Very vague at first, a low rumble, but slowly, steadily growing louder and closer. Lone recognized the sound. The approach of horses. Running hard.

He scanned his immediate surroundings. The terrain since he'd left the others back at camp that morning had stayed pretty much the same. Rolling hills, none too high though several sharply crested and cut by twisty gullies here and there; infrequent, oddly shaped rock outcrops small to moderate in size; scattered stands of aspen and cottonwood. A short ways off to the right of where Lone had stopped rose a medium high hill with some spikes of reddish brown rocks poking up at the top. Deciding it would make a suitable, quickly accessible vantage point, he swung Ironsides in that direction and gigged him once more into motion.

At the base of the hill, Lone reined up and vaulted from the saddle. Leaving Ironsides with a command to stay, he grabbed his Yellowboy from its scabbard and clambered up the slope of the hill. Reaching the top, he swept his Stetson back off his head, leaving it to hang by the chin string across his shoulders, and fell in behind the rocky spikes.

The view now provided, looking south out across a long, wide open expanse, was one of rippling low hills studded with a few trees and a handful of rubbled rock ridges. The expanse seemed to roll out in a kind of sweeping, natural presentation that culminated in the ominously grand display of Devil's Tower thrusting high and massive in the near distance. Lone had been seeing the distinct butte for some time now but not until he stopped and drank it in from this unencumbered perspective did he realize how close it was and how truly impactful the damn thing could be.

But now was hardly the moment for pausing to appreciate a piece of nature's handiwork. Somebody was in trouble.

Three riders were pounding hard across the wide expanse Lone looked down upon. Here was the source of the shooting and shouting he had initially heard. One rider, thirty or forty yards ahead of the other two, was hatless and in possession of no apparent weapons. It seemed clear he was fleeing desperately from the other two. One of the latter had a pistol drawn and was waving it in his right hand, though no longer firing it. The man riding next to him wore a gunbelt with a still-holstered sidearm, and both had the butts of repeating rifles thrusting up from saddle boots.

Lone knew with instinctive certainty he was seeing Padre Pete, the defrocked priest, being pursued by two members of the Eccles gang who had abducted him.

Damn.

Marshal Bourbon's words flashed through Lone's mind, the ones about maintaining the element of surprise—the one slight edge they had—for as long as possible before confronting Eccles' bunch. That was all well and good, a sentiment Lone had supported fully. But you could hang on to the element of surprise only so long before you had to spring it...and some-times you got a nudge that forced you to do so a little sooner than might be ideal.

It felt to Lone like the plight of Padre Pete was giving him that nudge. He didn't see where he had much choice but to expose himself and try to help the fleeing man. And there was something more, another feeling Lone was suddenly aware of, a stirring deep in his gut... the rage beast re-awakening. Was this it then? The long anticipated conflict that would finally unleash the full fury of unsatisfied retaliation for the death of Velda? The retaliation he'd been unable to deliver against her already-dead killers...or then against their possible substitute, Jack Swain, himself also turning up already dead before Lone could reach him. Were these murder-ous, robbing curs under the command of Fenton Eccles at last going to satisfy the craving, the demand? Was the abrupt resurgence of the beast somehow amplified by the thought and now the sight of this tormented former man of God being abused still further?

Lone didn't know all the answers to this sudden rush of questions and feelings. He just knew he had to act, and act fast.

No sooner had he reached this conclusion than the need to do so became even more urgent. As the fleeing man was nearing the hill Lone was positioned on the crest of, aiming his horse in what would have been a sweep around to Lone's left, the animal plunged suddenly into a grassy-edged old buffalo wallow and stumbled badly. The unfortunate beast's foot thrust into a deep hole and the crack of bones breaking in the attached leg was loud enough for Lone to hear clear up where he was. Shrieking in agony, the horse fell forward onto its chest and face, momentum causing its rear end to flip up high and fling the rider out into the middle of the wallow.

Double damn!

If not for this occurrence, Lone had been figuring he could remain behind the rocky spikes, wait for the pursuers to get a little closer and then pick them off in order to ensure their quarry's escape from them. That would have then left either Lone himself, or Bourbon and the others who were coming along not too far behind, to catch up with Padre Pete a little later on.

Now, however, Lone couldn't afford to let the pursuing riders get any closer before showing his hand. He had to get down there to more immediately assist the fallen padre while holding the oncoming riders at bay for both of their sakes.

CHAPTER THIRTY-NINE

Before quitting his stationary position atop the hill, Lone steadied the muzzle of his Yellowboy in a notch between a couple of the rocky spikes and got off three quick rounds at the chasers down below. The shots flatted out across the wide expanse. The first bullet gouged up a spurt of dust and dirt just in front of the pair; the second shot cut the air between them; the third drilled into the head of the horse being ridden by the pistol waver. The animal went down, instantly dead before it could make a sound, pitching its rider through the air like a rag doll with loosely flapping arms and legs.

Lone felt a pang of regret for killing the horse—far preferring it would have been the man—but there was no time to dwell on it. Having at least stopped the advance of the pursuers and thrown them into disarray, what he needed to do now was build on that. Which meant, for starters, moving to a new position from which he could protect both himself and the padre.

With a horse and one rider down and the second

one halted and dismounted to assist his partner, the pair was distracted enough to give Lone the best opening he was likely going to get for shifting his position. So down off the crest he went. Half-running, half-skidding, he began a rapid descent down the slope. At the bottom, he made a final sprint across ten yards of flat grass and then threw himself into the buffalo wallow just as two sharp cracks of a rifle let him know he was drawing return fire. The rounds passed well above his head, though, and thumped harmlessly into the slope he had just descended.

Staying low, crabbing across the floor of the wallow, Lone grabbed a still dazed Padre Pete by the scruff of his neck and dragged him along until they were pressed against the southern side of the depression, the one nearest the Eccles gang members. More bullets chewed the rim of the wallow just above their heads, kicking dirt and shards of grass down onto them.

This was enough to shake the padre the rest of the way out of his stunned condition. He rolled his widened eyes from side to side and then locked them on Lone. "W-who are you?"

"A friend," Lone replied tersely. "Keep your head down if you want to hang on to it."

Another slug gouged the rim, kicking more dirt and grass.

They were hunkered down right beside the padre's fallen horse, who writhed in pain and blew loud, ragged snorts to express its misery. "Oh, dear Lord," Peter murmured, reaching out to gently rub the flank of the suffering animal. "This poor beast is dreadfully injured."

"I know. And, sad to say, there's only one cure." After

jacking a fresh shell into the Yellowboy, Lone extended his arm to place the muzzle against the horse's temple and pulled the trigger. The beast gave a single jerking spasm and then went totally still.

"My God!" Peter gasped. "You killed him!"

"I put the critter out of its misery," Lone corrected. "It had no chance to survive, the only alternative was to leave it die slow while wracked with pain. I showed it mercy."

Peter sank back against the dirt. "Of course. I understand. But—"

A voice called from south across the expanse. "If I ain't mistaken, fellas, I think I just heard the sound of you boys saying goodbye to a horse. That about right?"

"Your thinkin' is about as good as your shootin'," Lone was quick to holler back. "What you heard us sayin' goodbye to was a snake that crawled in here with us. You know the type—one of those pissy little sidewinders. I blew its lousy head off as practice for more that I happen to know are squirmin' close hereabouts."

"So I guess that makes you some kind of holy terror when it comes to cuttin' down un-heeled critters, is that it, you horse killin' sonofabitch?" This was the anger-strained wail of a different speaker. The one who'd gotten his horse shot out from under him, seemed a reasonable guess. "How about you show the onions to stand up and face a critter who's got the iron to talk back in your same language? How much terror you figure you can dish out then, huh?"

"I'll never stoop low enough to speak the same language as a couple of backshooters who play two-to-one odds against an unarmed man," Lone sneered in response. "So take your phony sense of fair play and stick it up your ass!"

This brought the fully expected response of more bullets—half a dozen rapid-fire rounds—slamming and skimming across the rim of the wallow. But, as before, the only measurable harm done was to kick an additional spray of dirt onto Lone and Padre Pete.

Brushing bits of torn grass away from his face, Peter said, "Is it really a good idea to agitate them even more?"

"Maybe." Lone grinned. "If I rile 'em enough to make 'em so mad they ain't thinkin' straight, that could work to our advantage. Besides, in case you didn't notice, they wasn't exactly actin' friendly even before I said anything back to 'em."

"Yes, that is very true," agreed the padre. "They are decidedly *un*friendly men. At one time I might have called them evil. But that was before I encountered the real thing. Still, that doesn't make what's out there any less bad."

Lone wasn't quite sure what to make of that, so he sidestepped around it and said, "No matter what you call 'em, all we need to do is hold 'em off just a little longer. They ain't got near the bulge on us they seem to think. Reason bein', I got friends comin' up from behind who will have heard all this shootin' and will be showin' up any minute to give us a hand."

Peter's expression brightened for a moment but then quickly clouded over. "That's encouraging to hear. But I must warn you that those villains out there also have friends who most surely will be showing up soon to aid them as well."

"I ain't countin' on anything less," Lone told him. "The crew I'm ridin' with, see, headed by a U.S. Marshal named Charley Bourbon, has been on the trail of these varmints for weeks. Also, you might like to hear, a friend of yours from back in Reasoner's Gap has joined us—Reverend Farrow."

Peter's eyebrows lifted. "Charles? That's good to hear, but...but I hope he isn't exposing himself to danger on my part."

"It was his choice. He sort of insisted, matter of fact. He's a grown man, seems right set in his ways," Lone said.

"He's a good man. A man of strong faith. Not like..." Peter's voice trailed off and he didn't finish.

Lone spoke into the awkward silence. "Gettin' back to the rest of those comin' up behind, like I said we been on the trail of these varmints for a long spell now. We know exactly what they're made of and what to expect goin' against 'em. It's what we've been anglin' for. The double bad news for them is that they got no idea about us... But they're fixin' to find out real soon."

The voice of the Eccles man who'd been first to call out before hollered again, saying, "I hope you boys are getting comfortable bellying around in the dirt and dried shit of that buffalo wallow. If you ain't, you'd better be. 'Cause you're both damn sure on your way soon to a couple of *permanent* holes in the ground!"

"Especially you, you meddlin', horse-killin' bastard!" added the second one, still hurling his words in a strident half shriek. "Only you ain't gonna rate the nicety of no proper hole—you can lay out to rot and be left for buzzard and coyote pickings!"

Lone looked over at the padre, his eyes turning flinty and his teeth set on edge. "You know what?" he grated.

"I think I'm sick of talkin' to these lowlifes just with words."

An instant later, he twisted around, pushed up on his knees high enough to thrust his rifle barrel through the fringe of grass along the wallow's rim, and began cranking out shots as fast as he could lever home fresh cartridges. Five .44 caliber slugs blistered the air and either slammed into or skimmed tight above the horse carcass the two owlhoots were bellied down behind. Unfortunately, they had enough savvy to take advantage of that piece of misfortune and turn it into effective cover. They'd also thought to back off the still unharmed animal and force it to its knees behind a low, grassy hump so it was out of the line of fire. Had they not, one of Lone's notions when he rared up and unleashed his furious volley was to try cutting down the second horse, too, if there was a clear shot. He'd have hated doing it, but he nevertheless would have for the brutally practical sake of increasing the gang members' disadvantage. Still, a part of him was thankful the shot wasn't there.

When he dropped back into the wallow, Peter pressed close and anxiously inquired, "Did you get any of them?"

Lone replied, "Sorry to say, no. But I made sure they ducked their ugly damn heads low enough to chew some dirt. And I was able to see they ain't managed to creep any closer. Leastways not yet."

"So what now?"

"We wait." Lone's fingers were nimbly thumbing replacement cartridges into the Yellowboy. "Keep playin' cat and mouse until some backup shows."

Almost as if able to see this re-loading activity, one

of the outlaws called out with a new taunt. "Hey, meddler! You got so many cartridges to spare you can afford to waste 'em on an already dead critter the way you just did?"

"Thanks for your concern, backshooter," Lone hollered back, "but I got plenty. When the time comes, I'll only need two. Hell, if you and your empty-headed partner line up proper, I could do the job with just one."

"That'll be the day, you big talkin' bag of gut wind," crowed the second hombre. "Falls to me doin' you, I'll make damn sure *not* to do the job with just one. I'll nip off little pieces, a bullet at a time, until you're *begging* me to finish it!"

Lone issued a nasty laugh. "That's a big joke and we both know it. I know your type just by the weasely little voice. You ain't got near the onions for doin' a man in such a messy way. You'd give up a helluva lot sooner than you'd ever come close to gettin' a peep of beggin' out of me."

"You just wait and see, horse killer! You just wait and see!"

This last was emphasized by another barrage of gunfire, ripping and gnawing across the rim of the wallow.

When it was done, Peter brushed away fresh spattering of dirt and grass from his face and fought to keep the strain out of his voice when he asked, "Whose backup do you think will show first—theirs or ours?"

"Comes down to it, I expect they won't be appearin' too far apart," Lone answered.

"I hope not... I-I pray not." Saying this, Peter's voice abruptly took on a whole different timbre. "You may not realize how big a step it is for me to say that. Praying—

either in thought or deed—has become incredibly foreign to me. Once a man of the cloth who bent his knee dozens of times a day, in recent years I...I haven't... But that never meant..."

"It's okay, Padre," Lone told him. "Pray, don't pray. Whatever makes you feel better. I'll welcome all the help you can conjure."

CHAPTER FORTY

Twenty-five yards behind where Ames and Lasky were holding to cover in back of the horse carcass, angled a bit to the south and east, a cluster of cotton-woods and aspens thrust up out of a patch of bramble. After being delayed in order to clear the whiskey out of Eccles' eyes and stanch the flow of blood pouring from his nostrils, the gang leader and Luther now came riding hard, drawn by the sound of the gunfire. Quickly assessing the situation as they drew closer, Eccles steered them over to the bramble growth. There they quickly dismounted and, with rifles pulled from their saddle boots, took their own cover in amongst the trees.

From behind the rim of the wallow, Lone observed all of this. But there wasn't a doggone thing he could do about it. The new arrivals were too far away and too quickly obscured by the trees for any chance at a telling shot. But at least, with the same certainty he'd felt when he got his first glimpse of Padre Pete, he knew he had now laid eyes on Eccles. The man destined to pay the price that would hopefully satisfy the craving of the rage beast still lurking within Lone.

Once in place, Eccles called ahead to his men, "'Rillo! Bo! You two okay?"

Neither man had missed hearing the arrival of the rest of their gang. Responding now, calling back over his shoulder, Ames said, "We're pinned down in a kind of Mexican stand-off, Fen. Nothing serious, though. Wouldn't amount to much of nothing if he hadn't got one of our horses."

"A damn *good* horse!" Lasky added fiercely.

"Where did that crazy bastard get a gun?" Eccles wanted to know.

"Padre Pete? Ain't him got the shooting iron—it's that damn stranger who showed up and stuck his nose in."

"What stranger?" squawked Luther.

The cords in Ames' neck bulged visibly and it was all he could do to stay pressed tight behind the dead horse. "Jesus, Luther, if I knew who he was I wouldn't be calling him a stranger, would I? Whoever he is, him and the padre are packed into a buffalo wallow up yonder just ahead of that sloping hill. Now if you and Fen will kindly circle wide around and flush him the hell out of there so I can get my hands on him—"

"Not if I get mine on him first!" Lasky objected.

With strained patience, Ames finished, "I will gladly squeeze a formal introduction out of the sonofabitch so we all get to know him real good before we go ahead and fill him full of holes!"

"Everybody just take it easy," cautioned Eccles in a surprisingly calm tone. "We can't afford to let this get any more out of hand than it already has."

"So let's not waste any more time bringing it back *in* hand," Lasky agreed eagerly. "Let's swoop in like 'Rillo said and deal with that stinking horse killer, then drag the loco priest back where we need him to be and we'll have everything okay again!"

"That might be more trouble than it's worth," said Eccles, as if thinking out loud.

Ames craned his neck around, his dirt-smeared forehead puckering in disbelief. "What are you saying, Fen? All of a sudden the padre don't matter no more?"

"And what about settling with that stranger?" Lasky demanded.

"To hell with that stinking stranger. We got way bigger fish to fry than worrying about whoever he is," Eccles growled. "And as far as that crazy-ass padre, you all saw how he acted back there—you expect he's gonna reveal anything useful if we drag him back and he throws another fit like that? Is it worth the risk of somebody taking a bullet rooting him and the gunny out of that hole for only more of the same?"

"But I thought the padre was the key to the treasure," said a baffled Luther.

"A key ain't no good if it's busted. And that's what Padre Pete is—busted inside his head! Would've been easier if he wasn't, but the kind of riches we're talking about were never meant to be achieved easy." Even though Ames and Lasky couldn't see it and Luther was still too baffled for it to have full impact, Eccles' eyes took on an almost maniacal gleam. "Goddamn, boys! Didn't you *feel* it back there? I did. I felt it so strong I could almost taste it! We were practically on top of that treasure. We don't need no crazy goddamned padre to finish finding it. We can do it all on our own... All we gotta do is turn around and go back after it!"

"Is that really what you want to do, Fen?" questioned Ames, still unable to shake the disbelief from his tone.

"Yes!" the gang leader insisted. "Anything more we try to do here is just a waste of time and unnecessary risk, so get ready. When I give the word, one at a time, you and Bo drop back to these trees with me and Luther. We'll lay down cover fire. Bo, you first. Then you and your horse, 'Rillo. Okay, get set..."

It took only a handful of minutes for the fallback to be accomplished. While Eccles and Luther dutifully but unnecessarily poured a hail of lead across the top of the wallow, Lasky and Ames scrambled back to join them in the trees. Lone made no attempt to interfere with their withdrawal; hell, he welcomed the reprieve. He just kept himself and the padre flattened down and let Eccles and Luther burn powder to no avail. It wasn't like Eccles hadn't made it clear exactly where they were headed. If he wanted to put the backs of himself and his men to the north wall of Devil's Tower and make a stand there against anyone coming to try and pry them away, then that's how it would go down.

CHAPTER FORTY-ONE

CHARLEY BOURBON SET HIS JAW AND GLARED IN THE direction of Devil's Tower, looming in the near distance against a slowly churning gray sky. "So, like we been figurin' for some time," he said, "there's where it's gonna finish playin' out. After a long chase and some diversions and side squabbles along the way, it boils down same as almost always to a matter of rootin' the skunks out of their hidey-hole."

"If you say so," Lone allowed guardedly. "But these particular skunks have picked themselves a mighty formidable hidey-hole. With that big ol' slab of rock at their backs and all that open space in front, rootin' 'em out could prove a little tricky, don't you think?"

"Never said it'd be easy," the marshal grunted.

"What if we returned to Reasoner's Gap and formed a larger posse," Reverend Farrow suggested. "Might that not be a good idea?"

Near a half hour had passed since Eccles and his men, with Lasky riding double behind Luther, had departed the cluster of trees and headed back toward the Tower. Bourbon and the others, drawn by the gunfire as Lone expected, showed up at the buffalo wallow when the retreating gang was still a fading dust boil out on the flat. Giving immediate chase at that point had not been a viable option. Instead, the interim time had been spent bringing everyone up to speed on Peter's escape and rescue by Lone before turning to the issue of completing dealings with the outlaws.

In response to Reverend Farrow's suggestion about returning to town and forming a posse, Marshal Bourbon said, "There are times when roundin' up a bunch of brave, willin' men is a real good thing, Reverend. But this ain't one of 'em. Like McGantry pointed out, a force of men chargin' toward those rocks across that open stretch would get cut to ribbons. As long as they got ammo, Eccles' bunch could hold off a small army comin' at 'em like that."

"What does that leave then?" asked Bayne.

"Way I see it, comes down to two options," Bourbon answered. "One, we could wait 'em out, set up an ambush somewhere and hit 'em when they leave. Or two, we go in under cover of dark and get it over with. And I'll tell you right up front that my patience for dealin' with this pack is worn powerful thin. In other words, I ain't got a hell of a lot of wait left in me!"

"My feelin's run the same," Lone was quick to say. "We ain't gonna get a better, darker night than tonight. And we still got the element of surprise by them not knowin' we're behind 'em in any kind of force. They were willin' to write me off as just some do-gooder drifter who happened along. And, from the sound of it, Eccles himself is so crazy eager to get at the treasure he thinks is waitin' in there that he's pushin' the rest past takin' time to consider hardly anything else."

"There's that treasure talk again," Bayne piped up. "How long are we going to keep skirting around that? What's it all about? If Eccles knows about some kind of secret treasure, are we being short-sighted worrying over a few dollars' reward money if there's something bigger to be had?"

"We're in the business of runnin' down a pack of fugitives from the law," Bourbon stated loud and strong. "We ain't no stinkin' treasure hunters!"

"I'm in it for the money. I never made no bones otherwise," Bayne replied stiffly. "If there's more to be had one way as well as another, all I'm saying is maybe we ought not be so quick to ignore all the possibilities."

"Oh yes, you should. You should very aggressively ignore and avoid the treasure of which you speak." These words came from Peter, spoken softly, imploringly, yet immediately drawing the full attention of the others. His washed-out blue eyes met their inquiring gazes evenly and he went on. "I know that in recent years—via my descent into madness and alcoholism—I have ruined all credibility for almost anything I have to say. But in this instance I beg you to listen to me. Thanks to the patience and care Charles has been showing me these past months and then the jolt I got earlier today when I saw where those men were returning me, my mind is once again clear enough to face the reality—and yes, even the horror—of what I experienced. And if that means speaking out for the sake of others, even knowing how much of what I say may be met with ridicule and disbelief, then I'm ready to face that, too."

"Look, Pad–er, Peter," said Bourbon, "if you know something we ought to know before we go ahead with our plans, then by all means we want to hear. But just try to get straight to it, okay?"

Peter looked somewhat tentatively at Reverend Farrow, who nodded his head and encouraged gently, "Go ahead, Peter. Take your time. Tell us what you feel is so important for us to know."

The former priest took time for a sip from the canteen someone had handed him earlier. Then he proceeded. "It's true. There is an ancient treasure buried in near the base of the Tower. To my great sorrow and regret, I've seen it with my own eyes... And then I saw the unearthly horror associated with it, the force guarding it, that gets directed toward anyone who dares tamper with it."

"Oh, of course," sneered Bayne. "What's an ancient treasure without some kind of curse attached to it, right?"

"You wanted to hear this, Emmett. Let him speak," said Rena.

Seeing the sincerity and raw willpower Peter was displaying to at last fully relate the experience that had tormented him so, to finally get it off his chest, Lone rasped, "She's right. Everybody shut up and let him tell it."

Peter swallowed and resumed. "You all know by now that I first came here some years back intent on building a mission in near the north wall of the Tower. The area was already dubbed by some as the Bad Circle or the Bad Section, allegedly because neither crops nor cattle seemed to flourish very well in the soil or on the grass. But I was looking to cultivate souls, so that was of little concern to me. I arrived with a fully equipped crew of four hired skilled laborers from the Laramie area and half a dozen Cheyenne Indians from the reservation to the west. The laborers were strictly in it for the wages, the Indians were already converted to Christianity and eager to see the mission succeed so others of their tribe could be introduced to the word of God.

"Things went well for the first week. The men, red and white alike, got along good and I was very pleased with our progress. We plotted the layout of the court-yard and the chapel, began digging foundations and even started erecting some sections of wall." Here Peter paused and it was evident he was struggling to go into the next part. But he overcame the restraint and began talking again. "And then came the afternoon when, as some of the men were hammering out slabs of rock for the wall, they broke through into a narrow cavity that reached back into the base of the Tower. First a horrible odor rolled out, like something putrid sealed up for decades, centuries. Then, once the stink abated, we stuck our heads in for a closer look and there was the treasure...gold and silver bars, coins, artifacts, all strewn back for several feet."

Peter paused again, this time to let the impact of what he'd just described sink in. When he swept his gaze over the faces looking back at him, he saw nothing but rapt attention.

Continuing, he said, "You no doubt won't under-stand what I did next, but I immediately ordered the cavity to be covered over and left alone. Somehow I sensed the spoils were forbidden and that any tampering with them would end in tragedy. The Indi-ans, who had little or no personal interest in gold and had seen too many times what the white man's greed for same could lead to, obeyed without question. The laborers, naturally, were less willing. But in the end they complied with my demands. I knew it likely wouldn't be the end of their resistance, but I underestimated how soon it would show again. It didn't last the night.

"A few hours after I retired, I was wakened by the sound of scraping and digging and voices arguing. I knew right away of course what was happening. No sooner had I dressed and was preparing to leave my tent than a fierce wind suddenly arose, shrieking and furiously blowing things asunder. And from out of the terrible wind also came an unearthly howling, as if from the throats of massive wolves... And then there was the terrified screams of men. I mustered all my courage and emerged from my tent. In the darkness and whipping wind I could make out shapes—not clearly defined, yet huge and shaggy in outline. Fiery red eyes. Flashing fangs. Demons! I only caught a fleeting glimpse of this horror before I was struck and knocked unconscious by some brute force."

Peter paused again, obviously needing to gather himself for a moment. A sheen of sweat covered his pale forehead in spite of the chill air, and his breathing was quickened. And then, steadying his voice, he finished the telling. "When I came to, it was morning. Daylight. All about me the camp was torn to unrecognizable shreds. The Indians, I later came to hope and pray, had escaped. The remains of the laborers were...horribly maimed. Nothing but streaks of blood and gore painting the rocks everywhere I looked. The only living thing was me.

"I left there at once. Aimlessly. Recklessly. Beginning my descent into madness. Walking, staggering, crawling at times. I don't know for how long. At least a day and a night. A horrible night, fearing what might come after me in the darkness. Finally, I found myself stumbling down the street of Reasoner's Gap. People gathered around to aid me. God only knows what gibberish I was mumbling by that point. And then someone put a bottle of whiskey to my lips. To settle me. That was the next big step down. Down toward oblivion, numbness, abandonment of all hope and of my faith. Living only for the next swallow of poison to blot out the sounds and memories... Until blessed Charles began to gently pull me out. And then the shocking events of today that jolted me—whether I was ready or not—the rest of the way into a clarity I haven't known for a long, long time."

Reverend Farrow reached out and put a hand on his shoulder. He said, "You were ready, Peter. You're strong enough now to face it."

Peter gazed back at him mournfully. "Am I truly? Am I strong enough to continue holding up, to face the disbelief and ridicule I know will come...and to work to turn others from the tragedy I know awaits if they don't listen?"

"God gave people free will, Peter. You know that," Farrow told him. "Even His son was met with ridicule and disbelief. All you can do is try to guide with the truth and hope that more than not will listen."

Turning suddenly to Bourbon and Lone, Peter said, "Then I beg *you* to listen to me! Please do not follow those men in close to the Tower. Especially not at night. If they're deserving of punishment for their foul deeds, then trust me—the punishment they will receive in there if they go after that cursed treasure will far exceed anything they could face out here!"

Bourbon shifted uncomfortably under the intensity of Peter's pleading. "Now see here, padre. That's quite a tale you just told, though I got no basis to discount your claims. You've obviously been through a lot. But none of that changes the job I got to do. Me and these folks ridin' with me have traveled a lot of hard miles to capture these scoundrels and see they get served justice. The punishment part ain't for us to decide—even if I fully expect this bunch will get the permanent kind. Still, that gets handled by a judge and jury, not left up to... well, something else."

"Is upholding the law worth risking the lives of yourself and the others in the terrible way I've described?" challenged Peter.

"I been riskin' my life upholdin' the law to the best of my ability for more years than I want to think about," Bourbon replied stonily. "These others can drop out if they wish, but I'm goin' ahead. I cut you slack for your beliefs, padre, seems it'd be the Christian thing for you to allow a body the same."

Farrow touched Peter's arm. "The marshal's right. He needs to do his job as he sees fit."

Peter hung his head. "Yes. Yes, of course."

"But you two," Lone spoke up, "can make it back to Reasoner's Gap by nightfall if you double up on the reverend's horse and get a move on."

"That's a good idea," Bourbon was quick to agree. Then, turning to Rena, he started to add, "And, all things considered, I think it'd be another good idea if—"

But she didn't let him finish. "Stop right there. I've

been in on this from the start, I'm not turning back for no curse or anything else. I put in those hard miles you spoke of with no complaints or favors asked, and I threw my share of lead back on Hacksaw Highway. I'm sticking with the rest of you all the way!"

Bayne grinned. "That's my girl. And with reward money *and* a buried treasure in the pot, you know damn well I'm not folding my hand either."

Bourbon frowned. "Never figured you would. But I need the guns you've got backin' that hand, so I guess that's the way it'll have to be."

"You better know better than to ask if I got any turn-back in me," Lone said when Bourbon cut a glance his way.

"A-course I do," came the grunted reply. "Only thing I'm askin' you is if you got another one of your plans for how we're gonna work in close and unseen so's we're ready to clamp on those polecats come dark…"

CHAPTER FORTY-TWO

"THIS IS PART OF A WALL, NO TWO WAYS ABOUT IT. IT comes to a corner right up there." Fenton Eccles thrust out an arm, pointing. "And over across is another section. See it?" A growing excitement crept into his voice. "Yeah, I can picture more and more now. It all starts to be plainer. Do you fellas see what I'm talking about? Those grooves in the ground running off in straight lines, all blown over and mostly filled in now? I'm betting they were once foundations dug for more walls."

"Yeah, I *am* seein' it, Fen," Amarillo Ames replied, his own tone sharpening some. "By God, you're right. Once you get the idea, it all starts to fall in place. That crazy old priest and his crew had it all laid out and outlined."

"And we're standing right in the middle of it. We're here!" declared Eccles. "That means the treasure can't be far—maybe only a matter of feet from any one of us this very minute!"

The four outlaws were indeed sitting their horses in

the midst of the mission as plotted by Father Peter and his men years past. They had ridden in a sweeping pattern back and forth across the north face of Devil's Tower, gradually working in closer, until this late afternoon hour when they at last had spotted the indicators now producing their excited responses.

"Hot damn!" exclaimed Bo Lasky. "I never really doubted you, Fen, but I gotta admit I was holdin' back some from getting my hopes too high. Not no more, though. Holy shit! I got shivers runnin' through me, I swear."

"I hear you," said Eccles, grinning. "But don't go thinking that gold and silver is gonna jump into our arms all on its own. We still got some hunting and digging to do before that comes."

"Speakin' of diggin'," called Luther from where he'd reined up a ways apart from the others, "looky over here. See the gouged out area up in the side of this slope? Off yonder"—he pointed—"is another one. Ask me, I'd say that's where the bunch from before was breakin' out the rock slabs for those wall sections. Reckon that's where they might've ran across sign of the treasure and, if we're gonna commence diggin' ourselves, where we maybe oughta start. Wouldn't you say?"

The faces of the others turned to him and then tracked to the dug out areas he was indicating.

"By God, Luther," responded Eccles, "that's a damn sharp eye. And, you bet, I'd say that's a damn good idea for where we should commence our digging. I feel it stronger and stronger by the minute—it ain't gonna be no time at all before El Dorado is ours, boys!"

"Before that, though," said Ames, "I'm thinking

what's gonna be ours is a faceful of wet, cold rain. That sky's been threatening all day and now it looks to me like it's puckering plumb serious enough to cut loose pretty quick. And nightfall's gonna come soon behind. Being filthy rich ain't gonna do us no good if we all catch pew-mony and croak before we can enjoy it."

"Jeez, 'Rillo, you can put a damper on things even quicker'n a cold rain," muttered Lasky.

Ames shrugged. "Go ahead and stand out in it if you want. You say you're shivering already, have yourself a double dose for all I care."

Scowling skyward, Eccles said, "Damper or not, 'Rillo makes a good point. We ain't got time to get no work started yet today nohow. So being smart about getting through the night and the rain is our best bet. Come morning, though—rain or shine, mud or flood—you can bet your asses I'm gonna be out doing some digging!"

"You ain't gonna be alone," Lasky assured him.

"Alright. Me and Luther will break out our soogans and that big tarp from the gear. Spreading it over that wall corner should make a pretty good canopy. You two," Eccles directed, "see to the horses and then scrounge up some firewood. At least we can meet a wet, cold night with some hot coffee and beans in our bellies."

———

WHEN THE RAIN CAME, it was fairly light and without wind; more a dense mist of small, icy droplets that bit like tiny teeth against bare skin. Huddled under a tarp in the half built wall corner, wrapped in battered but efficient soogans with a crackling fire before them, the Eccles gang was reasonably comfortable as night descended around them. Mixed with their barely contained excitement over the perceived nearness of the treasure, however, was also a vague sense of uneasiness as the blackness outside their canopy thickened.

Ames finally put it into words when he lowered his coffee cup after a sip of bitter brew and said, "Anybody but me done any thinkin' back on some of the crazy shit that old priest said just before he went jackalope loco and flung that whiskey bottle in Fen's face?"

"Not if I can help it," responded Lasky. "Why dwell on the babblin' of an idiot?"

"I don't think about his words," growled Eccles, reaching up involuntarily to gently touch the heavy scab on the bridge of his nose, "but I sure think about the way he flung that bottle. The sneaky little sonofabitch! The one regret I have about leaving him and that meddling stranger back at that buffalo wallow is not taking time to wring Padre Pete's scrawny neck first. But, seeing how it's turned out where we're sitting now, I guess I can live with it."

"Hell," said Lasky, "when you get rich as holy blazes, you can hire a pack of the blood thirstiest cutthroats to be had anywhere and have 'em bring ol' Pete around for neck wringing or whatever else suits you."

Eccles smiled around a puff of his cigar. "Yeah. I could, couldn't I?"

"I dunno," muttered Luther, looking particularly glum. "I been ruminatin' sorta the same as 'Rillo. What that holy Joe spouted was crazy talk, sure, but, all the same, some of it was still...well, bothersome. He spoke of a place in Hell so deep the fires burn black! Man, that's a creepy damn thing."

"How can it be creepy when it's so crazy as to be ridiculous? How can fire burn black?" Eccles wanted to know. "Jesus Christ, Luther, there's a fire right there in front of you. You see any black flames?"

"Nobody's saying it wasn't crazy talk," said Ames. "Still, there was a wildness in the way it whipped up ol' Pete that sorta jars a body when you see it. And some of the other stuff he said... I've heard about folks who are touched in the head all of a sudden 'speaking in tongues', as the saying goes—but am I the only one who caught Pete making noises like no words I ever knew before?"

Lasky broke into a mocking chuckle. "Now you've really stretched it, you poor dumb heathen. 'Speaking in tongues' might also mean just talking in another language, ever think of that? In this case it was Latin, which ain't surprising for a crazy former priest to break into."

"Latin? What the hell is that?" said Eccles.

"It's sorta the official lingo of the Catholic church," Lasky explained. "They use it in all their masses and official doings. Everywhere else it's considered a dead language."

Ames arched a brow skeptically. "And you know this how?"

Lasky chuckled again. "Because I was raised Catholic, that's how. My earliest memories are of my old man pounding that doctrine into my skull morning and night. The old fool actually had dreams at one time of me becoming a priest. Hell, he might've been one himself if he didn't like diddlin' women too much—my ma, and any other slut he could get to spread for him. Hah! That's the only part of his teaching that took with me. Even though I actually did a couple stretches as an altar boy, if you can imagine that."

"What I can imagine," Eccles chuffed, "is how that probably gave you your first easy pickings by dipping into the collection plate."

"You wouldn't be wrong," Lasky confirmed with a wide grin.

"Getting back to that lingo Padre Pete was spouting," said Ames, looking thoughtful, "are you saying you understood some of it?"

Lasky sighed. "Christ, 'Rillo, you got a way of sometimes getting stuck on one note like a broke piano, you know that?"

"Did you understand any of what he said or not?"

Frowning, Lasky said, "Well, I'm a little rusty, let me think... Yeah, he only babbled a few words, I reckon I got most of 'em. He talked about a curse, he said that much, then he called it *Aureus Maledictum* in Latin. Maledictum means curse. Aureus, I ain't quite... Money? Fortune? Something like that."

"So a cursed fortune, or a cursed treasure. That would fit, wouldn't it?"

"It might fit, but that don't mean it makes any goddamn sense," growled Eccles. "We're talking about the rambling of a whiskey-addled idiot, remember. The fortune, the treasure is the constant—that's the only part we need to care about. And how can wrapping your arms around a fortune be a curse?"

Lasky shrugged. "He didn't say much else in Latin anyway. *Corpus Lupus*—the Guardian Wolves. That's the only thing more I recall. And that makes even less sense than the other."

Luther's eyes shone bright in the flickering firelight. "There could be wolves around here, though, couldn't there? I mean, there are wolves of some kind most everywhere in open country where there ain't a lot of people. Right?"

"So there might be a mangy wolf or two somewhere in howlin' distance. So what?" demanded Eccles. "There are probably coyotes and jack rabbits and pissants, too —what difference does it make? The baddest bastards the rest of 'em need to worry about is *us*! On top of that, we're only a few hours and a few feet from being the *richest* bad bastards anybody ever saw. Now are we gonna spend the rest of the night worrying how the Big Bad Wolf might come knockin' on our door, or are we gonna get back to worrying how we're gonna spend all that stinkin' treasure?"

CHAPTER FORTY-THREE

An eighth of a mile west of the outlaw camp, part way up a rocky slope just back from the rounded northwest corner of the Tower, Lone McGantry lowered the rain-dotted pair of binoculars he'd been peering through. Gathered close behind him, pressed in under the meager shelter provided by a stubby rock shelf jutting out above their heads, were Bourbon, Rena, and Bayne. All had their hats pulled down low and the collars of their slickers turned up around their necks and ears. The patter of small raindrops tapping on the rocks and the fabric of their slickers made a low, steady hissing sound.

"Well?" said Bourbon. "They all in there?"

"Every blessed one. All four," answered Lone, "snugged in under a tarp drinkin' hot coffee."

"That takes the goddamn cake," grumbled Bayne. "Those lowlife scum sitting dry and warm and us—the ones on the right side of law and justice and all that's supposed to be proper—freezing our asses out here with nothing but cold rain trickling down between our shoulder blades."

"Look on the bright side, gambler. Gives you something new to bellyache about," Lone told him.

"Real funny. Tell me you're enjoying this."

"I plan on gettin' me some enjoyment when we bust up that cozy little nest," Lone grated.

"Same here. And the sooner the better," said Bourbon. "This rain, miserable as it is, and the fact they're bein' cocky enough to post no lookout, gives us leave not to have to wait a whole lot longer. You agree, McGantry?"

"Like you said, the sooner the better."

Bourbon wiped a palmful of rain from his face. "You got us in this far, but unless you got something else in mind, I'm thinkin' the way we went at things back on Hacksaw Highway wouldn't be too far off from workin' here again."

"Don't see why not." While there'd still been light and once Reverend Farrow and Peter Misner were off on their way back to Reasoner's Gap, Lone had directed the others in a wide sweep to the west and then curling south so they were able to approach the Tower without risk of being spotted by Eccles' bunch. The arrival of the rain and darkness had aided the rest of the way in bringing them unseen to their current position. Continuing his response to the marshal's suggestion, Lone said now, "I suppose that badge of yours means you got to do a call-out, let 'em know who you are and give 'em a chance to surrender."

"That's the way it works."

"You know how they'll most likely answer, don't you?"

Bourbon shrugged. "Still don't change it none."

"Okay. So that puts me up high again, off-angle on that slope above their camp. Suit you?" said Lone.

"Sounds good." Bourbon nodded, though it was mostly lost in the gloom. "I'll 'front 'em straight on, just outside the light of their fire. I'll be able to see them but they won't me. Probably won't matter to the dumb bastards—they'll likely still try to kick out the fire and make a break. If and when they do, we'll have 'em in a crossfire."

"What about us?" asked Bayne.

Bourbon answered, "You and Miss Rena hold off to the side. Hopefully by their horses, if we can locate 'em in the dark. If the gang breaks they'll try for their mounts. Any make it clear of me and Lone, you're the final stoppers."

There was a long moment of silence. Only the monotonous hiss of the rain.

Until Lone said, "Okay, I best get a move on. You won't be able to see me and I won't be able to signal, so give me a little while to get in place. It'll be up to you to set 'er in motion, Charley. Use their campfire as a locator. But don't stare into it too long or hard."

———

LONE GLIDED THROUGH the inkiness with surprising surefootedness. His pulse and mind raced in unison. He felt a strange sense of calm, determination. And a conviction that it was all finally coming together like the point of a spear. His craving—the craving of the rage beast prowling inside him—for retaliation against some*one* or some*thing* in answer to Velda being so cruelly snatched away might at last be slaked. As well as achieving retribution for what had been taken from Ma Sharples.

Here, in this unlikely setting, against a looming slab of rock named after the devil, it was going to conclude...

Breathing hard, sweating inside his shirt under the sodden outer garments, Lone reached a suitable location about thirty feet above and slightly off-center of the outlaw camp. He looked down on the tarp canopy, faint glow of the campfire showing through the wet canvas. He sat and leaned back against a flat boulder, willing his breathing to level off. Resting the Yellowboy across his thighs and pinching his shirt closed tight at the throat so no excess rain would dribble down inside, he tipped his face up to the cooling wash of droplets. After a minute, he tipped his face back down and palmed water away from his eyes.

Ready when you are, Charley. Call down the thunder.

As if bidden by this thought, a sudden change filled the air. Not thunder, but wind. And not wind out of the west or north or any compass point such as might ordinarily release that manner of change, but a wind that seemed to rise up out of the very earth. A fierce, gusting, whirling, roaring wind that turned the misty rain into horizontal slashes of icy pellets sweeping with them bits of sand and gravel that stabbed like dagger points. Clods of dirt were driven like pounding fists. Had Lone not been sitting against the flat boulder, this assault hit hard enough to likely have knocked him off his feet. Even as it was, he had to scramble frantically, twisting and throwing his arms around the heavy boulder to keep from tumbling down the incline.

What in hell! What in the name of—

The words of Padre Pete, Father Peter, streaked through Lone's mind. *A fierce wind suddenly arose, shrieking and furiously blowing things asunder...* Could it be? Was it possible? Lone didn't want to believe it, yet he had never experienced anything remotely like this before. The wind buffeted him, tried to tug him away from the boulder. Bits of gravel tore into his face.

He tried to shout. "Charley! Rena!" But the wind instantly took the names and flung them into nothingness, smothered in the deafening roar.

And then, above that roar, there was an even louder sound.

A howling.

And from out of the terrible wind came an unearthly howling, as if from the throats of massive wolves!

Lone could no longer deny it. Everything was happening exactly as Father Peter had warned. The curse of the ancient treasure was striking once again!

But Lone was damned if he would succumb easily. Fighting back was second nature to him, woven tight through every fiber of his being. And if there were demonic forces on the outside, then another demon—the rage beast so long pent up inside him—was ready to also be unleashed against them.

Lone shoved away from the boulder and struggled to stand. He had to lean into the driving wind at nearly a forty-five-degree angle to remain upright. His Yellowboy was gone, fallen and skidded away down the slope. But now, from below, he could hear the crack of gunfire and the harsh voices of men cursing—and then starting to scream.

The screaming and howling rose to an ear-piercing crescendo.

Lone slipped on the rainslick incline and fell onto one hip. He started to slide down closer to the source of the screams. He clawed to find a purchase to hold himself in place. And then shapes, indistinct outlines, began streaking near, first grazing him and then bumping harder. A foul odor came and went and next he felt the brush of leathery hide covered by bristly hairs. He balled his fists and swung blindly, furiously, striking back but slipping and sliding in a way that diminished the impact of any blows he landed. Snarling sounds, some coming from him, from the rage beast within, mixed with the howls and screams.

And then a fierce blow struck Lone and sent him reeling. He spun around and pitched headlong down the slope. He hit the muddy, gravelly ground, landing on his chest and stomach, and went into a skid that ended up slamming the top of his head hard into an upthrust ridge of rock. The howls and screams went instantly silent and Lone was enveloped by a blackness even deeper and colder than the rainy night.

CHAPTER FORTY-FOUR

"GALAHAD... CAN YOU HEAR ME?"

"McGantry... Damn it, man, come on... No bump on that thick skull of yours is gonna keep you down..."

The voices faded in and out. At times they sounded far away, other times quite close. What was never far away, unfortunately, was the throbbing pain in Lone's head. It pulsed relentlessly down through his neck and into his shoulders.

He knew if he tried to open his eyes it would only be worse. But squeezing them more tightly shut had the same effect.

"I think he's comin' 'round."

"Thank God."

Lone slitted his eyes slowly open at first, then all the way. It wasn't that bad—no worse than having hot knives poked into them. Once he got past that initial stab of fresh pain and the blurriness began to lift from his vision, he could make out two faces floating over him. Charley Bourbon and Rena.

"If I'm dead," Lone husked, "are you two blockin' my view of the Pearly Gates...or the other Doorway?"

"Neither one, 'cause you ain't dead," Bourbon told him. "But, if you ask me, I'd say we all got a close enough look at that other Doorway last night so's not to be in the mood for makin' any jokes about it now or anytime soon!"

"Duly noted," Lone agreed with a groan.

He turned his head slowly and looked around. It was daylight. The rain was done, the sky clear. The sun, only an hour or so risen above the eastern horizon, was pushing a wall of bright warmth across the land. Lone could feel it on his cheek. Reaching up with one hand, he could also feel on his cheek and elsewhere on his face various scrapes and cuts from last night's flying gravel and sand. Reaching higher, his fingertips grazed through blood-matted hair and gingerly traced the scabbed-over gash where the top of his head had hit the ridge of rock. Glancing again at Bourbon and Rena, he could also see where they'd been pelted and chewed plenty by debris.

Lone was lying on the slope where he'd been knocked unconscious. He was on his back now, having either rolled over sometime during the night or been turned by Bourbon and Rena. Pushing up on his elbows, he scanned down the slope to where the outlaw camp had been. There was no sign of the men, their gear, nothing. Only the wall remnant that had been erected there years earlier.

Lone's eyes darted to Bourbon. "Did they get away?"

The marshal's expression turned grim. "From us, yeah. But not from whatever came howlin' and rippin' out of the wind conjured by the night."

"You mean..."

"You know damn well what I mean!" Bourbon barked. "You saw, you was in the thick of it, man. It was just like Father Peter told us. Something—demons or guardians or whatever you want to call 'em—showed up to enforce the curse of their forbidden treasure. And they enforced it with the same bloody fury they did to them Laramie laborers all those years ago."

Lone wagged his head slowly back and forth. He knew Bourbon was telling it straight. He'd seen it and heard it, he *had* been in the thick of it. But still. My God...

His eyes cutting suddenly to Rena, Lone said, "Where's Bayne? What about him?"

Her expression went blank, wooden. So was her tone when she answered, "He's gone. They got him, too. We were off to one side, over by the outlaws' horses like Charley said. We were clear from the worst of the wind and howling and screaming. I–I was terrified, but I thought we were safe. Only then, suddenly, there were these *shapes* swirling all around us. Snarling, howling. They grabbed Emmett and jerked him away. One second he was there beside me and then he was gone, just vanished. I heard him cry out a single time, but after that there was... I never..."

Bourbon reached out and put a hand on her shoulder. "Steady, gal."

Lone pushed to a sitting position but then his head spun too wildly for him to try rising any more.

"I got knocked loopy, same as you. Not near as bad, though," Bourbon explained further. "I came 'round while it was still dark and rainin'. Managed to find Miss Rena on account of I had a pretty good notion where to look. Those *things* was still prowlin' around some and we had no idea how to get to you—or what condition you might be in anyhow. So we hunkered together in the protection of some bramble and rode out the night. Come mornin', we still might never have spotted you if not for that horse of yours. The big gray showed up and plodded right to you. Stood over you pawin' the ground until we came to see what he was fussin' about."

Lone looked around over his shoulder and for the first time realized Ironsides was standing there just a few feet upslope, eyeing him speculatively. Lone grinned. "Hey, pardner." He reached out his hand and the gray leaned down to have his velvety snout rubbed.

"At least one of us will have a ride back to Reasoner's Gap," Bourbon grunted. "The outlaws' horses are long gone for sure. And it's hard tellin' if the rest of our mounts we left picketed back at the Tower corner will still be there or not. Even though they was a distance off, all that wind and howlin' might've spooked 'em to hell and gone."

Rena looked up at the looming prominence of Devil's Tower and said somberly, "Spooked them *away* from hell would be more like it."

Lone frowned. "What I don't get is why are we—us three—left behind to fret about how we're gonna be leavin' at all? Don't get me wrong, I ain't complainin', but why didn't the demons or whatever they were wipe us out like the rest?"

"I been wonderin' the same thing," said Bourbon, scrunching up his face. "But I wasn't sure I wanted to know the answer."

Rena's eyes danced back and forth between them.

"Do you really not see? Don't you get it? We were spared because we came here neither coveting nor intending to violate the ancient treasure. Everyone else—the laborers from the past, Eccles' gang, even Emmett—had become obsessed with what is forbidden. Father Peter, his Indian helpers, us...the curse did not extend to our purposes for being here."

Bourbon's jaw sagged. "By God, that might be right. It makes a kind of cockeyed sense, about the only thing that does."

"We came for reward money, but didn't get caught up in the whole treasure thing," echoed Lone, musing the notion aloud.

"As far as the reward," said Bourbon, "I'll be reportin' how the Eccles gang got killed resistin' arrest and you two deserve pay-out for aidin' me in the fight against 'em. Might take a little longer to get your money that way, but I'll do everything I can to see you do."

"Somehow that doesn't seem as important as it once did," Rena murmured somewhat dully.

"You earned it. Plus, you'll have the need for it in order to carry on," Lone reminded her.

"Speakin' for myself, my biggest need right now is to get the hell away from this place." Bourbon made this declaration glaring up at Devil's Tower looming high above them. Then, cutting his gaze down to Lone, he asked, "You think you and that busted head of yours can manage to get up and sit a saddle?"

Lone squinted back in response. "Give me another minute, I can get up and walk. What's wrong with you, Charley—don't you see a lady present? If we're stuck with only a single horse, she's the one gonna ride."

While Bourbon looked momentarily taken aback, Rena smiled wanly and said, "No sense trying to argue with him, Charley. It's like I've been saying all along... He's Galahad."

A LOOK AT: DANGEROUS TRAILS
COLLECTED WESTERN ADVENTURES

PEACEMAKER AWARD-WINNING AUTHOR WAYNE D. DUNDEE DELIVERS ANOTHER MEMORABLE COLLECTION OF THE OLD WEST FILLED WITH TURBULENT EMOTIONS, POIGNANCY AND TONS OF NAIL-BITING ACTION.

From the Oregon Trail to the Civil War this collection of western adventures will take you on a non-stop journey! Blood will be spilled, lives will be lost, fresh wounds will be inflicted ... but the chance to heal old ones is what will keep everyone pushing forward.

"As usual, Dundee's writing is tough and well-paced. He's one of the best storytellers in the business." – **James Reasoner**

Dangerous Trails: Collected Western Adventures includes: Trail Justice, Trail Revenge, By Blood Bound, The Fugitive Trail and seven novellas.

AVAILABLE NOW

ABOUT THE AUTHOR

Wayne D. Dundee is an American author of popular genre fiction. His writing has primarily been detective mysteries (the Joe Hannibal PI series) and Western adventures. To date, he has written four dozen novels and forty-plus short stories, also ranging into horror, fantasy, erotica, and several "house name" books under bylines other than his own.

Dundee was born March 24, 1948, in Freeport, Illinois. He graduated from high school in Clinton, Wisconsin, 1966. Later that same year he married Pamela Daum and they had one daughter, Michelle. For the first fifty years of his life, Dundee lived and worked in the state line area of northern Illinois and southern Wisconsin. During most of that time he was employed by Arnold Engineering/Group Arnold out of Marengo, Illinois, where he worked his way up from factory laborer through several managerial positions. In his spare time, starting in high school, he was always writing. He sold his first short story in 1982.

In 1998, Dundee relocated to Ogallala, Nebraska, where he assumed the general manager position for a small Arnold facility there. The setting and rich history of the area inspired him to turn his efforts more toward the Western genre. In 2009, following the passing of his wife a year earlier, Dundee retired from Arnold and began to concentrate full time on his writing.

Dundee was the founder and original editor of Hardboiled Magazine.

His work in the mystery field has been nominated for an Edgar, an Anthony, and six Shamus Awards from the Private Eye Writers of America.

www.ingramcontent.com/pod-product-compliance
Lightning Source LLC
Chambersburg PA
CBHW010816250626
47156CB00011B/3096